By: Stanley L. Battle

THE SON OF SCARFACE PART 2

MOCY PUBLISHING
WWW.MOCYPUBLISHING.COM

Detroit, Michigan

Printed by CreateSpace, An Amazon.com Company

The Son of Scarface Part 2

ISBN 978-1-940831-29-9

Published by Mocy Publishing, LLC.
Website: www.mocypublishing.com
Email: info@mocypublishing.com

Shawn was sitting around the house doing nothing. The phone started ringing and he said to himself, "who could this be?"

"Hello?" He said answering the phone.

"Shawn my man," Sorcerer said.

"Sorcerer, what'ah surprise."

"Yeah I saw what happen to that police station, I could hardly believe it."

"Yeah thanks to my good friend Stone, we no longer have to worry about anyone connecting you to me."

"I'm glad it went well. You know Shawn, I would like to meet this Stone fella. How soon can you bring him my way?"

"I'll contact him tomorrow. We'll be down this Friday coming up."

"When you say we, I hope you're just talking about you and Stone?"

"You right again. No one else will be with us I'll make sure of that."

"Good, I'll see you when you get here Friday."

Shawn hung the phone up and dialed Alvin's number. The phone ringed five times. "Hello, Alvin speaking."

"Alvin my man, it's Bomoski."

"Bomoski my friend, don't tell me you have more work for me already."

"N'all not this time. I'm just calling to let you know the big man want to meet you in person. That's if you're willing to accept his invitation for this Friday."

"That sound cool to me, you just tell me when and where to meet you and I'll be there."

"Meet me at the metro airport at twelve-thirty noon. My pilot will be waiting there for us in my jet."

"I'll be there."

"Good I'll see you then."

Alvin hung the phone up and said to himself, "I'll be damn, the man himself wanna meet me personally. I got it made in the shade now. A few years from now I'll be as powerful as Bomoski. Nobody will be able to touch me, not even Bomoski. I wonder what made the big man want to see me; Bomoski probably told him about the job I did for him, and now he want to see how the man looks behind all this heart. Well, you gone get your chance and I'm gone get my chance to finally meet the biggest drug dealer in the world. I see some dream do come true; thanks Bomoski, you all right with me."

Friday, May 1, 12:30 P.M.

Alvin arrived at the airport first. He knew Shawn liked it when he's on time for his appointments.

Ten minutes later Shawn drove up and parked behind Shawn's car, and after he parked he walked over to Alvin and shook his hand saying, "come on, my pilot is waiting, that's him standing over there. He's a little up to age, but he knows how to fly the hell out of an airplane."

Mack smiled saying, "let's get this baby in the air."

Mack this is my good friend Mr. Stone."

"Nice to meet you Mr. Stone, you two just relax and I'll have y'all there in no time."

Shawn and Alvin fastened their seatbelts, Shawn smiled and said, "Alvin my man, with the money you gone be into you'll be able to own as many jets as you want too, and when you do start buying planes and shit, you make sure you buy yourself a good pilot like oh Mack here. And that's a must situation. Mack is always on time, never once has he been late."

"I'll remember that when I go shopping for me a jet," he said smiling.

(Nine-hours-later) Mack said landing the plane, "well boys we're here."

Sorcerer had his limousine driver waiting at the airport for their arrival. Two of his bodyguards followed in separate Mercedes Benzs' behind the limousine.

When Shawn and Alvin arrived to the mansion, Alvin said, "damn, man."

Shawn smiled saying, "its beautiful isn't it?"

"Beautiful ain't the word, this place is paradise. Although, one would think there would be guards all around here. I don't see any."

"Oh believe me they're around here trust me," Shawn said smiling.

5

"Once they got inside the mansion, Alvin noticed all the protection Sorcerer had on the inside of his empire."

The two bodyguards escorted Shawn and Alvin to where Sorcerer sat waiting for them in his favorite black leather chair that had his name written in gold letters at the top of its base.

Sorcerer smiled as he watched them enter his dining room, and said to them, "welcome men, how's everything with the family Bomoski?"

"They're fine, Gena sends her blessings. This man here is Alvin Stone, the man you wanted to meet face to face."

Sorcerer stood up and shook Alvin's hand, saying, "Alvin Stone, I heard so many good things about you."

""Likewise, I like your place. I can see you are a man of much class."

"I try to be and I can see that you are a man with plenty heart, I like your style. I saw your work on television; you got'ah lot of balls Stone. I think a man of your class should be in charge of his own organization."

Alvin nodded his head up and down and said, "I see you don't waste much time saying what's on your mind."

"A man like me don't like to waste time period. Time is money in my world and I would suggest you adopt that same attitude; that way you may be able to live like your man Bomoski here, who knows. Maybe even like me," he said spreading his arms out to display his home.

"I sure hope so," he said smiling.

"I'm sure Bomoski has taken good care of you for your service, and a friend of Bomoski is a friend of mine. Bomoski, I want you to make sure Mr. Stone has everything he needs to live comfortable in America from this day on out, and Stone, my doors are always opened to you. You are welcome to my home anytime you wish to see me. Since we are all one now, why don't we go down to my bar, I'm sure I can find something for us to seal our vows together."

Alvin said, "that sounds like a winner to me."

When they got to the bar Sorcerer made them all a drink saying, "I would like to make a toast." They all held their glass in the air. Sorcerer smiled, "too our new partner in the drug industry."

They all touched glasses in agreement and said at the same time, "too our new partnership."

They talked a couple of hours before Shawn said, "well Sorcerer it's been great meeting you, and I'm sure you'll be seeing me again."

"Drop by anytime, just let me know when to be expecting you. You men have a nice night. I'll have my men take y'all to the plane. I enjoyed our little meeting. Give my wishes to the family' Bomoski."

"I'll do that you take care."

Saturday, May 2, 7:00 A.M

Alvin and Shawn got back to Detroit early the next day. They shook hands and went their own separate ways.

Two hours later Alvin called Mr. Belvedere Real-Estate. After seeing how well Sorcerer lived, he made up his mind the way he wanted his house

7

built. He said to himself, "first I'll buy me a big piece of land in Romulus city and have his house built from the ground on up. Shawn will help me get this done since he knew what Sorcerer told him."

July 4, 1974 3:00 P.M.

Thirteen months later, Alvin had the house of his dream. His house was finally completed. He even had a lake built in the backyard of the big brick ranch-style home.

The day before the fourth of July, Alvin had called Shawn to invite him and his family over for dinner to celebrate the fourth of July with him. Alvin had never met Gena nor the baby. Antonio was walking now, and had teeth in his mouth strong enough to eat meat.

When Shawn pulled into Alvin's driveway, Paula said, "well is he married or single?"

"As a matter of fact he's single and I'm sure he gone like you Paula, you both have something in common."

"And what's that?" Paula asked.

"Well you both colored."

Gena laughed saying, "wow that helps a lot."

Paula laughed saying, "well he can be purple, Lord knows I need'ah good man. I just can't see no black man living this damn good, you joking ain't you Shawn? You got to be good and rick to live like this here."

Shawn smiled saying, "maybe he is rich, sometimes it's not about what you know, it's who you know, and obvious this man know the right peoples."

8

Gena smiled saying, "enough of the talk let's go on in. I smell barbeque cooking and it's making me hungry."

When they all got out the car and headed towards the front door, Alvin opened the front door saying, "it's about time y'all decided to get out the car. My main man, Bomoski, who these lovely folks here?"

"This is my lovely wife Gena, and this is her best friend Paula, and this my lil-boy Antonio."

"Nice to meet you all," Alvin said smiling. "My name is Alvin, since my good friend didn't bother to tell y'all. Not to be sarcastic, but don't I know you from somewhere Paula?"

"I don't think so."

"I know you from somewhere; I know where I know you from now."

"Where? Refresh my memory."

"I rather not say right now; let's wait till we are alone."

Shawn said, "well since you two already acquainted with one another, where's the barbeque?"

Alvin smiled saying, "all the barbeque y'all can eat is in the backyard, y'all just follow me," so they followed. "Y'all got to excuse the junk on the floor, I do live alone."

Once they got in the backyard, Alvin said, "you guys help yourselves, it's plenty to eat."

Paula said, "I'll have something to eat as soon as you tell me where you know me from."

Alvin smiled saying, "have'ah seat Paula and I'll tell you just where I know you from."

"I can't wait to hear this," Paula said sitting down.

"Okay Paula, first of all do you remember this girl name Cookie?"

"Bad as I hate to say it, but yeah, I remember Cookie."

"Since you know who I'm talking about, one day me and'ah friend of mine was over to her house taking care some business with her strung out boyfriend, and you was over there that day too."

"Damn I remember that day," she said with a look of shock. "Yeah I remember you now, you and yoe."

Alvin cut her off. "Wait'ah minute baby, let me finish telling you what happen before you go jumping down my throat for nothing. Now this what happened. Forgive me if this offends you, but you wanted some dope. You did use to do drugs if I'm correct."

"Yeah that's true, but that was years ago."

"Okay let me finish now, you wanted some dope, but on this particular day you didn't have no money, so you told me that you would sleep with me if I gave you a blow, and if you can remember, my boy kept saying, forgive my French, he kept saying, "don't give that bitch shit.""

"And you told him to shut the fuck up. By the way, he's dead now."

"Sorry to hear that," Paula said.

"Yeahhh anyway I gave you some dope, and you and I started grinding a little if you know what I mean."

"I catch your drift."

"Well anyway you changed all a sudden; something snapped inside your brain. I guess the dope I had at the time was too strong for your mind, you start yelling, "get off me nigga, why you raping me!"

Then I said, "bitch you crazy." My boy said, "I told you not to give that dizzy ass girl nothing you see how she tripping out on you."

You kept hollering, "why y'all raping me, I wanna go home." I just stared at you, and said to myself after you left, "I hope she come back to her sense, and don't bring the police back here. My boy didn't even touch you and you were going out on him too."

"So what you trying to tell me is that you was the only one who got some of this?"

"Yepp, that's right baby, I was the only one."

"Since you was the only one, I have what may be good news to you, or bad news, you can take it anyway you want too!"

"What's the news?"

"Well, my mind migh'uv played tricks on me that day, but I do know right after that incident I got pregnant. I couldn't afford an abortion so I decided to give my son to my mother to raise."

Alvin smiled happily, "you mean to tell me that I got you pregnant, and I have a son?"

"That's exactly what I'm saying, yes, you have a son. You say you were the only one who got this didn't you? I often wondered what his daddy was like, and now that I'm looking you face to face, he's your twin. Same kind of eyes, same face shape, same everything, watch this." She called Shawn and Gena over. "Come here for a minute you two."

Gena and Shawn walked over to where they were. "Let me ask y'all two a question. Who do Alvin look like in my family?"

Gena said, "I don't know anyone in your family besides your mother and. Oh my God," she put her hand over her mouth. "Alvin you look just like her son Stan."

Shawn said, "damn sure do, you two could go for twins. What's the catch here?"

Paula smiled saying, "meet my son's daddy."

Gena said, "congratulations you two. How did you guys figure this out?"

"You remember that little incident I was telling you about back at the center about Cookie. Well anyway, Alvin was there that day, and he just explained to me how I was stoned out of my mind. What I thought happened didn't happen."

Gena smiled, "Girl that's terrific now your baby has a poppa and a wealthy one too."

Alvin's grin grew bigger as he said, "this day is even more special to me now. I would like to see my son, you got to take me to see him Paula."

Antonio was busy running around in the backyard playing, and eating on a piece of barbeque chicken.

Paula said, "let me call my mother she's probably at home barbequing too. Can you show me to a phone Alvin?"

"Sure can, follow me. Be right back Shawn, the beer is in the cooler if you're thirsty."

Alvin showed Paula to the phone. Sharen answered on the other end, "hello."

"Mama this yoe baby I'll be out there in'ah minute, don't go nowhere. I got'ah big surprise for my son."

"Okay baby I'll be here see you when you get here. Bring mama something to drink too when you come."

"Bye mama."

Paula went back in the backyard and got Alvin, saying, "she's at home, I told'er we was on our way out there."

"That's good, Shawn you guys don't mind staying here for a few minutes while we run out to her mother house?"

"N'all, go right ahead, we'll be right here when y'all get back."

After the two of them got in the car, Alvin said, "so where too?"

"My mama stays on Bassett Street in Southwest Detroit."

"You kidding, that's my old neighborhood. Bassett, I pass by that street almost every day when I was living out there. I can't believe I have a son on that street. Damn this a small world. You know Paula, it seem like I've known

13

you all my life. And I must admit I wouldn't mind getting to know you a little better. I mean that's if you're willing to get to know me."

Paula's mind was on something else. Alvin smiled, "what's the matter baby my driving scare you or the cat just got yoe tongue?"

"No, I would like to get to know you better too, but I'm not quite ready for a commitment or nothing serious right now!"

"I can dig it baby, I understand. I'm not ready for nothing serious myself. I just wanna get to know you better, that's all!" He said smiling.

"I'm still going through a lot of changes. I had a little incident that happened to me a while back, and I just can't seem to get it off my mind!"

"Would you care to share your problem with me, I'm all ears?"

"You mean to tell me you didn't hear bout this man getting his throat sliced open down on the riverfront a year or so ago?"

"Exactly where did this happen?"

"On the riverfront down on Jefferson."

"Oh yeah I did hear about that. The man tried to rape this lady and she cut his neck off."

"Yeah that's the one that lady was me."

"So what did the law do to you about that shit?"

"The judge threw the case out. I was very relieved, I thought I was going to prison for the rest of my life!"

"I'm glad they threw it out."

"Are you?" She said smiling.

"Of course I'm happy for you. If you would'uv went to prison I wouldn't know I had a son in this world. And I still can't believe I'm not dreaming."

"Believe me this is no dream, that boy look just... like you."

"My twin huh, I can't wait to see myself that little again. Well this is Bassett, what house am I looking for?"

"Right across Visger Road, righttt over there where you see that lil-boy playing in the front-yard."

Alvin couldn't believe his eyes when he looked at his son for the first time. Alvin parked and said, "well I'll be damned. I can see from here that he's me all over again, my son."

"You gone sit in the car staring or do you wanna see your son. I told you he looks just like you."

"You sure wasn't lying," he said getting out the car. "I think I got my head on straight now."

Alvin and Paula got out the brand new red Mercedes Benz. Sharen was inside the house making her barbeque sauce when they pulled up. Stan was three now, three years old.

Stan recognized Paula and ran straight to her when she called out his name saying, "hey lil-man, where's granny?"

"In the house," Stan shyly said.

"You see this man right here."

"Yeah," he answered. "This man right here is your daddy."

"Hay man, I'm your da-da, can da-da have a hug?" Alvin stretched out his arms to pick Stan up. Stan pulled away from his mama to go to Alvin.

Paula shouted out, "mama what you doing in that hot house?"

"I'm in here getting my sauce ready. I'll be out in'ah second, let me put this sauce in the oven."

Alvin was busy playing with his son and thought to himself. "I couldn't deny you lil-man if I wanted too, you look just like me boy."

Sharen came out the front door saying, "I know you brought me something to drink?"

"Mama I forgot."

"Yeahhh I bet you did, who's this young man in my driveway playing with my baby?"

"I'm sorry mama, this is Alvin, Stan's daddy," Paula said smiling.

"You kidding, I thought you said."

Paula cut her off, "I did mama, but God works in mysterious ways!"

"That boy looks just like him too. That's definitely yoe child, same eyes, same nose, this is truly a blessing!"

Alvin smiled saying, "I didn't catch your name ma'am."

"I'm Sharen, I'm the mother that don't have nothing to drink for the holiday, thanks to my daughter here."

Alvin popped the trunk open and brought Sharen back a gallon of Remy cognac and said to her as he passed it to her. "Here you go Sharen, this is my favorite." He then pulled out his knot of money. "Here's a few hundred, take it and buy yourself something nice."

"Thank you son, "she said smiling.

"You more than welcome, and I really would love to stay and chat, but I got some people over to the house, but now that I know you Sharen I'll be dropping by to see you, if you don't mind!"

"You welcome to stop by here anytime you like. I'll be right here, me and my Martell."

Paula said, "so Alvin, would you like to keep your son, he need to get to know you, you his father!"

Alvin smiled saying, "I would love too, and don't worry bout packing his clothes. I'm taking him shopping first thing tomorrow. I promise you both I'll take good care of him when he's with me!"

Sharen was very happy for Paula and Stan. She tried hard not to show her emotion, but the tears slowly started rolling down her face as she spoke to her grandson saying, "give yoe granny a kiss before you go." Stan kissed her. "I love you, Alvin you bring my baby back to see me. I'm gone miss his bad butt!"

"That ain't no problem Sharen, I be out here all the time. Do you know any Stone's out here?"

"Yeah I know some Stones', is that your last name?"

"Yes, I'm a Stone."

"Oh yeahhh, you Alvin Stone. I heard about your little run in with the police, you did what you had to do."

Paula said, "what you talking about lady?"

"If you don't know, you want know not from me anyway, and that's for not bringing me no liquor like I asked you too. Now if Alvin wants you to know he'll tell you. Now, I'll see y'all later. I'm going in my house and enjoy myself."

Sharen kissed Stan goodbye and went and sat on the porch, and watched Alvin drive off.

Paula put her arm on Alvin's headrest saying, "what was my mother talking about back there?"

"Not too long ago I had to ice a few cops. I just beat them to the draw that's all. Luckily, I got'ah hold to the right person while I was sitting in that nasty ass jail. He paid my way out of that bull-crap. Actually, he paid the judge off that was handling the case or my black butt would still be sitting in that county jail. You see Paula, as long as a person got money, he got power. I think men like me are living better than some of these rich white men, and you know they don't like that. I got everything I need in life, and I'm gone make sure our son have everything he need too. You can't go wrong when you mess with Alvin Stone," he smiled.

Paula smiled saying, "I like the way that sound."

As Alvin continued driving, his mind went into a deep thought. "Even though you my son mother, I don't need you lying around me. I want get involved with you; we can be friends and nothing else. I like you, but not that much!"

When Alvin and Paula got back they found Gena and Shawn laying topless in the backyard trying to catch a tan. Antonio was playing with his toy far from them.

Gena smiled saying, "ooh I see y'all brought the baby back, that's good, he can keep lil-butt busy."

Alvin smiled and said, "yeahhh that's right. I'm glad you two love birds didn't let the meat burn up."

Shawn laughed saying, "ain't no way man, as much as I love barbeque, no way my man."

Antonio and Stan started playing together like they've known each other a lifetime. The elders just looked at them enjoying themselves.

Gena put her shirt on saying, "so Alvin, how are you enjoying your son?"

"Oh I'm enjoying every minute of this. I lov'em he's me all over again. I'm gone take'em everywhere I go. He knows I'm his daddy too."

Alvin had no idea that Shawn wasn't Antonio's daddy until Gena said, "little Antonio look just like his father too especially with that scar on his face."

Alvin said, "Shawn don't have no scar on his face."

Shawn said, "you see Alvin, lil-Antonio isn't my biological son."

"I truly didn't know that."

"I know you didn't, but I lov'em like he was my own. His father was killed."

"Oh yeah, what was his name, maybe I know'em," Alvin asked sipping his beer.

"His name was Antonio Montero," Gena answered biting into a piece of rib.

"Damn, Antonio Montero, I heard many things about that man; somebody put a contract out on him. I believe that was in seventy-two when this happened, I'm not for sure, but I do know he was a powerful man. I'm sorry Gena we'll get on another subject. I know you don't wanna hear about the past."

"Thank you, I rather no bring up the past. I have who makes my life complete," Gena said kissing Shawn.

Shawn thought to himself, "Yeahhh if you knew I was part of that hit squad that took Antonio out this world, you probably wouldn't speak to me anymore in life. Antonio was very powerful, but he didn't know how to follow orders. I hope we don't have that problem with you Alvin, I would hate to have to waste you!"

Alvin said, "well I don't know bout y'all, but I'm starving, let's eat."

Shawn laughed saying, "I'm with that program."

Nighttime had crept up, Alvin bought plenty of fireworks. Gena yarned and said, "call the kids Paula it's time for some sparkles to be lit."

Alvin said, "Y'all just sit there till I come back. I have something much exciting than sparkles, the kids' gone love this, I'll be right back."

Alvin went and got the fireworks and came right back and sat the box on the patio. Alvin put Stan on his knee so he could watch Paula and Gena light fireworks after fireworks. The kids' were definitely having fun, every time a firework went into the air changing colors, the kids clapped their hands saying, "yayyyyy."

Paula handed Stan a lit sparkle and asked Alvin, "would you show me where the bathroom is please."

"Yeah follow me," he said putting Stan on the ground.

Alvin walked her to the beginning of the stairs saying, "when you get to the top of the stairs make'ah left turn and another left, you'll run into it."

"Thanks, whoops, I forgot my purse. I got to get that, if you know what I mean," she said smiling.

"Well now you know how to get to the bathroom, take care yoe business."

Paula went back outside and got her purse, and as she headed back to the bathroom Alvin smiled saying, "don't get lost sweetheart."

Paula laughed saying, "I'll try not to, be right back y'all."

When Paula was done using the bathroom, as she was coming out, she got nosy saying to herself, "I wonder what his bedroom look like?" She opened the door to the room. "This is beautiful; he has this bedroom laid out. I wonder what's in that cabinet, a little peak ain't gone hurt nothing." She opened the cabinet door and couldn't believe her eyes. "My goodness it's enough drugs in here to supply every junky in Michigan. N'all I can't do it, I can't steal from my son's daddy, let me get my ass out'uv here."

Paula headed towards the door, but before she could touch the doorknob another thought entered her mind. "gone and take'ah bundle, he want miss it. Yeahhh why not. I'll just slip one bundle in my purse. Damn, why did I have to be so damn nosy?"

Paula put the kilo in her purse and raced downstairs to join the gang, and said to Alvin, "you know I had to get nosy before I came back."

"That's okay baby, did your eyes like what they saw?" Alvin asked.

"I love the way you got your bathroom laid out, a person could swim in that bathtub," she said smiling.

Alvin laughed, "everything in my house I had custom made for me, I even had the floors custom made, and when I take my son room apart all his stuff gone be custom made too. I want him to have the best, and to live a normal child's life. I'm gone enjoy being a father to my only child."

Shawn yearned saying, "well Alvin it's getting kind'uv late, and we have a long drive ahead of us. I truly had a good time."

"Well since you guys had a good time today, when y'all gone invite me out to y'all place for dinner?" He said smiling.

"You have my address don't you?"

"Nope."

"Here, take this card, and when you feel like driving come on out."

"I'll do that Bomoski. This has truly been a pleasure man."

Paula smiled and said, "this has truly been a special day for me and our son."

Alvin smiled saying, "yes it has been. I'm glad you enjoyed yourself, I'm glad we got the chance to meet each other. Hopefully, we'll get together and take our son somewhere nice like to a picnic or something. Would you like to do that sometime soon?"

"Yeah, anytime you feel up to it just give me a call."

"Thanks for reminding me, here's my card, my phone number is on it, and my beeper number. When you feel like conversating call me. I wish all y'all could stay a little longer, but I understand that it's a long ride. Come over here Stan and give your mommy a kiss. Lil-Antonio is sleep, so you can't say goodbye to him. Give Gena some sugar too. Now shake your uncle Shawn's hand. Sorry Shawn can't have my son kissing no man."

"Don't blame you; don't want my son kissing on no man either. Well I'll call as soon as we get home," Shawn said.

"I'll definitely be here, me and my lil-bodyguard here. Ain't that right son?" Alvin said smiling.

Paula said, "don't you let nothing happen to my baby."

Alvin smiled, "don't you worry about that baby, he in the best hands he could be in. Now you nice folks drive careful."

Alvin and Stan stood in the doorway watching them pull out the driveway. "Well lil-man they gone, daddy got to get you in the tub so you can get ready for bed."

"Yo name daddy?" Stan asked.

"Yepp, my name daddy," Alvin said smiling.

Stan watched his daddy run the bathwater, and Alvin could hear Stan saying, "fish."

"Those not real fish son, they just make the bathtub look good. Since you like fish, we going fishing tomorrow, you want me to wake you up, or are you gone wake me up?"

Alvin put Stan in the tub and watched him play in the water. Alvin began to think, "son I don't want you to be no drug dealer like your daddy. I want you to be a better man than me, maybe a lawyer or a doctor. Come on lil-man it's time to dry off. I love you son. Yesterday I was a man on my own, now today I'm a daddy, and I love every minute of it. You gone have to put one of daddy's shirt on for the night. You can sleep with me tonight."

As soon as Alvin laid Stan down in the bed next to him, Stan went straight to sleep. Alvin kissed him on the forehead saying, "goodnight son."

Alvin laid in the bed and thought back to his childhood; how he was raised without a father. His thoughts were interrupted by the phone ringing. "Hello." It was Shawn calling. "It's me Alvin, just letting you know we made it back safely, I'll talk to you later."

"Good night Bomoski," he said hanging up.

July 5, 1974 9:00 A.M.

Stan was the first to awake, and Alvin was awakened by his son's hand pushing him in his side.

Alvin yearned and smiled, "okay lil-man, I'm up, daddy up now, I know you hungry, let's wash up okay. This the last time you'll have to wear my t-shirt son."

When they got inside the bathroom, got him a toothbrush, and said, "here son, brush your teeth, daddy got to buy you your own toothbrush when we go shopping today."

Stan brushed his teeth and spit toothpaste in the bathtub. Alvin just looked at him and laughed, saying to himself, "yeahhh that's my son."

After they got dressed, Alvin decided they would eat breakfast at the shopping mall, and after they were done eating. Alvin bought Stan everything he thought a kid could want. Every time Stan would touch something in the store, Alvin would buy it; not caring what it cost, as long as his son was happy.

Alvin spent over two-thousand dollars on his son, and when they got back to the house Alvin said, "you ready to go fishing son, it's one o'clock, the fish should be good and hungry right about now. First let's call and see what your mama doing."

The phone ringed threw times, "hello, I'm speechless."

"Hey Gena, may I speak with you Paula?"

"Sure, just'ah moment," she calls out. "Paula.... telephone."

"I got it Gena, hello."

"Hey what's up?"

"I knew it was you," she said smiling.

"You knew right this time."

25

Paula thought to herself, "damn I hope he don't bring up nothing about them drugs in this little chit-chat."

"You never did tell me my son birthday."

"Is that's why you calling me? I thought you had something else in mind. Anyway, his birthday is November the seventeenth, nineteen, twenty-one."

"Damn, I'm a Scorpion too, no wonder he act so much like me when I was a kid."

"So you're a scorpion too?"

"Yepp, November the fifteenth. Well Paula that's all I wanted to know me and our son is on our way fishing."

"That's good I hope y'all catch some fish."

"Oh we will, let me let Stan say hi to you, I'll catch you later. Come here son, yoe mama wants you," Alvin put Stan on the phone to Stan's ear. "Say hi mama."

"Hi ma-ma," Stan said repeating Alvin.

Alvin took the phone from Stan's ear and said, "we'll talk to you later on, you have a good day."

"Okay then, I'll be here, have fun."

"We will, talk to you later."

As soon as Paula hung the phone up she reached under the bed and grabbed her purse. She reached inside the purse and pulled out the cocaine; using the tip of her long fingers to dip the powder. She filled each nostril with a few snorts and said to herself, "damn this some pure shit." Her eyes turned glossy and watery this dope is good. I shouldn't start this shit again. A little toot ain't gone hurt nothing, I can handle it."

Tuesday, July 8, 1974 6:00 P.M.

Gena was downstairs watching the news and wondering to himself. "Why haven't I seen Paula none today, she normally be down here with me by now watching television like we normally do every day. I better go check on her she must not be feeling to good."

When Gena got upstairs she opened Paula's door and got the shock of her life; she couldn't believe her eyes, and shouted out, "girl what are you doing?!"

Hesitating, Paula said, "it's just I can't lie to you, I picked this up when we was out to Alvin's house."

Gena looked at the bag of cocaine and said, "you mean to tell me Alvin gave you all that dope?!"

"He didn't give me nothing, I took it."

"I don't believe you Paula, you took it!"

"Yeah, I took it, what you find that hard to believe," she angrily said.

As Gena continued to stare at the bag of dope in front of her, her mind flashed back to the times she would snort cocaine all day long. The Temptations was eating away at her brain, until Paula said, "come on girl, try one line, it want kill you, this some good shit."

"I guess one lil-line want kill me, okay, one life." Gena tooted one line. "Damn, this is some good stuff, let me do one more. I haven't felt this good since I gave birth to lil-Antonio."

Paula smiled, "I know that's right girl, I have enough coke to last me for months, and besides Gena, we can afford it now, use to be a time when I had to sell my body for this stuff, but now I know where I can get it free. I'm blowed Gena high as hell."

"Yeah me too, I'm so glad Shawn took Antonio to work with him today. I can't believe I'm sitting here tooting cocaine, especially when I said I would never ever do drugs again. Look at me now, Antonio was right I'll always be a dope head."

"Fuck Antonio, he dead and you not, you not'ah dope head, you my girlfriend, and I love you. So fuck Antonio and what he said to you. Let's enjoy our life together Gena. Here, do another line, and this will be our last one, so you better make it a good one."

They did one more line and went downstairs to watch television, and as they sat, Gena said, "girl I got to get my act together before Shawn got here. I haven't even cooked dinner and it's almost seven o'clock. I'm too stoned to cook, you cook Paula."

"I'm too stoned too, but I know what we'll do, we'll just get them ribs out the freezer that was leftover from the holiday and put'um in the microwave and that'll be dinner."

"Good that'll be dinner."

"Good idea Paula, you are a genius, now why didn't I think of that."

Before Gena could put the ribs in the microwave, Shawn and Antonio were coming through the front door. Shawn smiled and said, "what's up you two?"

"Hi honey, how was your day?" Gena asked heading toward the kitchen.

"Actually it was pretty busy today at the center. It's not like it was when y'all were there."

Paula thought to herself. "if you only knew, me and Gena may have to sign ourselves back in at the rate we going. If you knew how high we were right now you'll probably put both our ass out of here. Damn I'm glad you can't tell."

"So what's for dinner?" Shawn asked.

"I thought you might like some leftover barbeque from the holiday, so I didn't cook anything."

"Oh barbeque sound good, you know I can eat barbeque everyday of the week."

"Good, I was just on my way to put you some in the microwave."

Shawn watched Antonio follow his mother into the kitchen then said to Paula. "So Paula, what you been up to all day, have you heard from Alvin?"

"N'all I ain't heard from him today, I tried to pull'em earlier, but didn't get no answer."

"Why didn't you page him?"

"Well I really didn't want anything I was just calling to see how him and the baby were getting along."'

"You know Alvin, he probably somewhere spoiling him," Shawn said smiling.

"Yeahhhh you right, after all I did tell him to keep'em as long as he liked, because I'm not ready to be no parent yet, I love my freedom to much. Don't get me wrong, I love my son, I rather for his daddy to raise'em. I remember it used to be the man running out on the woman, but now it's the other way around."

"Alvin ain't complaining, so don't you complain."

"Yeah I don't think you'll ever see Alvin complaining, he's a good man, and a good daddy. And I guess that's why you like him so much."

"Shawnnn you can come eat, it's ready," Gena called out.

"Excuse me Paula I do believe my wife is calling for me."

As soon as Shawn sat down in the kitchen to eat, Gena went to Paula saying, "what was you talking about, he didn't notice anything did he?"

Gena sighed, "forget about that, come on girl let's do one more line before Shawn finish eating."

Paula shook her head in a no motion and said, "see girl, that shit got you out yoe hook-up all ready, let's chill for right now, okay!"

"Come on Paula, just more line."

"Okay just one more and that's it!"

"I knew you wouldn't let me down," Gena said going up the stairs smiling.

The two of them rushed upstairs and quickly came back downstairs and sat on the couch to watch television.

Shawn and the baby had finally finished eating. When they got in the living room, Shawn sat down in his lounge-chair, saying, "damn, you two look like y'all are stoned or something."

Paula just stayed silent, and Gena said, "boy, do we look that bad; we shouldn't be drinking liquor Paula. I told you how it affects me, but I didn't think it was that noticeable."

Shawn smiled saying, "believe me baby, it is. I knew you two had been doing something the moment I walked through the front door."

Paula said, "well I feel good, I could use one more drink, how bout you Gena?"

"Sure, give me the usual, and what about you Shawn, would you like to join us for a drink?" Gena said smiling.

"Yes certainly would you make mine on the rocks please."

The three of them sat around the house laughing and drinking.. Paula said, "Shawn your eyes look just like mine and Gena now, all three of us look'ah like." Paula thought to herself, "damn he fell for this liquor shit, what'ah sucker."

Antonio was upstairs sleeping. "Would anyone like another drink?" Paula asked.

"I'll have another one," Shawn said.

Paula fixed Shawn a drink, and as she approached him, some of the liquor spilled in his lap.

"Ooh I'm so sorry," she said brushing the wet liquor off him. "I didn't mean to waste it on you, let me get some paper towels."

"That's okay Paula, I'll be alright, and besides I'm about to lay my behind down anyway. I'll see you two later on, goodnight ladies."

"Goodnight," they both said.

Wednesday, July 9, 1974 3:00 P.M.

Alvin had made plans with his son to take him to see his grandmother, and to check on Dino and some more people that was in his line of work.

When Alvin pulled into Sharen's driveway he said, "damn lil-man, yoe grandma coming out the house like she fix'n to go somewhere." Alvin got out the car. "Hi Sharen, how you doing?"

"I'm fine, where my baby?"

"He right here in the car, but I see you bout to go somewhere, can I give you a lift?"

"As a matter of fact you can. I was on my way to the liquor store."

Alvin thought to himself as he said, "get in."

"Damn this woman can drink her ass off, she couldn't-uv drunk all that liquor I gave her that quick."

Sharen got in the car saying, "this boy is knocked out. I see you got'em dressed real nice."

"Yeahhh that's my son, my mellow man, got to keep him looking good."

"Well I see you got'em looking nice and clean. It's a shame his own mommy don't wanna be bothered with him!"

"Well Sharen don't worry yourself about that. I'm in the picture now, and as long as I'm in his life he don't have to worry or want for nothing as long as Alvin Stone is alive, and that's the God heaven truth. I'm just glad you had the heart you got; taking care of him while his mother was sick!"

Alvin pulled into Tolbert's Liquor store saying, "don't worry about this drink Sharen, this one is on the house, and I do remember what kind you like."

"Thank you Alvin and don't forget my smokes, Newports please."

Alvin ran in the store and bought Sharen a half gallon of Cognac and a carton of Newports. When Alvin got in the car, Sharen saw all the stuff and said, "oh Alvin, you didn't have to spend all that money on me."

Alvin smiled. "I want you to always be happy, you my son's grandmother, and in my eyes that makes you a beautiful person."

Sharen smiled, "I like your kind'uv talk boy."

As Alvin pulled into the driveway, she grabbed the bag saying, "why don't you come on in for'ah minute and have a drink with me!"

"That sound good, I guess I have time for one or two drinks. I don't wanna get drunk, I got'ah drive yoe grandson home," he said smiling.

"Don't worry bout that, I want let you get that drunk."

Stan was still asleep, Alvin laid him down on Sharen's bed to finish off his nap while Sharen grabbed two glasses out of the kitchen, but before Alvin and Sharen could sit down good, Stan woke up and recognized where he was at, and ran straight to his grandmother.

Sharen picked him up saying, "there go granny lil-bad butt boy. Peewee been asking about you, come on you wanna go outside and play with your friends?"

Sharen put Stan on the front porch. She knew once the kids saw him, her porch would soon be flowing with kids. Once she put him on the porch she said to Alvin, "this boy has a thousand friends out here. You know that he's outside let me pour yo a drink. You can handle your liquor can't you?"

"Ain't no question, just put plenty rocks in my glass."

Sharen put the ice in the glass and said, "you have to pour yoe own troubles."

"That, I don't have a problem with."

The two of them poured drink after drink, until Sharen said, "Alvin you better slow your role, cause you can't out drink me, I been doing this for years by myself."

"Don't worry about me Sharen, I know my limit," he said smiling.

Sharen laughed saying, "I hope so, cause I can't stand nobody throwing up around me."

"I'm not gone get that drunk where it'll make me throw up."

"Excuse me for a minute I got to get out of these hot clothes."

Sharen went in her room and changed into a long pink silk gown that came down to her knees. She didn't bother to put on any panties, nor bra. When

34

she got back in the living room, Alvin noticed she wasn't a bra when she sat back down saying, "now I feel better, why don't you pour yo-self another drink."

Alvin thought to himself, "damn, I believe she want me to hit that ass."

Sharen walked over to the living room window to check on Stan and Alvin said to himself, "damn she ain't wearing no panties either, yeahhh she want me to screw'er."

Sharen said, "your son next door playing with about ten of his friends. He ain't thinking about coming home no time soon. Alvin did you miss me any while I was gone?"

Alvin could tell y her voice that she was drunk, so he just sailed and said, "yeah I missed you."

"Well why don't you come over here and give me'ah hug, I missed you too."

Alvin smiled saying, "you sure that ain't the liquor talking, cuss this ain't yoe grandson now."

Alvin leaned over and kissed her lips, and as he kissed her, Sharen gently touched him between his legs. Alvin's cock immediately got hard as he slowly laid her on the sofa on her back, pulling her gown up he could hear her saying, "come on baby get undressed, this pussy gone be here for you."

Alvin took one more look out the window to see where Stan was at, and after he saw him still playing with his friends, he quickly got undressed.

Alvin placed one of Sharen's legs over the couch, and the other one over his shoulder, and slid his dick inside of her cherry. She screamed out, "oow shit, damn that dick feel good." The more she called out his name, the harder he stroked her cunt. "Yes Alvin, tear this up, take it out and put it in my ass." She hollered louder as he put the head of his penis in her. "Damn you got'ah big dick, take it out." The more she said take it out, the more he stroked. " Oow shit, please take it out, oooh shit."

Alvin burst his nut in her, and got up thinking, "damnnn this old woman got some of the best pussy in the world. I ain't never had pussy this good before. I can't believe I screwed a woman damn near twice my age."

Sharen kissed him saying, "you sure do know how to work that thang for a young man."

"And you sure do know you have some good stuff between yoe legs for an older woman," he said smiling.

"Oh do I, well I hope we can do this again sometime."

"Anytime you need me, just call and I'll be here." Alvin reached in his wallet and pulled out his cards. "Here's my number again, just in case you need me. I'm definitely coming back to see you."

"For some reason I do believe you."

"Well as I said before, I'm out here on business today. I'm gone leave Stan here with you for a lil-while while I'm out here. I'll be back to get'em as soon as I'm done taking care of my business. Let me tell'em and let'em know I'm gone."

Stan was running as soon as Alvin called him. Alvin picked him up saying, "daddy will be back to get you in a lil-while okay," Alvin kissed him on the forehead. "Now you gone and have some fun with your friends. I'll see you in'ah few, be good son."

Sharen was standing in the door watching Alvin and Stan, thinking to himself, "I hope when you come back to get'em y'all spend the night out here. I want some more of that young dick."

Alvin got in his car and waved goodbye to Sharen, thinking to himself as he drove off," yeahhh I can get that pussy anytime I want now. I ain't never screwed an older woman, but I must admit I feel damn good about myself. Now my first stop is Dino's house."

As Alvin slowly cruised down Visger Road he spotted Dino's car parked at the pool room. Alvin pulled his car right in the front entrance, saying to himself as he got out the car, "fuck the parking lot, I got the sharpest car in southwest Detroit, niggas ain't gone steal my ride."

When Alvin got inside the pool room, Dino was shooting pool down on the other end of the pool hall. Dino spotted Alvin coming his way, and shouted out. "My main man Alvin Stone, what's up?"

Alvin smiled saying, "man you won't believe what happened to me today."

Dino smiled, "run it down on me and I just might believe you."

"Dig man, I invited a friend of mine over to the house for the fourth of July, and he brought his wife, and his wife's girlfriend. His wife girl turned out to be this broad I boned a few years ago. I didn't really recognize her at first till I heard the name Paula, and immediately I remembered who she was, and then me and her got to wrapping, and I explained to her where I knew her from. When I was done telling her where we ran into each other at, she told me that I had a son by her. And Dino mannnn, this lil-nigga looks just like me. So me and her drove from my house out to her mother's house where my son was staying so I could see him. When we got to her mama house, man her mother was'ah trip."

Dino said, "man just tell me what happened and quit beating around the bush."

"Okay, so after I meet her mother, her mother tells me that I was welcome to stop by her house anytime, so I was on my way out here today to catch up with you, but I decided to stop by Paula's mama house first so she could watch my son while I take care of this business, so when I got to her house she needed a lift to the liquor store. I ended up paying for the liquor out of the kindness of my heart since that's my son grandma. So I bought her a half gallon Cognac and drove her back to her house. She asked me to stay and have'ah drink with her. Mannn we got to drinking and the next thing I knew we was doing the grown-ups, fucking like mad minks, man I tore that pussy up; and to top that off lil-broh, I even boned'er in the ass."

Dino smiled saying, "you hit that ass too."

"Hell yeah, went up in there too. I know when I get ready to go get my son she gone want me to tap that thang again, and you know me man, I don't turn down no pussy."

Dino laughed saying, "shoot me a game man."

"What we shooting for?" Alvin asked smiling, and pulling out his knot of money. "You know I'm not shooting for my health."

Dino smiled, "you ain't said nothing but'ah word my brother, how bout a hundred

dollars a game."

"Now you talking, wrack man, wrack these bitches," Alvin said smiling.

Dino ended up winning four-hundred dollars from Alvin. Alvin watched Dino sink the eight ball and said, "you're a lucky motha-fucka."

Dino said, "man you know I do this kind of shit almost every day. You know you can't fade me when it comes to shooting pool. You play this shit every blue moon, thanks for the donation."

Alvin smiled, "so you hustled me?"

Dino grinned, "you might can say I played you that time."

"Yeah you did, Forget that though, take'ah ride with me right quick."

"Okay where we going?" Dino asked touching his mustache.

"You'll see when we get there." They walked to the car. "Get in man the door is open."

Alvin pulled off saying, "Look here man, I want you to be the godfather of my son. If anything happen to me I want you to make sure my son is well taken of, cause you the only one I trust in this dope game, and you know I'm dealing with some very powerful peoples."

"Mannnn fuck them people, they fuck with you, they fucking with me and my boys. The Ecorse gangsters gone always back you up one hundred percent, and you know this man. Those Italian motha-fuckas better stay on their side of the road, cause once they cross on my side, they out of place, and believe me, I'm not the one to fuck with!"

Alvin glanced over at Dino. "I'm glad you got'ah heart of steel, that's why I love you man, you too much like me. I know you'll take care business!"

"you got that right my brother. I'm your friend to the end. Now take me to see my god-son. I got to see this lil-warrior."

"You must'uv read my mind. I might as well pick his lil-butt up. His grandma was kind'uv fucked up when I left her good pussy ass."

Dino laughed, "damn man, yoe son might be drunk when we get there."

Alvin laughed, "he might be, I wouldn't bet on it."

Alvin pulled into Sharen's driveway saying, "wait here man I'll be right out."

Alvin knocked on the door. e could hear Sharen saying, "I'm coming, shit."

Sharen opened the door, Alvin said, "I'm back, I came to get the baby."

"Come on in, he back in the back there playing. You can grab'ah seat; you ain't got to leave if you don't want too."

"I got to go, I have one of my partners with me, he sitting in the car."

40

Sharen hollered to the baby, "Stannnn, your daddy here!"

Stan came running out from the back straight into Alvin's arms. Alvin picked him up saying, "give your grandma a kiss. We'll be back soon Sharen."

"Yeahhh you make sure of that."

"Oh you can bank on that, now you have a nice night."

When Alvin got in the car, Dino said, "mannnn I know her. Damn, you'ah smooth nigga, she's bad as hell for her man."

"Yeah, yeah, forget her, this my son, your godson."

"Man this lil-nigga look just like you, I mean just like you, same eyes, and everything. You can't deny this lil-man and that's for sure. What's up lil-fell, I'm your godfather."

As Alvin turned off Bassett Street onto Visger Road, Dino said, "you see that punk walking there, pull up next to'em, I got some business to take up with his wanna be slick ass!"

Alvin's face turned real serious as he asked, "what's up man with this punk?!"

"This nigga owe me about five gee's, and this my first time running into his ass since he booked up with all my shit. Stop the car."

Alvin stopped the car, Dino got out the car shouting, "hay Jay, what's up, long time no see, you got my bread, I hope so for yoe sake. If you don't I'm gone let you eat'ah few of these motha-fuckaz," he pulled out his nine-millimeter and placed the barrel in Jay's mouth. "Nigga you should'nah never ran off with my shit."

41

Alvin could see what was about to go down and quickly got out the car saying, "Dino, don't do it man, it ain't worth it man!"

"I'll kill this bitch ass nigga man."

"This ain't the right time Dino, look at all the people out here, now do you wanna go to jail over this piece of shit, I don't think so, put the gun away man. If you want do it for me, do it for my son, he looking dead at you man, I don't want'em seeing nothing like this man!"

Dino took the gun out of Jay's mouth and said, "God on your side tonight nigga, next time I see yoe trick ass and you don't have my money, you'ah dead man, you understand me nigga?!"

"Yeah man," Jay said trembling.

"Get yoe no good ass out of my face befoe I buss'ah cap in yoe ass!"

When Alvin and Dino got back in the car, Alvin said, "man what's wrong with you, you know it's too many witnesses out there to do that bum!"

"I wasn't gone kill'em. I just wanted to scare the hell out'uv him, that's all!"

Alvin laughed, "I think you did a damn good job of that, not only did you scare the hell out'uv him, you scared the hell out'uv me too. I thought you was about to blow his head off, let me hurry up and drop yoe crazy ass off to your car."

Alvin took Dino straight to his car, where they gave each other a handshake. Dino said, "peace out my brother."

"Yeahhhh tell your mama I said hello and you my brother, you got my address come check me out sometime."

"I'll do that, catch you on the rebound or brother."

Alvin watched Dino get in his car before he pulled off. They both tooted their horns going their own separate ways. Alvin thought to himself as he drove off, "damn you would think with all the money that boy is making now, he would stop driving them damn tagged cars. O'well that's my boy Dino, he ain't gone never change. Let me speed up some so I can get home and wash this pussy smell off my nuts."

When Alvin got in his driveway, he said, "wake up son, we home."

Alvin put Stan in the tub and while he played in the bathtub, Alvin decided to call Paula. Shawn answered, "hello."

What's up Bomoski, is Paula in?"

"Hold on a second," he called Paula. "Paula...telephone."

"I got it," Paula said speaking through the receiver, "hello."

"Hi Paula."

"Hi, I knew it was you."

""Oh yeah."

"Where's the baby?"

"I just put'em in the bathtub, and decided to call you while he's busy playing in the water."

"Well I'm glad you called. I was just sitting around here doing nothing. I had called y'all earlier, but y'all wasn't home."

43

"Believe it or not, we were out to your mom's house."

"Oh, and what was she up too, probably the usual, drunk."

"You guessed it. I see you know your mother," Alvin said smiling.

"That I do, that's all she knows how to do too, drink, drink, drink."

Alvin laughed, "I wouldn't say all that now," he thought. "She sure in hell knows how to screw."

"Hold on Paula, I think your son calling me; as a matter of fact he is. I'll just call you back tomorrow okay."

"Okay, talk to you later, give the baby a hug for me okay."

After Alvin dried Stan off, he put him in the bed, and said, "daddy will be right back lil-man. I got to get me'ah shower so I can smell good too."

Alvin got in the shower and started singing one of his favorite songs by Marvin Gaye (Trouble Man.) And while he was humming the song he thought. "I can't wait to see my son get old enough to stay home by himself. He needs him a good woman when he reaches my age; a woman he can depend on to be there when the going gets tough. A woman with'ah education, and most of all, drug free. He'll find'ah woman who's right for him. Ain't no woman out there right now for me; if it is I'll be glad when she shows her face. I know my son gone be a heartbreaker to the girlies."

Alvin dried off and went and laid down next to his son, and fail straight to sleep.

Chapter VIII

Friday, June 1, 1977 1:00 P.M.

Three years later a riot broke out in Detroit, the riot lasted seven days. No one was allowed to hang outside after seven o'clock. Many people were killed trying to protect their businesses; and lots of people who owned stores lost their stores due to people setting fires. Most of the people who lost their stores didn't have insurance on their property, and couldn't afford to rebuild. This wasn't a lost to Alvin at all, he knew people sell their property to him for a little of nothing just to avoid a total lost; so they jumped on the first reasonable offer for their property.

Alvin didn't waste any time, he wanted to own Visger Road, and everything on the strip. Alvin got with different owners and bought them out. He turned buildings into clothing stores, liquor stores, and a few markets.

Alvin's name started ringing all over Detroit because everything that was sellable in River Rouge, Michigan, and Ecorse, Michigan, he bought it!

The I.S.S had started closing in on Alvin, but somehow he got cool with one of the workers, slipping him a pay here and there to keep them off his back until he turned legit.

Alvin turned strictly into a one man business man, even owned his own car lot on every side of Detroit. The police stayed on his back, but couldn't figure out a way to bust this self-made billionaire. They even knew he was part of one of the biggest drug mobs in America. Alvin had become the biggest drug pusher in America since Amos Nitty.

Amos Nitty just disappeared into thin air it seemed to everyone, but police believe Alvin Stone may have had Amos body cut up into dog food.

Alvin was untouchable, always dressed sharp from head to feet, loved himself some alligator shoes, and long length leather coats, but he loved nothing more than he loved his six-year-old son Stan!

Alvin was always taking his son to baseball games, skating, and their favorite spot together was go kart racing.

Paula and Gena were always high on cocaine when Alvin would take Stan to visit. Alvin knew they were getting high, but dared to tell Bomoski about his wife uncontrollable desire to do drugs. Alvin always said to himself over and over again, "if Bomoski is that blind where he don't know, then he don't need to know."

Paula had started losing her figure, and Gena wasn't far from losing hers too. Alvin had gotten to the point he couldn't stand to be around Paula nor Gena; nor did he want his son around them. He often said to himself, "I'm so damn glad my son ain't around that slut mother of his, bitches like her and Gena need to be put to death. They don't give'ah damn about themselves anyway. I can't stand a dope fiend, hopefully one day Shawn will wake up and smell the coffee, and get rid of both them no good hoes. I feel sorry for Antonio, he's four now. I wish he was my son. It's a shame he got to grow up around two dope fiends, and a stepfather that's too blind to see that his wife is strung out on that shit!"

Wednesday December 30, 1977 12:30 P.M.

It had been months since Alvin had taken Stan out to Shawn's house to play with Antonio. Shawn called out to Alvin's house to ask him over for a little while. Alvin accepted Shawn's invitation. "I'll be out there about three Bomoski."

"Good, we have to talk, I'll see you when you get here," Shawn said.

Two-hours later Alvin and Stan were walking through Shawn's front door. Antonio was happy to see Stan; having not seen him in months was unusual for the both of them.

Stan smiled saying, "let's go play in our secret hiding place."

Alvin and Shawn could never find them in their secret hiding place no matter how hard they searched for them. Alvin and Shawn would just give up looking for them. Antonio and Stan would come upstairs laughing and playing, and Shawn and Alvin would ask. "Where was y'all hiding, we looked everywhere for y'all," Alvin asked.

Stan said, "we got'ah secret hiding place downstairs where nobody can find us."

Alvin smiled, "oh yeah, I remember when I used to have a secret hiding place when I was a kid, but everybody knew where it was."

Stan and Antonio acted like they didn't even hear the words Alvin spoke, and ran back downstairs to finish playing.

Shawn said, "o well, they didn't fall for that line, I guess we'll never know their lil-secret hideout."

"Yeahhh I guess you're right. Now what did you have o talk to me about?"

"Has Gena and Paula been acting strange to you lately?"

"Nope not at all, is that what you called me way out there for? Have they been acting strange to you?"

"They really ain't been the same since the fourth of July. I believe they drinking themselves to death. You know how it is when you use to do drugs."

"N'all man I can't say I do, I ain't never been on drugs before. Maybe they using the liquor to substitute for the drug habit they use to have."

"You know Alvin, that's exactly what I was trying to say to you. Enough about them two, look at you man, I have brought you a long way Stone."

"If you don't mind me saying, I brought myself a long way, and I'm still climbing the ladder. I will admit, you did play a big part in my success, and if I never told you before, thanks man, I appreciated everything you done for me. I'll never where I came from if that's what you thinking. If you ever need me for anything you know I'll be there for you, and I do mean anything. Oh yeah, one more thing before I forget, I got my own private jet now, and that reminds me, Sorcerer want me to fly down there this weekend."

"Oh yeah, I talked to Sorcerer the other day, he didn't say anything to me about you coming that way."

Alvin smiled, "I guess he trust in me enough to let me come down to visit on my own. He knows I'm the man here in the States, and can't nobody touch me now!" Alvin thought to himself, "not even you."

"So where is Gena and Paula?"

"They went shopping."

Alvin thought to himself, "yeahhhh I bet they did, probably for some more dope. I bet them two bitches don't have no shopping bag in their hands when they walk through the front door."

Before Alvin could get his next question out, Gena and Paula came walking through the door empty-handed just as Alvin had predicted. Alvin said to himself, "I knew it, I bet they're full of dope."

Paula smiled, "where's my son?"

Alvin said, "he's downstairs playing with Antonio."

Paula sighed, "so Alvin, what you been up too, we ain't seen yoe face out this way in awhile?"

"I ain't been up to nothing, just taking care of my son, that's all."

Paula felt a ray of guilt run through her heart as the words Alvin spoke registered in her mind. "My son," thinking to herself. "He's right, I've never been there for my own child, I can't argue with him about that comment he made about my son!"

"So Paula, what you been up too lately?" Alvin asked smiling.

"Nothing at all, just hanging on."

Alvin thought, "yeahhh you keep on doing that dope you want be hanging around too long."

Gena said, "come on girl let's go downstairs and see what the kids doing."

Alvin smiled, "I bet y'all two hundred dollars a piece y'all can't find them."

When Gena and Paula got downstairs they didn't see the boys nowhere in sight so they started calling out for them, but Stan and Antonio didn't respond as usual. Alvin and Shawn could hear them calling for the boys, and the more they called the boys, the more Alvin and Shawn laughed.

Alvin said, "I told you they wasn't gone find them, they in that damn secret hiding place."

After Gena and Paula had given up the search, they came on back upstairs. The boys came running up the stairs into the kitchen where Gena and Paula sat talking. Antonio said, "mama we hungry."

Gena said, "I know, where were you two at, we looked everywhere down there for y'all."

Stan said, "in our secret hideout place."

Gena smiled, "in y'all secret hideout. Well you two deserve a sandwich for us not being able to find y'all."

Shawn and Alvin sat in the living room discussing where they should build a skating rink.

Alvin said, "I need'ah drink, maybe that'll help me think a little better on where we could build this skating rink."

"You know where everything's at, help yourself, and while you at it fix me one too."

After Gena and Paula were done making the kids sandwiches, they eased upstairs one at a time, trying hard not to be seen, but Alvin was up on what they were trying to do. Alvin just smiled and said to Shawn, "Shawn, my man, I hate to runoff, but I got to make some more stops before it get to late."

"Damn man, you just got here, you leaving already?"

"Yeah man, I got to take care this business today," Alvin thought to himself, "I can't be around no drug addicts. I got to get the hell out'uv here. The fiends upstairs getting high. I know the score, my son ain't gone be around this kind of shit!"

Alvin handed Shawn his drink, and then chugged his down, and called for Stan. "Let's ride son, let me call yoe mama down so you can say goodbye, "Alvin yelled upstairs for Paula. "Paula… your son wants you."

"Okay, I'll be right down," she yelled out, wiping her nose.

Paula came downstairs and kissed her son on the lips saying, "you be good."

Alvin shook his head saying, "we'll see you good folks later, say goodbye to everybody son."

Shawn said, "don't stay away so long the next time."

"I won't, you take it easy, I'll be sure to tell Sorcerer you said hello."

"You do that, I'll call you when I think you made it home, drive careful, it's slippery out there."

Friday Jan 1, 1978 8:00 A.M.

Alvin arrived in Columbia around eight in the morning. Sorcerer had his limousine already at the airport waiting to bring Alvin and Stan to his home.

Alvin had no idea Sorcerer was in the limousine waiting on him until he heard. "Good morning Mr. Stone, how was your flight."

"it was okay I know you are wondering who this lil-fella is? This is my son, couldn't find'ah babysitter."

Sorcerer smiled, "I understand, well what I got in mind want take long to say. Alvin you have become a very wealthy man in your country, and I want beat around the bush, I think it's time you started branching out!"

"What you mean branching out?"

"I mean it's time to build in places like Chicago, Cleveland, and a thousand more places like that. I mean when I look at my map. I see that these places are right next door to you, and I think a man with your brain can pull off anything. Running other states shouldn't be difficult to do with the man power you have in the states!"

"I need some time to think about that!"

"I'm sure you will make the right decision Stone, because you are a smart man, and a smart man makes smart decisions!"

"What you say is very true, but I always size my opponent up first before I attack."

"And I'm quite sure you always come out a winner some type of way. Look Stone, you can become the richest black man to ever live if you do things my way!"

52

"I don't doubt that at all, but do allow me time to think matters over." Alvin started thinking, "damn, I don't like motha fuckaz making up my mind for me."

"Well Alvin, I'm sure you will find my way the best way, because without me, business in America would come to an end, and that's a matter of fact!"

"What exactly you mean by that?"

"It means if I wanted too, I could replace you at anytime. Now you think on that for a minute while you're making up your mind!"

Alvin smirked, "if I didn't know better. I would think you were threatening me!"

"No, no my friend, that's not a threat, that's a promise. Enough of the bullshit, the bottom line is you gone branch out or make damn good sure your son is in your will. I hope I make myself clear. It's been a pleasure talking with you. Do have a safe flight back to America!"

Alvin could tell by the expression on Sorcerer's face that Sorcerer meant all that he said to him. When Alvin got back on his plane he said to his pilot, "fly me to Chicago, I have a cousin there, he'll work for me."

Alvin's pilot said, "Chicago here we come."

As the jet got in the air, Alvin's mind went into a deep thought. "Sorcerer don't know me at all. I will smoke his ass in a heartbeat. Threatening me too, ma that's definitely a no-no. I don't need no drama right now; things are going to well for me. Besides, Sorcerer is the man with all the suppliers!"

Chicago 1:00 P.M.

When Alvin got to Chicago he used the payphone at the airport to call his cousin Pig. "Hello," the voice on the other end said.

"Yes, is Pig home?"

"Yeah this Pig."

"What's up boyyy, this yoe cousin Alvin," he said smiling.

"You bullshitting, man what's up. Damn it's good to hear yoe voice. I ain't talk to you in years," he said smiling.

"I need to talk to you man, I'm in Chicago at the metro airport."

"Don't say another word, I'm on my way, don't disappear."

Twenty-minutes later, Pig was walking through the airport looking for his cousin. Alvin spotted him, and called out, "hay Pig!"

Pig couldn't believe his eyes. He wasn't used to seeing Alvin dressed in mink coats, and alligator shoes. "Damn couz, is that you?" Pig asked smiling.

Alvin smiled, "yeahhh baby, this me, give me some love nigga," they hugged. "Come with me man, I got somebody I want you to meet, he over in that chair sleep. I guess the TV was too much for his butt, wake up boy, Pit this is my son, yoe cousin."

Pig smiled, "what's up lil-man, boy you look just like yoe daddy."

Alvin said, "dig man, I'm here to talk business with you!"

"Oh yeah, what kind'uv business."

"We'll talk, but first let's have lunch while we're eating I can fill you in on what I need you to do for me."

"That sound good to me, I know if you got something to do with whatever, money is certainly involved."

"You know I do," he said smiling. "Come on I'll take you and lil-cous where they serve the best food in chi-town."

"Cool, me and my son don't eat swine. The only pig I like is my cousin."

"Don't worry man, I don't eat pork either," Pig said smiling.

Pig took Alvin to a nearby restaurant called Pig Mama's Grill on the south side of Chicago. They ate in the no smoking area being that either one smoked. Alvin ordered his and Stan food, and told Pig, "order what you want man. Look couz, I won't waste your time, I need your help couz, and I'm telling you couz, you can get rich real quick messing with me man!"

"Damn couz, I like yoe kind'uv talk you know I love myself some green-back."

"You know I know," Alvin said with a long grin on his face, "we're first cousins, and you know I know you love yoself some money. I want you to hear me out. Here's the deal, I'll supply with all the dope you need to take over Chicago, and I guarantee you that you'll never ever want for nothing else in life. And besides man, I know you tired of fuck'n with them dime and nickel ass jobs. I know you have the smarts for this man, you can take over Chicago. You got my blood in you couz, ain't nothing you can't do. What I'm gone do for you first is to let you know I'm not bull-shitting is this here. I'm gone give you a half million dollars worth of yae-o, pure, untouched dope for free my cousin, and the only thing that I ask you to do for that dope is to cop from me, and me only. You see Pig, the people I'm dealing with have so much of that shit, but they don't know how to get rid of it, and that's where you and me come in at. A few more men like you and me, and we gone run this world. You hear me man, we gone run this motha-fucka!"

"How quick can you get me the shit?!"

"As quick as you can drive me back to my jet, and I did say, my jet!"

"You brought the stuff with you?"

"Yepp, sure did, it's on my private jet, just'ah waiting on you to come get it."

"Man…. You mean to tell me your own your own jet?"

"Not one jet Pig, I own two jets, and you can own yoe own jet too man once you start doing business with me. Now do you know how the law operates around here?!"

"Don't worry about the law man. If you can supply me like you say you can, I want have no problem with the law!"

"Ain't no "if" to this Pig. I'm gone supply you with the dope, and I'm gone supply you with it today. That's why I'm here. I'm gone give you a million dollars worth of shit. A half million of it is yours, and the other half is mine. Mannn it's good seeing you again Pig. I'm full as hell, let's ride, we got business to take care of!"

Pig smiled, "that sound good to me, I know a short cut to the airport from here, it won't take us no time to get there, should'uv took it coming here."

Alvin had his pilot to load the dope in Pig's trunk, and as the last package was being put in the trunk, Alvin said, "well couz, here's my word, both of my numbers are on it, feel free to dial me up if you need my help for anything, and I do mean anything. I got to go, I got more business to take care of. It was damn good seeing you again!"

"It was damn good seeing you again too. And teach that boy of yours how to talk. I ain't heard him say over there words yet," Pig said smiling.

"He ain't much of a talker he's an observer, which is better than talking. We out'uv here."

"One more thing Alvin."

"And what's that?"

"That lil-joka looks just like yoe ass."

Alvin smiled, "I know, now gone get rich, we'll be seeing-ya."

After the jet got in the air, Alvin thought to himself, "Sorcerer is right, I do need to branch out. Pig thinks just like me, I know he gone take over Chicago!"

When the jet landed in Detroit, Alvin checked his watch, it read 5:30 P.M.! Stan vomited all down the stairway of the jet as he was getting off the jet.

The pilot said, "damn, he throwing up all over my damn steps!"

Alvin got angry. "Look here man, you don't own'ah jet in this world. I pay you to fly this motha-fucka not to make complaints. Now make sure you clean my steps good. Come on son let me get you home, You feel any better since you throw up?"

57

Stan nodded his head, "yeahhh!"

"Good, that's my boy. Damn lil-man, I'm surprise we ain't got no snow yet."

"I hope it snow daddy."

Alvin smiled, "why you hope it snow?"

"So we can make'ah snowman."

"Yeah that would be fun son, but since we don't have any snow, what would you like to do, you name it, we can do it, okay!"

"Let's go make'ah birdhouse in the backyard."

"We can do that, let's go by the store first. You know what lil-man, I almost forgot today was New Years. I tell you what, how about me taking you to the show, and we can build the birdhouse tomorrow. Don't you wanna go to the show?"

"Yeahhhh."

After the show Alvin went home and called Sorcerer. "Gone run your bathwater son, I'll be up in a minute."

"Hello," Sorcerer answered.

"Yeah this me, Alvin. I flew to Chicago today, and everything went well. I got in touch with my cousin there. He's on our line now!"

"So Stone, how do you know we can trust this cousin of yours?!"

"He has my blood in'em, and besides, it would be my lost!"

"That is where you are wrong Alvin, your lost is our lost, don't you ever forget that!"

"Look man, I know you are a powerful man, but I'm the one taking all the risk. If anything go wrong I'll be the one behind bars, not you, so I would really appreciate if we can start seeing eye to eye. I would hate to have to get out the business!"

"Mr. Stone, you don't quite understand, there is no getting out, once you're in, you're in. Unless you would like to be eliminated from the business, the business way!"

"You mean to tell me if I wanted to get out, I couldn't get out?!"

"That is exactly what I mean. You see Alvin, you know too much bout my business to get out. And besides, you like it too much to wanna get out. So you have a goodnight and one more thing before I hang up."

"What's that?"

"Happy New Year."

Alvin listened to the dial tone come in the phone. He was still upset from the words Sorcerer had spoken. He slammed the phone down, and called out for Stan. "Where you at son?"

"I'm in the tub dad."

"Make sure you wash behind your ears."

Alvin went on upstairs and laid across his bed and fell asleep. After Stan got out the bathtub he passed by his dad's room and noticed his daddy had fall asleep with all his clothes. Stan took Alvin's phone off and turned off his light, and laid beside his daddy, and fell asleep too.

Thursday Jan 28, 1978 9:00 A.M.

Shawn left the house early that morning going jogging, something he loved to do in the winter time.

Gena and Paula was up having a cup of coffee together when Shawn walked out the door saying, "I'll be back in a few."

"Okay honey," Gena said.

"Come on Gena let's do something we ain't did in awhile."

"Girl you ain't said nothing, but a word. Well just don't sit there, undress me if you want some of these goodies," Gena said smiling.

"You lay yoe sexy self on the kitchen table so I can get busy then."

They started kissing and sucking each other all over. The only sounds that could be heard were: "oooooh, yeahh, yess, yess, suck this cunt."

Meanwhile, while Shawn was jogging he tripped over a hole buried in the snow and twisted his ankle, and as he limped home, he said out loud, "damn, how in the hell I miss that big ass hole." And as he continued to limp towards home, one of his neighbors was driving by and offered him a ride.

"Hey Mr. Bomoski, thought that was you. Twisted your ankle huh. Get in I'll drop you off."

Shawn sighed. "Mannn, Mr. Reed you don't know how happy I am to see you, you couldn't-uv come along a better time."

"yeahhh I know how them spranged ankles are. Whelp, you home now. Make sure you soak that ankle in some Epsom salt it works for me."

"Thanks for the ride Mr. Reed!"

"No problem, you have'ah nice day."

Shawn got out the car saying to himself, "damn, I ain't got my key. I hope this damn door ain't locked." He turned the knob. "Good, it's open. Let me get me a hot cup of coffee before I do anything else."

Shawn walked in on Gena and Paula making out. He couldn't believe his eyes and said, "what the fuck is this?!"

"Shawn!" Gena yelled out in shock. "You, you're."

Shawn cut her off, "Don't say shit, yeah I'm back early. What's this shit here? I would take a wild guess and say you two are exploring the hell out of each other company!"

"I'm sorry Shawn, I!" Gena said.

"Shut up Gena, don't say another word. Just answer me this one question, how long this shit been going on under my nose?!"

Paula was too embarrassed to say anything, so Gena said, "every since she's been staying here."

"I kind'uv figured you two was doing some shit like this!"

Deep down in Shawn's mind he'd already known they were having sex with each other, but couldn't prove it until now.

"So this been going on every since she moved in huh?"

"Yeah, but it's not what you think," Gena said buttoning her blouse.

"What the fuck you mean it's not what I think huh? What you take me for Gena ah fool? I come home and find you two sucking each other pussies, and you tell me it's not what I think. Who in the hell you think you talking too

Gena, Antonio? I know what my eyes seen, just get dressed before Antonio come down here!"

Shawn limped over to the refrigerator and Gena said, "what's wrong with your leg?"

"I sprung my foot, what's it to you?"

Shawn looked over at Paula and thought to himself, "damn, Paula body is looking good."

Gena walked over to Shawn and grabbed his dick saying, "Shawn, make love to me right now, I want you." Shawn's cock got brick hard. "Paula would you give me'ah hand with this, it's too much for me to handle."

"Girl… I'll love too."

The two of them undressed Shawn, and gave him the freakiest time of his life. Shawn thought to himself, "damnnn this feel good, I wish I could'uv busted them years ago."

After Shawn burst in Gena's mouth Gena said, "as you can see Shawn, I would do anything for you to make you happy. I love you Shawn, I hate you found out about me and Paula the way you did, and I hope this don't come between us, I don't wanna ever lose you!"

"Don't worry baby, this won't come between what I feel for you, and Paula you are still my wife best-friend, and you are welcome to have a piece of my wife anytime. At least I don't have to worry about her cheating on me with another man."

Paula laughed, "well we all better be getting dressed before lil-Antonio wake up. I'll check on him on my way up to the shower. See you two lovebirds later."

Paula peeked in on Antonio, he was still sound asleep. Shawn and Gena stayed downstairs talking. Shawn said, "I'm a very lucky man, in fact, I'm the luckiest man in the world."

"What makes you say that?"

"Because I have you in my life."

Gena smiled, "I'm glad you feel that way about me Shawn Bomoski. I feel the same way about you!" Gena hugged him, and they kissed. "How does your foot feel?"

"With all the good loving going on baby, I actually forgot I had'ah sprung foot. Oh, before I forget, did I tell you I had Antonio name put on all my inheritance. If anything should happen to me, all of my businesses and money goes to him and to you of course!"

"That's very beautiful of you to think of Antonio in such a way. He has a long way to go before anything happens to you. And besides that, Antonio has a long way to before he's grown."

"Well Gena darling, when he does get old enough and I'm in the ground, he's set for life. I love Antonio, he's like my own son. I would do anything in the world for him!"

"I understand! Shawn, hold me tighter."

Shawn held her gently in his arms and said, "O Gena I almost forgot, I got to call Sorcerer."

"Shawn I wish you and me could have another child, I'm probably trying too hard to get pregnant."

"Gena baby, when it happens, it'll happen, don't worry yourself about that."

The two of them could hear Antonio calling out for Gena. Shawn said, "lucky we wasn't you know what."

Gena laughed, "we're in the kitchen."

Antonio walked in the kitchen saying, "mama I'm hungry."

"Mommy gone feed you right now."

Shawn said, "come here lil-man and talk to your poppa, poppa love you, you love poppa?" Antonio shook his head in a yes motion. "If daddy ever has to go away, I want you to be the man of the house, okay." He nodded yeah. "That's a good lil-man, now gone eat your cereals daddy got to make a phone call."

Shawn limped over to the phone and called Sorcerer. Sorcerer answered the phone. "Hello Sorcerer speaking."

"Yeah, it's me, Shawn."

"Shawn my man, I was just about to call you, but I see you beat me to the punch."

"So what's up with you Sorcerer?"

"Business as usual. You know there's a large shipment coming your way, and I need you to be on tip of things."

"No problem, just tell me when it's coming in and I'll take care the rest."

"It'll be there Saturday. It's not as large as the last shipment."

"Well just how big is it?"

"About two-billion street value."

Shawn had no idea his phone was bugged, and he was under surveillance by the F.B.I! "Don't worry, I'll take care of everything, talk to you later."

"Good day Bomoski, give my love to the family."

Shawn hung up saying, "that's strange, sounded like two people was on the other end of the phone. O'well let me hop my tired ass up these stairs and get me a quick shower."

As Shawn was going up the stairs, Paula was coming down the stairs. Shawn smiled saying, "you were good Paula."

Paula smiled saying, "I know, and just think, it didn't even cost you this time. Really I always wanted to do that with you and Gena."

"What... are you serious?"

"Yepp, every since I heard you stroking Gena that one night in y'all bedroom when I first got here."

Shawn smiled. "I'm flattered to hear that, perhaps the three of us can do it again one day soon."

"Maybe, we'll see," she said smiling.

Shawn just smiled, and thought to himself as he watched her go down stairs. "Damnn that girl got'ah big ass on her."

While Shawn showered, Gena and Paula were downstairs talking. Gena said, "girl you see how easy it is to manipulate a man?"

Paula smiled, "yeahhh girl, now we don't have to pretend anymore, everything, everything is in the opening now. Shawn knows that we are dikes."

"Do you remember what I told you back in the days about Shawn?"

"Nope."

"Well let me refresh your memory, I told you back at the center that I had to do what was necessary to make a life for my son."

"Oh yeah, I do remember you telling me that. So what are you getting at?"

"Don't you get it? You think if I truly loved Shawn I would'uv let what went down earlier happen? Let's be for real!"

"I get the picture now..."

"Fuck Shawn, I just want my son to have a good life, that's the only reason I married his soft ass. Don't get me wrong, I do have some feelings for him, but not in the way he thinks. Where is Antonio?"

"I don't know, but I'm right here."

Gena pulled Paula closer to her and slipped her tongue in Paula's mouth, and when they were done kissing, Gena said, "come on girl, let's watch some tube."

Thursday 10:00 P.M.

66

Alvin was home watching the ten o'clock news, he couldn't believe his ears as he listened to the news spokesman.

"Today in the city of Ecorse, it was learned that the leader of the Ecorse gangsters was shot several times while sitting on the front porch of his home. He is listed in critical condition at the Outer Drive Hospital." Alvin couldn't believe his ears. "Witnesses say four men in a blue Chevy car drove down the one way street and fired several shots at the victim. Still no one is able to identify any of the shooters, leaving once again, no suspects in what appear to be a brutal tragedy. If you have any information as to the shooting, please call 911, I'm Bill signing off for channel seven action news."

Alvin knew there was nothing he could do tonight, but maintain a level head till morning. He began to think. "Who could'uv done this to Dino? Lord don't let'em die. I know his mother is having a fit. I'll see her tomorrow at the hospital."

Alvin sat up half the night watching television until he fell asleep.

Friday Jan 29, 8:00 A.M.

Alvin woke up the next morning and got Stan ready for school, and after he dropped Stan off at school, he drove straight to the hospital to check on Dino.

When Alvin got to Dino's room the first person he saw was Dino's mother. She sat next to the bed shedding tears as she looked at the life support machine connected to her son's throat.

"Hi, Ms. Jones."

"Hi baby, this'ah shame, my baby!"

"He gone be okay Ms. Jones, he's a strong young man!" Tears started to fall from his eyes. "I heard what happened on the news last night. I can't believe this happened, who would wanna hurt Dino?"

"Only God knows son, he'll be all right. I'm putting it in God's hands. I told Dino over and over to leave that gang mess alone, he won't listen to his mother, now look what done happened!"

"You know he love you Ms. Jones. A man will always be a man, he been leading that gang for years, they part of his family. It makes a black man feel like somebody; makes him feel important. Dino is a very strong man, he'll pull through!"

"I pray to God he do Alvin!"

"Did you see what I just saw, his mouth moved. I told you he was gone be all right." Alvin started talking to Dino. "Dino, can you hear me, it's me, your brother Alvin, can you hear me?"

"His mouth moved again, he's trying to say something."

Alvin put his ear to Dino's mouth saying, "talk to me Dino, who did this to you? Do you know who did this to you?" Alvin could hear him trying to say something. "Say it again Dino, who did this to you?"

"Jay."

"Sound like he said Jay Ms. Jones. Jay did this to your son!"

Dino squeezed Alvin's hand as tight as he could, indicating that Alvin was right.

"Do you know this Jay boy that did this to my son?" She asked.

"I believe I do, I got'ah go."

"Alvin don't you go getting into no trouble. I don't want you to end up in here too or maybe even worse than this, let God handle it!"

"You hang in there my brother," Alvin said to Dino. "See you later Ms. Jones I'll be back Dino, I got work to do!"

"Bye son, and do be careful!"

Ms. Jones knew how close Alvin and Dino were to each other, and she knew in her heart that Alvin was going to kill whoever did this to her son.

Alvin drove around in Ecorse looking for any member of Dino's gang, and Chico one of the members recognized Alvin's car and flagged him down. When Alvin pulled over to the curb, Chico said, "do you remember me Alvin, I'm Chico, one of the Ecorse gangsters. I know you here to take care of business."

"You got that right, what you know about the shooters?"

"I don't know nothing, everybody around here is scared to talk."

"It don't matter bout everybody else, I know who shot Dino."

"Who, tell me so we me and my fellaz can take care our business."

"This pussy motha-fucka go by the name Jay."

"Jay, yeah I know that clown, that's who did the shit?"

"Yeah that's who did it, so you know'em."

"Hell yeah I know'em, him and Dino had'ah beef with each other over some dope."

"Yeahhh he's definitely the nigga I'm talking about. How can I catch up with this nigga?"

"You don't have to, let me and the gangsters handle this one. You can rest at ease now Jay is one dead motha-fucka, and you can bank on that!"

"You need me to do anything?"

"Nothing at all, you just let me handle this okay. Damn I'm glad I ran into you. When you go see Dino, you can tell'em Chico the lieutenant got everything under control. Halloween is tonight if you know what I mean."

Alvin smiled, "you be cool lil-bro and be sure to be careful. Here's my card, call me if you need me, I'll be around."

Alvin knew in his mind that Chico had a heart of steel from working him before on a job they did together on the first precinct.

Chico went straight home and called all the gangsters over for a meeting at four o'clock. Chico knew all Jay's hangouts, and Jay didn't have a clue that Dino was still alive.

Alvin decided since he was in the old neighborhood he'd stop by and check on Sharon. Alvin pulled into her driveway. The next door neighbor yelled out from his built in porch, "she left about ten minutes ago."

"Thank you sir, if you see'er tell her Alvin Stone was by. You have a nice day."

"You too."

Alvin backed out the driveway, saying to himself, "o well, guess I'll go by Homespun Restaurant and grab some of Mr. Jones chili."

70

As soon as Alvin stepped foot in the restaurant, Mr. Joe said, "well, well look what the wind done blew in here."

Alvin smiled, "yeahhh how bout fixing me a bowl of that good oh chili. Mr. Joe when you gone sell me this place?"

"Can't do it son, this place is all I got left, ain't much, but it's mine."

"Yeahhh and you got plenty of business too. Well I wouldn't sell either if I was making yoe kind'uv money."

"Here's your chili son, enjoy it, it's on the house."

"Thank you Mr. Joe!"

After Alvin finished his chili off, he wiped his mouth, and left a twenty dollar tip on the table saying, "well..... Mr. Joe that was the best chili I ever tasted. I got to get going, got to stop by Outer Drive Hospital and check on a friend of mine."

"Do I know this friend of yours?"

"You might, his name is Dino?"

"You not talking about the Dino on Ninth Street are you?"

"Yeah that's the one."

"What's wrong with him son?"

"You mean to tell me you ain't hear about the shooting on Ninth Street yesterday, it was all on the news."

"Lord no, I was in Chicago yesterday. I just got back this morning. You mean to tell me somebody shot Dino. How's his condition son?"

"The doctor says he'll live. Well Mr. Joe it was nice seeing you again. I'll be back soon for some more of that good chili, and maybe some of that beef stew too. I'll bring my son with me next time so you can meet'em."

"Boy you mean to tell me you got a son now, damn, it really has been a long time ain't it."

"Yes it has, he's almost eight years old. I'll bring'em by one day and let you see'em."

"I'll be looking forward to that, you have a good day son, and give my blessing to Dino!"

"I sure will."

Mr. Joe watched Alvin leave out and said to himself, "now there goes a good man." He smiled picking up the tip.

When Alvin got back to Dino, Dino was looking much better to Alvin than he did earlier. Alvin held Dino's hand saying, "everything is take care of. We gone get that sucka for you man, your boy Chico is on top of everything. You just hang in there, you'll be on your feet in no time. I love you man, I can't lose you, you my ace man. I got to leave right now, got to pick your godson up, I'll be back to see you man!"

The doctor told Alvin that Dino had slipped into a coma. Deep in Alvin's heart he didn't think that Dino would pull through. Tears rolled down Alvin's face as he said, "God, help my brother, God bless you Dino!"

Alvin was a few minutes late picking Stan up from school. "Sorry I'm late lil-man, I got stuck in traffic."

"Dad can I spend the night over my grandma house?"

"Sure can, let's go by the house first and get you some clothes to wear."

"We ain't got no school Monday daddy, here's the letter."

Alvin read the letter. "Y'all ain't got to go back to school till a week from now, y'all on y'all winter break. You can spend your winter break out to your grandmother house, that'll give me'ah chance to take care some of my business. What you want to eat lil-man?"

"I ain't hungry."

"Me neither, I just got finished eating me a big bowl of chili."

When Alvin got home he called Sharen. "Hey Sharen, it's me, Alvin."

"Hi, Alvin."

"Yeah I had stopped by earlier, but you wasn't home."

"I know, Ike told me, he's the man you talked too, he watches my house when I ain't here."

"That's good, well the reason I called you, your grandson want to spend some time with you. He's out of school for his winter break."

"You ain't got to say another word, bring'em on out I'll be here, and when you come."

Alvin cut her off, "let me guess, bring you something to drink."

"Damn you good and a pack of Newports please. I'll see you two when y'all get here."

"Okay we on our way," Alvin hung up. "Get your stuff packed man, you out'uv here. Make sure you get enough clothes to last you a week."

73

Alvin drove straight to the liquor store, and when he got to Sharen's house he said to her, "I would love to stay and chat with you, but I got'ah lot of things I got to do today. One of my friends is laying in the hospital in a coma, he got shot'up yesterday!"

"I'm sorry to hear that."

"Yeahhh, well I'll be back to get him next week, unless something else come up and I can't make it. I doubt it though. You take care. Come here son and give me a hug before I go. You too big for me to be kissing on now. You be good man, daddy will see you later. Take care your grandmother."

Sharen smiled. "Alvin you be careful out there and thanks for the drink."

"No problem, I'll see you later."

Alvin drove back to the hospital to check on Dino, and when he got there he found the doctor checking Dino's heartbeat.

The doctor smiled saying, "how are you feeling today young man?"

"I'm fine doc, how's my brother doing?"

"He's the same; he has a very strong heartbeat. I'm sure he'll pull through this in a matter of time."

"I'll take your word on that doc. Doc would you do me a little favor, take my card please. Give me a call or a beep if there's any change in him."

"I'll do just that son. You go home and get you some rest."

Alvin drove straight to the Hip-Hop Lounge and when he got inside he ordered a mug of beer.

Hours passed by, and Alvin's beeper started vibrating. He checked the number on it and said, "damn, I wonder who this could be? This must be the doctor calling."

Alvin dialed the number, and the voice on the other end says, "Doctor Fisher's Office."

"Doctor Fisher this is Alvin, the young man at the hospital earlier with his brother."

"Oh yeahhhh, well I have some good news for you, your brother has come back."

"Are you serious?" Alvin asked in disbelief, and smiling at the same time.

"Of course I'm serious, why don't you come see'em now, he been asking for you and his mother."

"I'm on my way doc."

When Alvin got to Dino's room he smiled saying, "what's up lil-brother?"

Dino said, "ah little dizzy, but I'm still here."

"I'm glad you pulled through man. I thought you wasn't gone make it there for a minute lil-broh. And what lil situation is being taken care of!"

"I want that bitch dead!"

"Don't say another word my brother your lieutenant got all that under control. Chico told me to tell you that."

"Yeah that's my boy, he the lieutenant of the gangsters."

Alvin smiled, "you make sure you watch the news tonight, and if it don't go down as planned tonight, I'll handle it myself tomorrow, but I'm quite sure Chico handle it!"

"Oh he can, that's why he the lieutenant."

When you hurt man, I hurt, and your mother is a very strong queen. I got to give her that much; the average woman would'uv been on broke down, but not yoe mama, she still going strong."

"Yeahhh I love that old lady too death. I wanna get her a house in the suburbs, but you know mama, she refuses to leave Ecorse."

"Well know how that go, she been in Ecorse all her life, Ninth Street is all she know; you or nobody else can talk her into leaving her home in Ecorse."

"Yeahhh you're right, I wish you wasn't, but you are."

"Well my man, it's time for me to ride." Alvin pulled on one of Dino's tubes coming from his arm. "Enjoy your meal."

"You welcome to have some."

Alvin laughed, "I don't think so, I'm on my way down to Mr. Joe's place an order me'ah broiled steak."

"Don't tease me like that man."

"I would kiss you goodbye, but you know me man," he said smiling.

Dino smiled, "get out'uv here man."

"I'll see you tomorrow man, and don't you eat too much."

Dino smiled as he watched Alvin walk away. Alvin felt relieved knowing Dino was going to be all right. After Alvin had eaten dinner at Mr. Joe's, he decided to drive to his favorite bar J.R. Lounge.

Alvin sat the bar ordering Budweiser after Budweiser celebrating Dino's recovery.

Two men walked pass Alvin, and one of the men bumped into Alvin's seat, and that bump caused Alvin to spill his beer on his lap. The man kept walking until Alvin said, "hey my man, its'ah word for what you just did!"

"You talking too me?" The man asked.

"Yeah, its'ah word for what you did."

"Yeah, you exactly right, it is'ah word for what I just did, and it's called fuck you!"

"Look man I'm not looking for no smoke, all I want is a simple apology for you making me spill my drink."

"Nigga fuck you!"

Alvin gripped his Budweiser bottle saying, "o that's how you feel about the situation?!"

The bartender said, "ohhh shit," as he saw Alvin hand grip the bottle hitting the man in the head.

The man's head started bleeding instantly as Alvin threw blow after blow to his head. The man's friend ran up and hit Alvin from the back with a barstool. Alvin fell across the table in front of him. The man was about to strike Alvin again, but the bartender fired a shot in the air from his shotgun, and said, "it was all good when it was one on one, but two on one in my place is a no-no. Now back up off'em and get the hell out my place before y'all find y'all selves being chalked!"

The men left out saying, "yeah nigga we'll see you again."

Alvin smiled, "I hope so! Thanks for the hand JR."

"Yeah man, anytime, you one of my favorite customers, you do spend money when you come in my place. Them two bums sit around on one drink all night, and start plenty shit. I knew you wasn't buying it; they beat'ah man damn near too death just last week in here. If it would'uv been for Jake they would'uv killed the poor fella in here."

"Well if I run into them on the outside you won't have to worry about them two no more. I'll have them two punks head sent to their mammies in a cardboard box. If there's one thing I hate, it's a bully, I can't stand that!"

"I couldn't disagree if I wanted too, I hate'ah bully too."

"I guess I'll take my butt on home now, I'm kind'uv tired. That lil work out there did me in," he said smiling. "

Alvin put a twenty dollar tip on the bar saying, "you take care JR."

"Take it easy Alvin, and do drive careful. Watch your back!"

Alvin got in his car and turned the radio station to WJZZ and listened to the Jazz. And as he drove he thought about when him and Dino use to be kids, how they couldn't talk to grownups without saying yes sir and no ma-am. Alvin smiled at the different old thoughts that entered his mind back in his childhood days. His mind traveled all the way back to the time his daddy caught him peeing out the backdoor into the snow. He could hear his daddy cursing him out. "Boy that ain't no damn bathroom, you wanna pee in something, pee in something that's yours, piss in your pants, shit you don't own them either. Hell piss on yourself anyway, but don't be pissing out my backdoor. Now get your lil ass out my face before I kill'ya." Alvin laughed, shaking his head to the beat of the music, and saying, "I miss you dad. Life is short; I hope I don't have to go through that with my son."

When Alvin got inside his house he said, "dammn my back hurt, that nigga knocked the hell out of me with that stool, lucky it wasn't my head. I better take me'ah couple-uv aspirins for this pain."

Alvin turned the television on and kicked back on the couch, waiting patiently for the news to come on.

Chico and six of his men loaded up in a red 1977 van that Chico had gotten from a friend of his across town. Chico knew no one would recognize the van in their neighborhood. Chico drove straight to Jay's hangout, which was at the pool hall on 11th Street and Visger Road.

Chico parked saying, "well my brothers we're here. Everybody know what to do, we doing this for Dino, we don't wanna leave a soul living. Anything breathing in there got to die. I'm gone pull up to the front door, y'all ready? Put y'all mask on, let's do this shit!"

They put their Halloween masks on and burst through the pool hall door. Chico yelled out, "y'all know what time it is!"

The rack man said, "what's this shit?"

"Your death wish," Chico said tuning his oozie machine gun loose, shooting the rack man in his chest numerous times.

Jay was at the opposite end of the pool room looking at what had just happened to the rack man. Chico looked at Jay saying, "Jay tonight ain't yoe night gangsters, handle y'all business!"

The Ecorse gangsters started opening firing on everything moving in the pool room, killing all, but one woman until one of the members said, "what about this bitch here?"

Chico said, "is she breathing?!"

All of them pointed their guns at the woman and cut loose on her shivering body, killing her instantly.

Chico said, "now blow this mothafucka up!"

The last two men coming out of the pool room threw two grenades in the pool hall, and quickly ran out to the van. Within seconds the pool hall went up in flames. After the explosion Chico drove off saying, "hell yeah, that's what I'm talking about, good damn job. Always remember this fellas, no witnesses, no jail. Remember that, now we can rest in peace, our mission is completed. All we got'ah do now is dump this van and guns in the river. Y'all already know, never ever do we keep murder weapons after we do'ah job."

Chico dumped everything they had in the Detroit River and got in another van that was parked a block away from where they dumped the red van. Chico drove everybody back to where they all met up, and he gave order for them not to say a word about today, and they all made their hand sign as to being in agreement with what Chico ordered.

Alvin was still at home in front of the television sound asleep. Dino also had his television on back at the hospital, but the news didn't have a story about the pool hall, so Dino turned the television off and went to sleep knowing that his men would never let him down.

Saturday, Jan 30, 1978, 11:00 A.M.

The next day Alvin took a quick shower and headed up to the hospital to see Dino. When Alvin got to the hospital he found Dino in his room watching television and said, "what's up boy, how you feelings?"

"I feel all right, pull up a chair my brother. The news is talking about what went down at the pool hall."

Alvin and Dino listened closely as the newscaster said, "I'm standing here today at a spot that once was known as the neighborhood pool hall. So far the fire department has managed to come up with eleven dead bodies. There is still no identity to any of the brutally burnt bodies. Police believe this tragedy was drug related, and the killings were done by gang members. There are no suspects as to these killings yet. Police are doing a full investigation; we'll have more on the killings later on, on our six o'clock news. I'm Val Clark, signing off for channel 9 news."

Alvin looked at Dino and said, "hell yeah, yoe boys took care of business, I like that."

"Chico ain't no joke. I knew he was gone handle that," Dino said smiling. "We all brothers Alvin, if one is in trouble, we all in trouble, that's the way it is with the Ecorse gangsters, and that's the way it's gone always be. We all got to stick together man no matter what big brother!"

"you definitely my lil-brother and you definitely right. I like your style man, that's why I'm here with you now, show you that I care about you man. I'm gone visit everyday till you get yoe crazy ass back on your feets."

"You all right with me Alvin Stone. I'll do anything in my powers to help you my brother, and you know this!"

"I feel the same way about you lil-brother. Have your mother been up here today?"

Dino could see his mother coming through the door, and started smiling. "You talked her up, turn around."

Alvin turned and Ms. Jones smiled saying, "what you two up too?"

Alvin smiled, "hi Ms. Jones, I was just asking about you."

"Well... mama here now." She kissed Alvin o the jaw and did the same for Dino. "How's my little pootsie wootsie?"

Dino smiled saying, "mama... I'm a grown man now, you ain't got to pootsie wootsie me no moe."

"O boy please, you just don't want Alvin to know you're a big baby, mommy understand. Alvin knows you my big baby, don't you Alvin?"

"Yepp," Alvin said laughing.

Dino said, "mannn get out'uv here. I'm not no baby. Mama did you hear about what happened to the pool hall?"

"No she answered. "It burned down."

"Lord no!" She said in disbelief.

Alvin said, "yeppp, it was just on the news a minute ago."

"Did anybody get hurt?" She asked.

"Yeah about eleven people," Alvin answered.

"That's a shame, what is the world coming too. People dying every day in fires and shootouts, I thank God for letting you live through this Dino," tears started running down her face.

Alvin and put his arm around her saying, "everything gone be all right Ms. Jones!"

Dino said, "Mama please don't start that crying, you make me wanna cry."

"I just can't help it. I already lost one son in a shooting, and this happen to you. Lord knows I just don't know what to do anymore. I pray for you children day and night, but y'all still don't wanna listen to me. I try to get y'all to come to church with me on Sunday, but y'all don't want that. I hope this'll open up y'all eyes!"

"I'm fix'n to go get me something to eat, would you like to join me for lunch Ms. Jones?" Dino asked smiling.

"I would love to Alvin, but I just ate, thank you anyway."

"Well Dino my man I'll catch up with you later on today."

Dino know in his mind that Alvin was getting away from his mother preaching, and said, "okay man, see you later on."

Alvin gave Ms. Jones a kiss on the cheek saying, "I'll see you later, you have a nice day."

"You too. Be careful out there son, and please don't get into no trouble."

"I won't," Alvin said walking out."

When Alvin got to his car he said, "I'll be damned, a damn ticket. I didn't know this was'ah handicapped spot. O'well I'll pay the ticket whenever. Now today is Saturday, where can I go? I wonder do that white girl still stay where I dropped her off that night. She should be glad to see me; after all I did save'er life. I believe her name is Lora if I'm not mistaken. I know she stay on Maple Street. I'll drive by there real quick and see if she remembers me."

Ten minutes later, Alvin was in front of Lora's house blowing his horn. Lora peeped out her living room window and said to herself, "who could that be?"

Alvin saw the curtains move, and said, "she's home. Let me get out the ca maybe she'll recognize me."

As soon as Alvin stepped out the car Lora recognized him, and said to herself, "o my God, that's Alvin." She quickly opened the door. "Long time no see, come on in," she said smiling.

As Alvin started walking towards the house, she said to herself, "dammn that's a sharp fine ass black man." Alvin got to the front porch. "Gosh, I thought I would never see you again, I'll never forget your name, Alvin Stone, I'll never

84

forget you." Alvin walked in her house. "Have'ah seat, and where you been hiding yourself Alvin?"

"Well I've been around. I was in the neighborhood and said to myself, let me see if Lora still stay on Maple Street, and you do, so here I am visiting you."

"I'll never forget what you did for me that night."

"I'm just glad I came along when I did," he said smiling.

"Not as glad as me," she said smiling. "Would you like something to drink?"

"Do you have any beer?"

"Yeah I only have Budweiser."

"Shood that's my favorite."

"Mines too, I'll grab us one. What are you doing so sharp?"

"Oh this ain't anything, it's a habit. I dress like this every day."

Lora got the beers and came and sat down next to Alvin saying, "just how long has it been since that incident?"

"Who cares baby, as long as you okay."

"I was just about to make lunch, are you hungry?" She asked smiling.

"Believe it or not that's where I was headed before I thought about you."

"Do you like corn beef?"

"Are you kidding, do I like corn beef, that's one of my favorites."

"That's good, we can lunch together then. You can come in the kitchen with me if you like."

"So tell me, are you still taking the bus?" He said smiling.

"No way, I followed your advice and bought a car two days later."

"That was a good move for you. And before I say anything else, you looking beautiful today yourself. I love a woman in a skirt; it looks real nice on you, even though I believe you would look good in anything you wear. You are a very attractive woman Lora!"

"Why thank you," she said smiling.

"I'm only speaking the truth, you don't have to thank me."

Lora smiled, "I'll be honest with you, when I saw you walking towards my house from your car I said to myself, damn that's a fine black man."

"I'm glad I stopped by."

"Me too," she said smiling.

When they were done eating, they went to the living room and watched television, and as they watched television Lora said, "would you like to see a tape or you just gonna watch regular television? I have a couple-uv good drama and romance movies. I even have a few triple-x movies."

Alvin smiled. "Now you saying something, throw on one of them triple x movies."

"How about deep throat?"

"It don't matter baby."

As the tape started playing, Lora said, "you can take your shoes off if you like."

Alvin took off his shoes and gazed into the television set, his penis brick hard. Lora's pussy started heating up; her legs rocked back and forth to the sound of the screwing on the video. Alvin knew this was the perfect time to say what was on his mind.

"Why don't you come a little closer to me, I'm not gone bite you."

Lora smiled and slid closer. Alvin placed his arm around her shoulders running his hand up and down her hair. Lora placed one of her hands on Alvin's thigh, and worked it slowly to his penis until she touched it. Alvin started kissing her on her neck, and working his way to her lips.

Lora pulled away saying, "make love to me Alvin."

They made love on the couch until Alvin had finally burst his second nut. Alvin laid back thinking to himself, "I got this girl!"

"You don't have to leave, you can stay the night with me if you like."

"I got a better idea, we can spend the rest of the day together shopping and you can spend the night at my place if you don't mind?"

"I don't have a problem with that."

"Good, don't bother getting a change of clothes. I'm gone buy you something pretty to wear for me."

Alvin and Lora jumped in the shower together and Alvin thought, "damn for the first time in my life, I think I'm actually in love. I can tell how tight her pussy is she ain't been with a man in a long time, plus she work too. I couldn't ask for a better woman."

The two of them got dressed and headed for the shopping mall, but when they got ready to get in the car, there were neighbors sitting on the porch that didn't take to whites dating blacks. Alvin could hear them saying, "nigga lover, why don't you stick to your own kind!"

"Don't pay them no mind!" Lora said getting into the car.

Alvin wasn't going to say anything until he heard one of them say, "I bet your mammy worked a lifetime to buy them shoes you got on nigga boy."

Alvin got in the car and popped the trunk from the inside. Another man yelled out, "what's the matter boy, you forgot your screw driver?" Everybody on the porch started laughing

Alvin bent over in the trunk and came back up holding his oozie machine gun saying, "there ain't nothing in this world worse than poor white trash and cheap hoes. Now any of you red necks brave enough to crack a smile now so I can blow yoe fuck'n teeth out your heads?" They didn't breathe a word. "I didn't think so. Now if you bitches would excuse me, I have'ah date to go on1"

When Alvin got in the car Lora said, "you are crazy man, those guys will kill you!"

Alvin smiled. "I ain't never known a man yet crazy enough to wanna die."

When Alvin pulled off, one of the men on the porch said, "that's one crazy son-of-a-bitch, he got to be high on some strong shit man."

Three hours later 3:00 P.M.

88

Chapter IX

Shawn was on his way to the boat dock to pick up the shipment of dope that had been there waiting on him to get there since two o'clock. Shawn was doing way over the speed limit, and when he exited the expressway he checked his watch saying to himself, "damn I'm late."

Shawn had no idea he was being tailed by the F.B.I! The closer he got to the dock, the more he checked his scenery saying to himself, "everything looks good from the ground. I'll get the binoculars and check things out from the above when I get on the ship."

Shawn went aboard the ship and said to his workers, "gentlemen, I'm sorry I'm late, I took the long way today."

One of the workers said, "that's okay, we don't get paid by the hours no way."

"Well you gentlemen know what to do, I'm gone go to the top dock and check things out from up there."

When Shawn got to the top deck he scanned the area with the binoculars. He spotted a plane police car coming their way. He looked further down the road and spotted a convoy of F.B.I cars coming their way also. Shawn hollered out to his workers, "blow the ship!"

"Are you sure?" One of the workers asked puzzled.

"Do as I say, blow the fuck'n ship now… and set the timer for five minutes and get the hell out'uv here."

Two of the men let the ramp down on the ship so they could drive off, but before he could pull off, police cars had him blocked in. they drew their weapons for Shawn and the men to step out their vehicles with their hands in the air. Shawn got out the car with his hands in the air saying, "you men got about ten minutes exactly to get out'uv here unless y'all wanna go up in flames like that ship is about too. I say'ah minute now."

The leader of the F.B.I posse yelled out, "move out mens, the ship is about to blow."

Cars were squirving and swerving getting out the parking lot. Shawn knew he had gotten away from what could have one of the biggest drug raids in history. About a block down the road Shawn pulled up to one of the F.B.I cars and said, "sorry, better luck next time, no drugs, no case."

The F.B.I agent was about to say something back to Shawn, but was interrupted by the exploding ship. Shawn drove off saying, "good day gentlemen."

Shawn got on the expressway thinking to himself, "Sorcerer ain't gone like this shit at all. How I hell they know about this shipment of dope? Fuck Sorcerer, I had to do what I had to do, I ain't going to prison for nobody. If he can't understand that, then the hell with him!"

When Shawn got home Gena noticed he was looking worried about something and she asked, "what's wrong honey?"

"I had to blow up three billion dollars worth of drugs today. What in the hell am I gone tell Sorcerer?"

91

"Tell'em the truth. I'm quite sure he'll understand."

"You don't know Sorcerer like I do. I mean, how do you tell'ah man you fucked up three billion dollars worth of dope. He depends on me to run things and I screw things up for him."

"Shawn darling, you had to do what you had to do."

"I know that Gena, but I still don't know how the feds knew the day of the big shipment."

"Who knows, maybe the phone is bugged or something."

"You might be right," Shawn pushed over to the phone and started talking it apart. "Bingo." He spotted the small device and shook his head. "Those bastards had my phone tapped. Ain't no telling how long either. They had to follow me to the ship from here. Well I'll just be damned?"

Shawn slammed the phone on the floor and ran upstairs to check the other phones. He went into a rage and started snatching the phone cords out the wall.

Paula ran downstairs asking, "what's wrong with Shawn?"

"He fucked up a shipment of dope and now he's worried about what his boss man Mr. Sorcerer gone do."

"Damn Gena, can you blame'em, you know he's playing a dangerous game. Them Cubans don't play especially when it come to their money!"

Shawn drove to a nearby payphone and called Sorcerer. Sorcerer knew it was him calling. "Hello Bomoski, I already know about your fuck up."

"Wait'ah minute before you jump the gun on me, hear me out."

Sorcerer went into a rage. "Hear you out? How in the fuck can you explain three billion dollars of my shit going down the drain? You fucked up!"

Shawn goes into a rage. "Will you shot the fuck up and listen to me. I'm sick of your bullshit talk; listen to me for a change."

"Right now Bommosk, I don't wanna hear shit you got to say. I need some time to think about what I'm gone do about you, and don't call here again unless you get word from me!"

"What you saying?"

Sorcerer slammed the phone and all Shawn could hear was the dial tone in his car. When Shawn got back home, Gena asked, "are you okay?"

"Yeah, I talked to Sorcerer; he didn't wanna hear shit I had to say."

"Give'em some time. I'm sure he'll forgive and forget. He needs you; without you he can't do business in America."

Shawn smirked, "yeahhh you're right. I'll give'em some time to cool off, then I'll call him again. Who knows, maybe he'll call me first. I'll be back in a lil while."

"Where you going now?"

"I got'ah go buy some new phones. I messed up the other ones remember."

"Take Antonio with you. I been promising him all day I was gone take'em to get him some rock candy. And Shawn darling, please try to cheer up some."

Shawn kissed her on the lips and said, "I'll be okay!"

After Shawn and Antonio got in the car, Shawn said, "you know son, one day you gone be a powerful man."

"Like Batman daddy?"

Shawn smiled. "Yepp, like Batman. You too young to understand me right now, but one day you'll see. You got your daddy blood, and your daddy was very powerful. I know you don't know what I'm talking about do you?"

"Nope."

When Shawn and Antonio got inside Fairlane Shopping Mall," a hand touched Shawn from behind and Shawn turned around to see who touched him. It was Alvin, Shawn smiled. "Well Alvin Stone, what you doing in this neck of the woods and who is this pretty young lady?"

"This beautiful young lady is Lora, Love meet my good friend Shawn and his son Antonio."

Lora smiled saying, "nice to meet you Shawn. Hi Tonio, you so cute."

Shawn said, "say hi Tonio."

"Hi," Tonio said looking at Lora.

Alvin smiled, saying, "boyyy you getting big."

"Where's Stan?" Tonio asked.

"He's out to his grandmother's house. I'm not gone hold you up Bomoski. You don't look happy, is something wrong?"

"I need to speak to you alone for a second," Shawn said.

"Excuse me for one second baby."

Shawn and Alvin stepped a few feet away from Lora and Shawn explained to Alvin everything that happened. Alvin put his hand on Shawn's shoulders and said, "Don't worry about it. You did what you had to do. I would'uv did the same thing if I was in your shoes. You'll be okay!" Alvin smiled, "I better get back to my date before lil-Tony steals her from me. You take care, I'll be seeing you."

Alvin walked away knowing in his mind that Shawn's mistake was going to open up another door for him. "Sorcerer would probably ask me to take over Bomoski's position after a fuck up like that one."

Alvin smiled saying, "where to now baby?"

Lora put her arm inside his arm and said, "let's go somewhere where they serve crabs and lobsters."

"That sounds good to me. Red Lobster here we come," he said smiling.

When Alvin and Lora got in the car Alvin said, "you never did tell me what kind of work you do."

"I'm a nurse for Lynn Hospital. What about you, what kind of work do you do for a living?"

"Do you really wanna know?"

"Yes, I really wanna know."

"I'm not gone lie to you Lora and I hope you sill like me when I'm done telling you. Here goes, I'm a pusher man."

"Ah who?" She asked.

"I'm a dope pusher; I sell drugs for the meat I get. That's how I make my living baby. Now do you still feel the same about me?"

"It doesn't matter to me what you do. I like you for you. If selling drugs is what you do, then go right ahead."

"I'm glad you approve. Tell me something Lora, have you ever been in love before?"

Lora smiled, "I think I'm in love right now!"

"Is that right," he said smiling.

"Yeahhh that's right. What about you Alvin, have you ever been in love?"

"No, but I'm beginning to feel like I'm in love with you!"

Lora leaned over from the passenger side and kissed Alvin on the jaw. He smiled and thought to himself, "damn, I can't believe I'm falling in love with a white woman."

Lora was thinking the same thing. "I'm in love with a black man. I cannot believe it."

They both were silent for a minute until Alvin said, "whelp, we're finally here. Now all I got to do is find a parking spot, this place is packed."

Alvin found a parking spot and parked, popping the trunk at the same time so he could put her oozie back in the trunk, and grab his smaller gun, the 45 revolver. As Alvin placed the gun in his coat he said to himself, "I don't need no drama with the white folks out here in this all white neighborhood. I'm with'ah white woman too, know they don't like that!"

After they'd gotten inside and were seated, all eyes were on them, Alvin said, "mannn are we that popular. I'm gone act like I don't even see them. Now what would you like baby?"

They both ordered the combination special. As they sat eating, Alvin smiled saying, "it seem like I have known you all my life."

"I feel the same way too. You sure you met'ah mind reader?" She said smiling.

"No, not at all, but why don't we get out'uv here before I turn into one of them lobsters if you know what I mean." Alvin left a fifty dollar tip. "I enjoyed being the centerfold, let's go to my place."

"Sounds good to me," she said smiling.

Alvin and Lora went to Alvin's place and made love like never before and after the third go round, Lora said, "damn I'm sore," running her fingers through Alvin's hair.

Alvin laid his head on Lora's chest and thought about what Shawn had told him earlier. Alvin could hear the sound of light snoring coming from Lora's mouth.

Sunday, Jan 31, 1978 12:00 P.M

Lora was the first to awake. Alvin was still asleep while Lora went to the bathroom to shower.

Alvin was awakened by the telephone ringing. He answered it, "Hello." It was Sorcerer on the other end.

"Alvin my man."

"I knew it was you, I had a feeling you would be calling me today. So what's on your mind?"

"For now on Alvin, I want you in charge of all shipments coming that way."

"What about Bomoski?"

"Fuck him! He fucked up for the last time with me!"

"I think you should give it one more thought. Every good man deserves another chance."

"I have heard you out, but my decision is final. You listen to me and listen good; I cannot afford anymore fuck ups. I will give it some more thought on the strength of you, but do keep in mind what we talked about. Now you have a good day."

"Yeahhh you too." Alvin hung up thinking to himself. "This shit is getting to deep for me."

Lora came waking in the bedroom butt naked saying, "well, it's about time you got your behind up."

Alvin smiled. "Girl you better hurry up and put some clothes on before old…"

Before Alvin could speak another word Lora was jumping in the bed with him saying, "before you what?"

"What time is it baby?"

"It's twelve-thirty" she answered.

"Damn I didn't know it was that late. Time is flying, let me get'ah shower."

"Ohh Alvin, I almost forgot. My mother calls me from San Diego every Sunday at four o'clock, and if I'm not there she'll be worried sick."

"Don't worry baby, I'll have you home in no time. Soon as I get out the shower we can leave."

"Take your time it's only twelve-thirty. We have a few hours and besides you can spend tonight at my place today."

"Yeah I guess I can do that."

Lora smiled. "Oh you guess."

Alvin laughed, "okay let me rephrase that. I will spend tonight with you. Now... are you satisfied?"

"Yes I am."

"Good, now don't you go nowhere, I'll be right back."

"I guess I can do that."

"O you gonna," Alvin said smiling.

"I'll make you breakfast while you're in the shower."

"That'll be nice," he said heading towards the bathroom.

Lora cooked sausages and eggs for him. Alvin got dressed and joined her in the kitchen.

Two hours later Alvin was pulling in front of Lora's house. Lora couldn't believe her eyes as she looked at her living room window from the car. Somebody had written 'nigga lover' all over her picture window and car window. When they stepped out the car they could hear voices yelling out. "No niggas allowed, go back to your own kind!"

Lora shook her head, saying, "look what they did to my windows and my car."

"I'm sorry I caused all this trouble for you baby!"

"You don't have o be. Who are they to tell me who I can date? I don't bother them and they shouldn't be bothering me. Look at my windows, they're ruined!"

"Let's gone in, I'll help you clean them, but I don't think it'll be a good idea for me to spend the night here. I wouldn't want them throwing cocktails through the window on account of me. Your neighbors ain't friendly at all!"

"Forget them," she said with teardrops falling from her eyes.

"Look Lora, I don't need no trouble right now because if I stay here tonight and somebody do something to me or my car, I'm going to prison and I know it, and I know you don't want that to happen to me. I'll be stopping by to see you from time to time. You got my beeper number and my phone number to my house. If you need me, call me. I'll see you later on."

"I will….be calling you tonight Alvin, so do be home."

Alvin kissed her on the lips and said, "I'll be there baby."

"I'm gone be real upset if you don't!"

Alvin smiled. "We wouldn't want that now would we?" He kissed her again on the lips and headed to his car.

"I thought you was gone help me with the windows."

"It ain't nothing, but soap. It'll come right off. You don't need me, I'll see you later."

Deep in Alvin's heart he was ready to kill. He drove slowly down the one way street hoping somebody would mess with him, but nobody did. He drove straight to the hospital to see Dino.

When Alvin got to the front desk to get his pass, the desk clerk recognized him and said, "I'm sorry you come up here for nothing. Mr. Jones was released four hours ago."

"That's good, thank you man," he said smiling.

"You're welcome. Have'ah nice day."

"You too," he said rushing out.

Alvin drove straight to Dino's house and when he got there he found out that Dino still was unable to walk. Dino was glad to see Alvin and said, "I bet yoe ass was shocked when they told you I was at home. Man you don't know how good it feels to be back home."

"Where you mama?"

"She's taking'ah nap."

"So how long you think it's gone take you to get back on your feets, start walking again?"

"Give me a couple'uv weeks and I'll be back to my old self."

"I hope so because I need you bad man. This dope shit is getting bigger than I anticipated."

"So what's the problem?"

"The big man called me this morning wanting me to take over all the shipping."

Dino shook his head saying, "so what's so hard about that?"

"Well really it's not'ah problem. It's just that the man's place; he wants me to take to the man who got me on my feets."

"So don't do it then."

"You don't understand my brother. You just don't say no to the big man when he asks you to do a job for him. He expects you to do that job. I hope he give my man his job back."

"I know it ain't my business man, but why did he get rid of your boy?"

"Dino man, you my boy. I can tell you anything. I trust you more than I trust myself. Bomoski fucked up a big shipment of dope yesterday. Three billion dollars worth to be exact."

"Damnnn three billion, I would get rid of his ass too."

"I don't know who and what caused that shipment to go sour, but I don't think it was Bomoski fault. That's why I'm hoping the big man reconsiders giving him another chance, and besides, we doing just fine the way things are being run right now."

"Yeahhh you right, things are smooth the way it is now."

"Pretty soon man we gone have money coming from state to state. Things are what you might say, branching out for us."

"All that sounds good to my ears. Damn man, what you do, put some lady perfume on before you came over?"

"Hell n'all man, I just took Lora home. She was all over me in the car. You know how women are; they just gotta sit up under you while you trying to drive," Alvin said smiling.

"Yeah I know how it is, lov'um and leav'um," Dino said smiling.

Alvin smiled saying, "you sure we not blood brothers? Seriously though man, I met this bad ass snow game, I mean bad as hell. Farrah ain't got shit on her. She stays in River Rouge. I'm gone make her my main lady."

Dino smiled, "I'll be damn, the man done fall in love with'ah white woman."

"Man o man, do you know how hard it is to get'ah white woman to go out with'ah black man? Almost impossible, but'ah nigga like me done squoze one, and have'er under control too. I know how to lay this pipe boy."

Dino smiled, "yeah, yeah, but you know them white folks don't like no black man fuck'n with their kind. You better be careful man!"

"I stay on my guard. You ought to see'er man. You wouldn't believe how pretty she is, and she got'ah body."

"All I can say is be careful man. Them white folks don't play when it come to'ah nigga messing with one of their. They rather kill'er first then let you be with her. Trust me an, I know what I'm talking about!"

Alvin shook his head up and down in a yes motion saying, "I know you right, but don't worry about no man. I can take care of Alvin Stone. You just get yoe crippled ass well so we can double date sometimes."

Dino smiled, "do it look like I lost any weight?"

103

"Yeah ah little, but with a couple of yoe mama home cooked meals you'll pick back up in no time. That liquid shit they was feeding yoe ass through your veins ain't no joke. You can't help, but to lose weight."

"You ain't lying, I'm glad I ain't got to put up with that no-moe. I miss the hell out'uv mama cooking. All the fellaz gone be over here in'ah few. Getting cussed out by mama for making noise. She hate when all of us get together. She told us we sound like'ah Elvis concert."

Alvin laughed, saying, "man I'm out'uv here. I'll catch up with you later on. Tell mama I said hello. You take it easy man, and don't eat too much."

"I want you to take care of yourself out there, and don't forget what I told you about that white girl."

Alvin got in his car and said to himself, "since I'm out here in the neighborhood, I might'as well go check on my son. It's too cold for him to be outside playing. He probably got a house full of kids over playing in the basement knowing him. First let me stop by the liquor store."

Sharon heard a car pull in the driveway and peeped out the window, saying to herself, "that's Alvin, I know he got me something to drink." She opened the door, "I know you got something for me to drink in that bag?"

"As a matter of fact I do, you know I didn't forget about you."

"Thank you Alvin."

"Any time for you. Where's my son?"

"He's a couple'uv doors down the street playing with his friends. I'll go get'em if you want me too."

"N'all that's okay. As long as you two are okay I'm satisfied. I just dropped by to bring you that bottle. I wish I could stay and chat, but I got some very important work to take care of. Tell Stan I'll see'em next Sunday."

"I'll do that. You be careful out there in them streets."

Alvin knew that if he stayed around Sharen would want him to make love to her, and that's why he lied to her about having important business. Alvin left Sharen's house and drove straight to JR Lounge."

Alvin walked in ordering. "Give me a Budweiser JR."

"What's up Alvin? You remember two thugs you got into it with?"

"Yeah, what about'um?"

"You ain't got to worry about them two starting no more trouble with nobody else. Man they tried that same shit they tried on you with another fella in here yesterday. All I remember was them two punks stepping outside with the man who turned their lights off permanent. I called the police after I heard about six shots. When I got outside them two niggas was dead as hell, stretched flat out on the sidewalk."

Alvin smirked, saying. "o well that's two less punks I ain't got to worry about. Now do you remember the little fox I left out'uv here with not too long ago?"

"Alvin man, how in the hell you expect me to remember what woman you done left out of here with, when every time I look up you leaving here with'ah different woman out'uv my place."

Alvin smiled, "well this girl name is Honey."

"O yeahhh I remember her, man I haven't seen her since that day you left out of here with her. Did she have some good pussy?" He asked smiling.

"It was okay, nothing to brag about. I just thought she might'uv come in here looking for me, being that I got the twatt and put her ass out my house."

JR laughed saying, "I bet she cussed yoe ass out didn't she?"

Alvin laughed. "Well… yeahhh, how you guess that?"

JR smiled, "I know Honey, she ain't nothing to play with. She'll cuss'ah nigga out in a heartbeat."

Alvin laughed, "yeahhh she can go. I had to burn rubber getting away from her crazy ass. She's a trip. I'm done messing around with all these women. I get me one now that I truly like, and to top it off she's white."

"Man is you crazy, ah white woman? Nigga you done lost yoe mind; them white folks will kill you man. You better stick with your own kind man. You know how the white man is about they own kind!"

"Yeah I know, but the white man don't scare me man!"

"I hear you son, but do be careful. I would hate to see you in'ah pine box over some white woman!"

"Don't worry about me man, I'll be all right. My last name ain't Stone for nothing. I'm a mountain that can't be moved and I'm not gone let no man, white or black stop me from doing what I like to do best."

"I hear you man, and I admire your courage. Just be careful, that's all I ask you to do for me. You remember Sweet Pea don't you?"

"Yeah I remember oh Sweet Pea."

"Anyway, Sweet Pea use to mess with this white girl from Taylor, Michigan until one day they found him and her ass cut up into small pieces in the back of ah garbage can truck. Had a note taped on the garbage truck that said, "we would of made dog food out of them, but even the dogs wouldn't want this waste."

Alvin shook his head up and down in a yes motion, saying, "I get the picture man, but that was years ago. Time is changing; a man has the right to date whoever he wants too."

"It just looks that way to you now son, but it ain't changed. I'm telling you for the last time, I like you Alvin Stone; do be careful about what you doing out there man!"

"I will, because I know you know and you ain't never talked this serious to me before. I'll keep in mind all that you said to me today. It's hard to cut something a loose that you care about!"

"I understand that son, just be careful, that's all I'm saying."

Alvin glanced at the clock on the wall and said, "Damn its five-thirty. I got to cut my wheels JR, you take care." Alvin left a twenty-dollar tip.

"You be cool Alvin, and don't forget what we talked about."

"I want," he said heading out the door.

When Alvin got outside he looked at all the blood on the sidewalk and said, "it's a shame brothers are dying like flies around here. Man when will this world come to an end? Soon as Alvin got on the expressway he could see the state troopers through his rearview mirror. "I hope these motha-fuckaz don't pull me over."

Before Alvin could get the words out the blue lights was flashing for him to pull over. Alvin pulled over to the side of the road. One officer got out the car, while the other one stood back behind the passenger door with his gun pointed at Alvin's head.

"The officer said, "do you know what you did wrong back there boy?"

Alvin wasn't the type of man to answer no sir and yes sir to white folks. "N'all tell me boyyy?!" He said staring at the officer with the hate in his eyes.

"O you'ah smart nigga. I just might run you in for having'ah bad mouth boy!"

"You do what you got'ah do or leave me the fuck alone!"

The other officer that stood with his gun pointed at Alvin's head said, "Fuck'em Bill, we got'ah breaking and entering going on one minute from here. Let the nigga boy go his way."

"Get your tail light fixed and consider today yoe lucky day."

Alvin got back on the expressway saying to himself, "crazy ass police. I thought I did something wrong. They punk ass ain't never around when the real shit go down. I'm glad he didn't get too focused on me. If he would'ah heard my name he probably would'uv shit on himself. I know they ain't forget about Alvin Stone taking out their kind. If they would'uv had any idea I killed three police officers, my ass would probably been arrested just on GP!"

When Alvin pulled into his driveway he could hear the telephone inside the house ringing and said to himself, "I bet that's Shawn."

The phone continued ringing, Alvin picked it up. "Hello."

"Hi, it's me Lora, what are you up too?"

"Ohhh nothing, just getting in from out the way. I had stopped by JR Lounge for a few hours, and now I'm here talking to the beautifulest woman on earth."

Lora smiled. "You just saying that, I'm talking to the handsomenest man in the world though."

"Well I guess we are fortunate to have each other."

"I guess we are. What's your sign?"

"I'm a Scorpion."

"So you're a Scorpio, Scorpio's love to make love."

"You know your signs I see."

"I'm a Leo."

"So you're a lion?"

"Lora smiled. "Nope, I'm a kitten, can't you tell?"

"I guess."

"There you go again guessing."

"It's just a figure of speech baby."

"Anything you say Alvin. Anyway, I have to go to the grocery store to pick up a few things. Is there anything you want me to pick you up while I'm out shopping?"

"Yeah grab me a case of Budweiser."

"I think I can handle that, is that all you want?"

"Yeahhh, you."

She smiled saying, "you got me. I'll call you later on when I get back from the store."

"I'll be right here, talk to you then baby," he said hanging up.

After Alvin hung up he said to himself, "Damnn what other people say, I like this girl, and ain't nobody gone keep me from being with her."

Alvin kicked his shoes off and laid back on the couch watching television for the rest of the day."

Chapter X

Friday, Feb 26, 1978, 8:30 P.M.

Dino was finally back on his feet's and in good health. Alvin took him to JR's Lounge to celebrate his recovery. After hours of hanging out together, night time had finally crept up on them. They both were pretty high from drinking beer after beer.

Alvin downed his beer saying, "Dino, man I don't know about you, but I'm fucked up."

"Yeah me too, man take me home so I can sleep this shit off, I'm blowed."

They marched out the bar with their arms around each other, laughing and talking loud all the way to Alvin's car.

When they got in the car Alvin said, "whatever you do, don't throw up in my car."

"Mannn you just don't hit nothing with your drunk ass. You don't drive that good when you soba."

As Alvin drove off he said, "I wanna stop by Lora house before I take you home."

"Man I don't care what you do as long as you don't crash while I'm in this baby."

"Cool, let's go see what my girl up too."

When they got to Lora's street they could see police and ambulance lights flashing. As they got closer Alvin could see that they were in front of Lora's house.

Alvin got out the car asking, "what's going on?"

The officer said, "somebody slit the girl who stays here throat, and threw'er out the living room picture window. Do you know the lady?"

"Yeah she was my girlfriend. Can I see'er before y'all take her away?"

"Sure," the officer said.

Alvin stared at Lora's body and the tears rolled down his face when he saw that they carved, '**nigga lover**' on her forehead.

Alvin cried out, "whyyy, why?"

Dino grabbed him, saying, "come on man, ain't nothing we can do about it right now. Come on now, let's get out of here!"

"They didn't have to kill'er man, I loved that woman!"

"I know man, let's handle it later. I'll drive man."

"I'm gone get them red neck sons of bitches!"

Let it go man!" Dino put him in the car and drove off. "I'm gone spend the night with you man, because I don't want you to do nothing crazy man!"

Alvin sat on the passenger side speechless for a few minutes before saying, "why can't we all just live in peace man?"

"I wish I had the answer to that question man, I really do."

"It ain't right man, that girl ain't did nothing to nobody!"

"I know man, I know. And I know you hurting right now. When you hurt man, I hurt!"

When they got inside Alvin's house Alvin said, "Dino man, you ain't got to stay here with me. I'll be okay."

"Right now man you need somebody to talk to you, and I'm gone be right here for you. I'm not going nowhere till I think you okay so you mine as well get use to seeing my handsome face in the place."

"I'm not gone argue with you, do what you like, but I'm telling you I'm all right."

"Alvin man I seen that look on your face to many times. You look like you ready to kill the world man, and I can't leave you here in that state of mind. Now you kick back and relax while I go and pick us up something to munch on right quick. I got'ah taste for some Chinese food, how about you?"

"I'm not hungry man. I just wish I could get my hands on one of them bastards that did that shit to Lora!"

"I know man, I'll be right back."

As soon as Dino pulled off, Alvin started punching the wall and kicking furniture around, crying out, "why they have to kill'er?"

Alvin walked over to his bar and helped himself to a fifth of Jack Daniels. He turned the bottle up taking gulp after gulp trying to get drunk, but all he could picture in his mind was the carving on Lora's head that read '*nigga lover.*' He turned the bottle up again to down it.

When Dino got back he saw Alvin downing the liquor and said, "Alvin don't do this to yourself. Getting stoned out yoe mind ain't gone change nothing."

Alvin was drunk, and Dino could tell by the tone of his voice as he listened to Alvin say, "I just wanna die. Why don't somebody kill me? I'm tired of living, I just wanna die."

Alvin started staggering over furniture and steady talking crazy. Dino grabbed him and said, "come on man, sit down before you hurt yourself." Dino guided him to the couch.

Alvin sat on the couch for about three minutes before passing out. Dino sat down eating his Chinese food, and called his mother and explained to her everything that happened to Alvin.

Ms. Jones said, "you stay with him till he gets back to his right mind!"

"I will mama, talk to you later."

"Bye son and I'll be praying for you both."

Dino laid back on the love seat catching the news, and saying to himself. "I'm glad Alvin sleep. He don't need to see this. Damn stuff about that white girl on every damn station in Detroit tonight. I know my boy Alvin; he'll feel better about things tomorrow when he wake up. I love that nigga, I'm glad I was with him tonight. He might'uv been in jail tonight, maybe even dead if I wasn't with him!"

Tuesday Mar 3, 1978 12:30 P.M.

On the day of the funeral, Alvin knew he wasn't welcome to attend the wake or the funeral so he had flowers catered to the wake.

Alvin parked across the street from Woodmere Cemetery watching the blue hearse lead the way through the gate of the cemetery, saying to himself with tears running down his face, "I'm gonna miss you Lora. I tried to be here for you, but you know how things are." Alvin drove off, "I guess I'll go home now and wait for my son to come home from school."

Ten minutes later Alvin got home and the phone ringed. "Alvin speaking."

Bomoski said, "What's up Alvin, where you been? I've been trying to call you all morning. Let me guess, you went to the funeral didn't you?"

"Yeah something like that."

"Anyway, I'm thinking about calling Sorcerer."

"Why don't you do that, I'm sure he'll be glad to hear from you."

"You think so?"

"Yeah man, he can't stay mad forever."

"You right, he can't do nothing, but cuss my ass out."

"I doubt it man, gone and give'em a call."

"I'm gone call'em right now. I'll call you back later and let you know how it went."

"You do that, I'll be right here."

After Shawn hung up from talking to Alvin he took two quick shots of Scotch to help boost his courage up to call Sorcerer. The Scotch went to work right away. Shawn dialed the number, and the phone rang three times. The voice on the other end said, "Sorcerer speaking."

"Hello Sorcerer it's me, Bomoski."

"Bomoski, I was just thinking about calling you, but I see you beat me to the punch, we need to talk."

"Yeah that's why I called you, hear me out. True enough you put me on the map and you put this organization together, but I'm not some small time punk you can just kick to the curve and shit on man!"

"Bomoski, have you been drinking?"

"Never mind all that bullshit, you owe me an apology."

"What you mean I owe you an apology?"

"Just what I said, you owe me an apology for talking to me the way you did." Shawn took another sip of Scotch.

Sorcerer got angry. "Bomoski, don't you ever call my house telling me what I owe you. If I owe you anything it should be a free trip to your grave for fucking up that shipment. So you just calm the fuck down and listen to me. Now I'm gone give you another chance, but don't never ever call me and tell me what I owe you again. Now do I make myself clear? I said do I make myself clear?"

"Yeah."

"Good, welcome back to the family."

"I'm glad to be back."

"What you say?"

"I said I'm glad to be back."

"And Shawn, please, no more fuck ups!"

"Don't worry, I'll be real careful about the way I do things from here on out."

"I'm sure you will Bomoski."

"Look Sorcerer, I was thinking, why don't you get away from Columbia for a weekend, come to the city."

"Are you inviting me to your home?"

"That's exactly what I'm doing, how soon can you come down?"

"Well me and my wife anniversary is coming up in a couple'uv weeks, and she has never been to the states before. That will be her anniversary gift from me. I'll be there March twenty-seventh on our anniversary. Have your wife cook us up one of her delicious meals. Me and my wife will see you all then."

"Good, I'll have something set up for the two of you. What time should we be expecting you?"

"Around noon."

"I'll see you at the airport around noon then. Good day Sorcerer."

Shawn held the phone in his hand for a few seconds saying to himself. "That wasn't hard at all. Let me call Alvin."

Shawn dialed the number and Alvin answered, "hello."

"It's on again man, I got good news, I'm back in man. And guess what, him and his wife is coming down for dinner on their anniversary which is the twenty-seventh of this month. I want you to be there too man. It'll be nice to have you there with me."

"I don't think so Bomoski. I got a lot on my mind right now, maybe some other time."

"I understand, but you know you welcome in my home anytime."

"Yeah I know man."

"It's Lora isn't it? You can't get her off your mind."

"I'm trying hard Bomoski, it's not easy. I think about her day and night. I wish I would'ah never went by her house that day. I wish I would'nah never met'er!"

"It's not your fault Alvin; it's these sick ass people in this world. Don't blame yourself: we can't change the color of our skin to please others."

"I know that, but they killed'er because of me, and I got to live with that on my conscious till the day I die." Stan was coming through the front door holding his books. "Well Bomoski I have to hang up, but my son is home from school, and I know he's hungry, cause I am."

"Hey dad," Stan said.

"Well call me back when you get a chance, and don't go doing nothing crazy," Shawn said sipping his drink.

"I'll try too, later man." Alvin hung up. "What's up son?" The phone started ringing. "Hello."

Dino said, "what's up my brother?"

"You tell me," Alvin said.

"I'm just calling to check on you, you doing okay? I can tell by your voice."

"Yeah I'm okay, how bout you?"

"I'm just laying low making this money as usual. You know me man, got to make that money."

"Be careful man, our names getting to big around here. Watch your ass; I don't want nothing to happen to you!"

"What you mean?"

"You know yourself; it's some jealous ass motha fuckas around here. If they think you got some money they'll kill yoe ass, and you stay loaded with a bankroll in your pockets."

"Man I don't carry that much cash on me, just enough to get me through the day."

"Yeah, but everybody in southwest Detroit know you the man out there. Just be careful man."

"I see what you saying man; I'll be on my guards."

"Thank you, that's what I wanted to hear you say."

"Where's that son of yours?"

"Probably in the kitchen eating. He just got his behind home from school about ten minutes ago.

"So what you gone do the rest of the day?"

"Probably chill out around here, ain't nothing I really wanna do today."

"Well I got to take mama to the store, and you know how she shops. I might not get back home messing with her butt till tomorrow night."

Alvin laughed, "have fun."

"Yeah later man."

Alvin hung up and went in the kitchen saying," what's up man?"

"Nothing, what's up with you?"

"Ain't nothing up with me, you got any homework to do today?"

"Nope."

"Damn, why you don't never have homework to do?"

"I don't know."

"One day soon I'm gone pay yoe teacher a visit, and if I find out you been lying to me you can forget about hanging out with your friends this summer."

"I'm not lying."

"All right, just don't let me find out you are."

"I do my homework at school."

Alvin laughed. "Yeah I know that's the same line I use to run on my old man until he found out I was lying. He tore my ass up in front of all my classmates." Alvin thought to himself,"I hope he buy this story, I'm lying my ass off. Now you wouldn't want that to happen to you?"

"N'all I wouldn't want you to come to my school and whoop me."

Alvin walked out the kitchen saying, "well that's what's gone happen to you if you don't do right in school."

120

As soon as Alvin got out of sight Stan jumped up out his seat and ran to the garbage in the kitchen and got his homework out the garbage.

As the day grew old, Stan was upstairs sleeping, and Alvin was downstairs drinking and looking out the window thinking about Lora, and the more he thought about her, the madder he got. He slammed the glass of liquor down on the floor and ran to the cabinet in the hallway and grabbed one of his machine guns, and three grenades saying to himself, "I'll show those red necks!"

Alvin rushed to his car and put the machine gun in the backseat, and the three grenades on the passenger seat. He headed off for revenge, and knew exactly what house he wanted to blow up.

Alvin got on the expressway heading 75 east, and as he turned the radio on, the DJ was talking. Alvin's heart was full of hate until he heard the DJ saying, "hello you folks out there in radio land. I hope you people out there dig this next new tune; it's by one of our newest artists Marvin Gaye. Y'all check it out, this tune is called 'War is not the Answer,' y'all check it out."

The song started playing, "brother, brother, brother, there's far too many of you dying. War is not the answer. You know we got to find a way to bring some loving here today." The more Alvin listened to the words to the song, the calmer he got. "Tell me what's going on?"

Alvin said to himself, "this song got'ah strong message, let me take my ass home. I got to get that record. You right Marvin, war ain't the answer." When Alvin got back to the house he was feeling real good about himself saying, "thank you God for that song tonight. Now I know for myself you do work in mysterious ways."

Alvin went upstairs to check on Stan and Stan was still sound asleep. Alvin just stared at his son while he slept and said to himself, "I hope when you get grown life will be different. I love you son." He cut the light back off.

Alvin went to his own room and fell straight to sleep. Meanwhile Gena and Paula was too busy snorting line after line to go sleep. Gena had snorted so much her nose started bleeding. They kept a bottle of liquor on the table next to them just to throw Shawn's mind off of what they really was doing. He never suspected them to be doing cocaine again.

Paula said, "I don't know bout you girl, but I'm done for the night, and you should be too, yoe nose is bleeding bad."

"One more line and I'll be done too."

"Just one more and that's it Gena, I don't want you to buss your heart. Too much of this shit at one time can kill yoe ass, and you know this."

"Yeah I know, now please hold your voice down before you wake Shawn up."

"Oops I forgot he was home, my bag."

The two of them stayed up a little while longer watching television before going upstairs to retire for the night.

Wednesday March 3, 1978 8:00 A.M.

Stan's alarm clock sounded off, he rolled over on his back and stared at the ceiling for a second, saying to himself, "mannn, school, I'll be glad when we get our summer break."

Stan got on up and peep in on Alvin, he was still sleep. Stan washed his face and brushed his teeth, then got dressed for school. After he ate his breakfast he went back upstairs and woke Alvin up. "Dad I'm gone."

"Okay son, I'll see you when you get home, and try to bring that homework home with you."

Stan smiled, "yeah all right."

Stan had a crush on one of the girls in his class. Tangela like him too. Stan would bring candy to school for her almost every day. He would carry her books to the bus for her after school. He had met her one day after school about to get beat up by a boy who called himself liking her too, but she didn't like him. Stan came to her rescue; he ran over to where they were pushing each other and said to the boy, "why you got to fight'ah girl? Fight me, I'll kick yoe ass."

The boy pushed Stan, and Stan bit him in the eye as hard as he could, and the fight was over just that quick. Stan took Tangela's books out of her hands saying, "come on let's go, I'll walk you to the bus stop."

The two of them been going together every since that day. Stan definitely had his daddy attitude when it came to fighting and women.

"Heyyy you, you got that homework today," he asked smiling.

"Yeah, dad do I have'ah uncle my color?"

"Funny you asked me that. I was just thinking about my brother, your uncle. Yeah you got'ah uncle your color, but he's dead now."

"He died dad?"

"N'all man, your uncle Howard was killed before you were born. Women loved that nigga to death. I miss that boy; he was my only brother by my mother. I wish he was still alive."

"Who killed'em dad?"

"Some jealous ass punk over'ah woman. I'll never forget that day. Me and Howard was laying right beside each other in the bed that night, talking and joking with each other; then he said he was about to go over to one of his women houses. Told me he'll see me when he got back. Alvin's eyes got watery. When he left that night he never made it back! I could hear mama talking to the police. They asked her if she had a son named Howard Stone. She said yes. That's when the bad news came. He said ma'am I have some bad news. I thought he was about to tell her Howard was in jail or something, but he said, ma'am your son was murdered tonight. Mama just burst out screaming and crying. I started crying. I couldn't believe my brother was dead. Come to find out that the woman he went to see that night had him killed; all because he was seeing other women. I tell yo son, when you get older try not to have over one girlfriend."

Stan smiled saying, "I got'ah girlfriend now."

"Oh yeah, what's her name?"

"Her name is Tangy, short for Tangela."

"Well you just try to hold on to Tangy and leave them other girls alone," Alvin started smiling. "I'll be damned, my son got'ah girlfriend, Anyway, I just don't want you to end up like your uncle did. Now gone and eat, and get to that homework."

After Stan went in the kitchen Alvin said to himself, "yeah son I didn't tell you they never caught the punk who killed my brother."

Alvin went in the kitchen saying, "I'll be back in a minute son. I'm going to the record shop and pick up this song I heard last night on the radio. If anybody call me get their name and tell'em I'll call-um when I get back, and make sure you do your homework."

"I will, bring me back some rock candy dad."

"All-right."

Alvin drove straight to Norman's Record Shop in southwest Detroit. Herman had his back turned when Alvin came through the door saying, "well I'll be damned, if it ain't oh Herman himself."

Herman turned around to see who was talking to him. He smiled and yelled out. "Alvin Stone, man where the hell you been hiding yourself?"

Alvin laughed, "I've been around. And since I'm here let's talk some business."

"What you got in mind?"

"I wanna buy this record shop from you."

"Shiddd you ain't said nothing but'ah word. Give some digits."

"I'm serious man; I wanna buy this place from you."

"I'm serious too, give me fifty-thousand and it's yours."

"You got it."

Herman smiled, "man you know this place ain't worth no fifty thousand. I got to get at least one hundred thousand."

Herman thought Alvin was gonna back out, but Alvin just smiled and said, "you got it, I'll have your money here tomorrow first thing, and all you'll have to do is sign the shop over to me. I'll get somebody to run it for me."

"Alvin my man you got yourself a record shop."

"That's right, now look up on that shelf and give me that Marvin Gaye tune."

Alvin reached in his pocket to get the money out, but Herman stopped him saying, "you can put your money back in your pocket son, this yoe record shop now."

Alvin threw twenty dollars on the counter anyway, saying, "give me some of that rock candy you got back there."

"When you start eating rock candy?"

"It's for my son."

"Yoe son, man I didn't know you had kids."

"Yepp, sure do, lil joka look just like me too," Herman passed him the candy. "You be cool Alvin, and I'll see you first thing tomorrow."

"Yeah, I can't be nothing, but that. I'll see you tomorrow."

When Alvin got in his car he said to himself, "nigga will sell their mama for the right price. I guess'ah man got to what'ah man got to do."

When Alvin made it to the house Stan said, "this man called, he say he yoe cousin from Chicago."

"Yeah that's yoe cousin Pig, he didn't wanna give his name over the phone, which was a smart move on his part. Did he say anything else?"

"He just said call'em."

"Let me put this record on and give'em a call." He put the record on and dialed Pig's number.

Pig answered saying, "what's up cous?"

Alvin said, "damn man how you know it's me?"

"You'ah business man and you the only one with my number. Anyway, fuck that shit, man business is booming down here. You can pick yoe ends up whenever you like, and bring me'ah hundred birds when you come." Pig called kilos birds. "I need them birds no later than tomorrow."

"Be at the same spot tomorrow, you'll see a man dressed in all white with black gloves on, give him the money. Be there at eleven tomorrow morning, you got that coming to'ya."

"Cous man, I love you, you looked out for me big time, and you know I appreciate it."

"That's what family for man, you take care cous, I'll be hollering at you."

As soon as Alvin hung the phone up, he walked over to the stereo and the phone ringed. "Hello," he said answering it.

"Hi Alvin, it's me Paula."

127

"Well what'ah surprise, what made you dial this number?"

"I do have a son there, remember."

"Oh yeahhh, that's right you do, I almost forgot. He don't hear from you till you high on that shit."

"High on what shit?"

"You know better than I do."

"I don't know what you talking about. I ain't seen no drugs since I left the center."

"Cut the bullshit Paula, you high right now, and I don't give'ah damn, just don't bring that shit around my son. I don't give'ah damn about what you do over that way, it's none of my business, but when it come to my son, that's my business. Don't get me wrong, I don't mind you calling here talking to'em, but until you can stop doing what you doing, I won't have'em around you!"

Tears started falling from her eyes as she said, "look, I have just as much rights to see my son as you do!"

"And that's true Paula, but I will not allow my son to be around two dope using ass women."

"Two dope users."

"Yeahhh two, I know your girl Gena is back to using too, but my lips are sealed, just don't fuck with my son while y'all on that stuff. And that's my final offer, because I wouldn't want to explain to him how his mother really is, and I'm more than sure Shawn don't have'ah clue. I'll let you talk to'em, that's if he has anything to say to you. He don't even know you, and that's a shame. Hold on," Alvin called out for Stan. "Telephone son, it's your mother."

Stan took the phone out Alvin's hand saying, "hello."

"Hi Stan, how you been?"

"Fine."

"You wanna spend the weekend with your mommy?"

"I wanna go over my grandma house and spend the weekend, all my friends over there."

Paula's heart was crushed. "Okay, then, I understand. Well mommy got to go, I love you. Tell your grandma I said hi."

"I will, you wanna speak back to my daddy?"

"N'all tell'em I'll talk to'em later."

"I will."

"You be good now, okay."

"Unn huh."

"Bye, bye," she sadly said.

After Paula hung the phone up she started crying, Alvin asked, "she gone?"

"Yeahhh."

"You finish that homework yet?"

"Yepp."

"That's good, come sit down next to me I wanna talk to you about something. You know I love you don't you?"

"Yeah," he answered. "The reason I want you to graduate from high school is because I want you to do good in school is because I want you to graduate from high school, so you can make something out yourself. I don't want you to be like me son. I didn't finish school. I wish today that I did, but I didn't. You have an opportunity to get your education, and that's why daddy be on you tough about your homework. That's all I wanted to tell you. Now give me five on the dark side," They gave each other five. "Now get out'uv here so I can relax."

Alvin kicked his shoes off and laid back on the sofa listening to Marvin Gaye.

Thursday March 4, 1978 7:00 A.M.

Alvin woke up the next morning and called his pilot telling him to meet him at the airport at 9:30 A.M. Alvin drove to his warehouse and bagged up the dope, and as he was bagging the dope he said to himself, "I got to find me somebody to transport this stuff for me. I ain't got no business being a delivery boy."

After he was done bagging up the dope he hurried back to the house hoping Stan hadn't woke up before he got back.

As soon as Alvin got in the house he could hear Stan's alarm clock going off. Alvin ran up the stairs to Stan's room saying, "dig lil-man, I'm about to make'ah run, I'll see you when you get home from school. You be cool in school, I'm out'uv here."

Stan looked out his bedroom window and watched Alvin drive off. When Alvin got to the airport his pilot was already there waiting on him. Alvin parked his car and walked over to the jet saying, "I see you early too."

"Yeah better early then late."

"That's why I like you Coyd, you think like I do."

"Well I'm done with the inspection, this baby is ready to flap her wings, and I'm ready if you are Mr. Stone."

"Let's do this."

The jet landed in Chicago at ten-thirty. Alvin's eyes scanned everything moving. He checked out the scenery from the jet, and said to himself, "everything looks cool so far."

Alvin was dressed in an all white double breasted suit, and a full length white mink, and white alligator shoes that shined like diamonds. The only black thing he had on was his black leather gloves.

Pig had no idea Alvin would be the one delivering the package, and as soon as he saw Alvin getting off the jet he walked up to him saying, "man you didn't tell me you was gone be the one in all white."

"I know I wanted to surprise you."

"Well you damn sho done that. Here's the money, a million plus. Hell I need me one of these furs you wearing."

Alvin smiled, he trusted Pig. "I'll send you one for Christmas, your stuff on the plane. I'll have my pilot load it in your trunk."

Pig saw the boxes and said, "why didn't you use two or three suitcases?"

131

"Boxes are better, trust me."

As soon as Coyd finished putting the dope in the trunk he smiled saying to Alvin, "all done boss man."

"Good, we out of here, you know where I'm at if you need me."

"That I do know, take care couz. I still dig the hell of that hook up you wearing."

"You can afford this kind of shit, so get with the program. Peace out, we out'uv here."

Pig smiled, "peace, and the next time you see me couz I'll be dressed like you, but I'll be in all black."

Once the jet got in the air Alvin relaxed and thought, "my cousin Pig, you just don't know the bigger you get, the bigger I get. One day I'm getting out the dope game. Sorcerer just ain't gone let me quit. I got to have a plan, and a damn good one."

When Alvin got back to Detroit, him and the briefcase went straight to Herman's record shop. Alvin opened the briefcase up in front of Herman, and counted out one hundred thousand dollars to him then threw him an extra thousand for being late getting there.

Herman quickly passed him the deed and said, "it's all yours man."

Alvin knew Herman loved quick money, so he threw him another thousand saying, "find me somebody to run this place."

"Shit that ain't no problem, what I wanna know is how can I double this money?"

Alvin smiled, "for some reason I knew you would get around to that question. I'll tell you what, since I know you love to make money, for the hundred thousand I just gave you, I'll you 28 kilos of uncut dope, and not only will you double your money, you'll triple it. You can't beat that with an egg beater."

"Hell yeah, when can I get them twenty-eight keys?"

"I'll have'um to you in an hour."

"Here then, here the money."

"You trust me man," Alvin said smiling and grabbing the money.

"Sure I do, a man in your line of work don't need no trouble."

"That's right, you sure know what to say. I'll see you in about an hour."

"I'll be here in your record shop and by the way, I already found somebody to run this shop for you."

"You have?"

"Yeahhh me, this record shop will be the perfect place for me to do a little business of my own, if you know what I mean."

Alvin smiled, "I know exactly what you mean. I'll see yo in'ah minute."

Alvin got in the car talking to himself. "I love it when a plan comes together. I know what I'll do, when I get I'll just call Dino up and have him to take Herman them keys."

As soon as Alvin got home he called Dino and had him to take Herman the keys, and as soon as Dino was done dropping off the keys he drove out to

Alvin's house. The two of them sat around the house drinking beer and talking junk. Dino was happy to see Alvin back to his usual self.

Alvin rocked his head back and forth to the beat of the music on the radio and said, "yeah man, own me'ah record shop, and that reminds me, I want you to hear this record I got by Marvin Gaye."

Alvin put the record on, and Dino said, "O hell yeah, that's the jam, I got to get that one myself."

"Just go by the shop on your way home and pick you up one, it's on the house."

"Mother, mother, mother, there's far too many of you crying, brother, brother, brother, there's far too many of you dying. You know you got to find a way to bring some loving here today.

Yeah, yeah, yeah....

Father, father, we don't need to escalate. You see war is not the answer, falling in love can conquer hate.

You know we got to find'ah way to bring some loving here today.

Oh, oh, oh picket lines, and picket signs don't punish me with brutality. Talk to me, so you can see, ohhh what's going on, what's going on, yeahhh what's going on? Ayee what's going on?

Mother, mother, everybody thinks we're there, but who are they to judge us, simply because our hair is long.

Ayee you know we got to find a way to bring some loving here today.

Ohhh, picket lines, and picket signs, don't punish me with brutality. Come on talk to me, so you can see what's going on, yeahhh what's going on, tell me what's going on? I'll tell you what's going on. Whennn, right on baby, right on.

"I'll do that, that's a bad ass song."

After the song went off Dino said, "I'm about to cut my wheels man."

"All right then, you be easy man, and thanks for taking care that for me."

"Anytime for you man, you know me, we brothers. I'll do anything I can to help you man, and you should know that by now!"

"Yeah I do, and you know I'll do the same for you, and you know that!"

"Now that we got that established I'll see yoe ass later," he said smiling.

As Dino was leaving out, Stan was coming in saying, "hayyy Dino."

"What's up lil-Al, give me five on the black side. You be cool."

Alvin said, "go wash your hands and get you something to eat. I fried some chicken, and made some hamburgers and French fries. Ain't no hamburger buns, you got to settle for bread till I go grocery shopping. I'll be upstairs chilling if you need me."

"All-right."

Chapter XI

Friday, May 26, 1978 7:00 P.M.

Shawn and Gena had been busy all day preparing for Sorcerer and his wife Maria anniversary. Gena had some last minute grocery shopping to do. Paula stayed home with lil-Tony while Gena and Shawn drove out to A&P grocery store to get what they needed to prepare tomorrow's dinner for Mario and Sorcerer. "

Shawn pushed the buggy while Gena's eyes scanned the can goods on the shelf. Shawn started teasing Gena saying, "get in the buggy baby, I'll push you."

Gena laughed, "I probably can't get my feets in that buggy, not to mention my thighs. You know I been really thinking, what kind of gift can we get them that they don't already have?"

"We'll get them a his and her shirt that says '*I Love Detroit*' on it."

"If we hurry baby we can catch Northland Shopping Mall before they close."

Shawn pushed the buggy into a Mexican man by accident, and turned and said to him, "ooops."

The American said, "oops didn't do it, it's another fuck'n word people use in America when they run into me!"

"By you being a man I thought you would shake that little ass bump off."

Gena said, "look sir, he's sorry, he didn't do it on purpose."

136

"I want him to say he sorry, not you. Somebody needs to teach him to say he sorry. He has no manners, he not man enough to say he sorry."

Shawn got tired of listening to the Mexican complain. He got upset and said, "somebody need to teach you some English."

"Fuck you," the Mexican said pointing his finger at Shawn's face.

Before he could put his hand down, Shawn punched him in the left eye, and then in the jaw. The Mexican's jaw broke as he hit the ground landing on it.

Shawn had no idea the Mexican was not alone until the isle got full of customers looking on. When the Mexican two brothers and cousin got on the scene, they saw their brother holding his jaw.

While the security guard was busy holding Shawn back, one of the brothers asked his brother, "is that the mothafucka who do this to you?"

Shawn started yelling, "yeah this me mothafucka, you want some of me?"

"You a dead man punk, nobody do this to my brother and get away with it. It's not over bitch, you ass is out, and you can bank on that amigo!"

Shawn smiled, "you jalapeno eating mothafuckas don't scare me. You'll get the same treatment yoe sissy ass brother got, and you can bank on that. I don't need no help for you coward mothafuckas. Y'all don't know who y'all fuck'n with?"

Gena said, "please Shawn, let it go, please."

The Mexican men grabbed their brother, and the one arguing said, "come on, we'll get you to the hospital."

Twenty minutes later, the security guards walked Shawn and Gena to their car, but they had no idea the Mexicans were waiting patiently for them to come out the store, the Mexicans followed them.

Gena said, "are we still going to Northland?"

"I'm tired we'll go in the morning."

"The truth is, you mad about what happen, ain't you?"

"Yeah I guess that's it, I should'nah hit'em like I did. It was all my fault too; I was in the wrong and couldn't admit it."

"It's done and over now, let's just concentrate on tomorrow."

"Yeah you right baby, it's over with."

As soon as Shawn turned into their driveway the Mexicans drove pass the house and parked a few houses down, and as soon as Shawn and Gena went inside the house, they doubled back and got the address. The cousin said, "we'll come back tomorrow and shoot this bastard house up. We'll teach him not to fuck with a Vandino amigo."

After Shawn and Gena got in the house Paula said, "you guys back kind'uv early, what's the matter? Couldn't catch the blue light special," she laughed.

Gena said, "Shawn got into a fight with'ah bunch of Mexicans at the grocery store."

"You kidding girl?"

"N'all honey I wish I was, he in the living room mad as hell at himself."

"What he mad at himself for?"

"Because he started the shit, he broke the man jaw for no reason at all. All he had to do was tell the man he was sorry for running into him with the buggy."

Paula laughed saying, "at least he didn't lose the fight."

"Yeah, but when you wrong you wrong, and Shawn was in the wrong."

Saturday, March 27, 8:00 A.M.

Shawn was the first one up, and he woke Gena up saying, "aye you still going shopping with me?"

"Yeah what time is it?"

"It's eight o'clock, let's get ready, they'll be here at noon. I wanna have everything set up for them."

Paula and Antonio was still sleep when Shawn and Gena left the house going shopping. Gena said, "stop at a restaurant somewhere I'm hungry."

Shawn got off the expressway and drove to a small restaurant called Old Country Kitchen. They ate breakfast and then drove out to the shopping mall, and two hours later they were back home. Paula was in the kitchen making herself a cup of coffee.

Gena walked in the kitchen where Paula was at and showed her the gifts they had gotten Sorcerer and Maria for their anniversary.

Paula looked at the shirts and said to Gena, "this was very thoughtful. I like them, y'all could'uv got me one."

As they stood talking the phone ringed, and Shawn yelled out, "I got it," it was Sorcerer, "hello."

"Well Bomoski we are here."

"You kidding, you guys are two hours early."

"Yeah I know, now will you come and get us, we freezing out here."

"I'm on my way," Shawn hung up and called out to Gena, "Gena! I'm on my way to the airport to pick up the guests."

Gena came out the kitchen saying, "my goodness they here already?"

"Yeah, they are a little earlier than planned."

"I thought you arranged for the limousine to pick them up?"

"I did, but he not gone get there for another two hours, so that leave me to pick them up myself. Straighten up a little around here, I'll be right back."

"Do you still want me to make some pasta?"

"Yeah sweetheart."

When Shawn made it to Sorcerer and Maria, Sorcerer said, "man you guys have some of the coldest weather. If I would'uv known it was gone be this cold I would'ah packed my long johns."

"I'm just glad you guys made it. Maria you looking lovely as ever, welcome to Detroit

My wife can't wait to see you again. I hope you two enjoy y'all trip here. I'm y'all host till you guys leave. I have something special set up for you two. You guys gone love y'all anniversary gifts Gena and me got for y'all," Shawn said smiling.

Maria smiled saying, "I can't wait to see what it is."

"Where y'all luggage?" Shawn asked.

Sorcerer said, "we didn't bring any, that one suitcase was enough. We planned on going shopping here in America tomorrow."

Shawn smiled saying, "that sounds good, we'll have plenty fun."

It got silent in the car for a brief moment until Maria said, "what was your wife doing before you left the house?"

"Making sure you don't forget your stay here in Detroit.

Maria laughed saying, "how can I, the weather here won't let me."

"You'll get use to it," Shawn said.

Sorcerer said, "I really don't think so, we won't be here that long. By the way, did you invite Alvin over?"

"Yeah I did, but he said he couldn't make it this time, and to tell you hello. Well y'all we here, this is the home of the Bomoskis'."

Maria said, "you have a beautiful home."

"Thank you," Shawn said smiling.

When they got inside the house Paula and Gena was in the kitchen, and Antonio was upstairs playing with his toys, Shawn hollered out, "we home."

Gena and Paula came running out the kitchen to greet Maria and Sorcerer. Gena was the first to speak; she smiled saying, "it is so good to see you again Maria."

"It's good to see you too Gena," Maria said smiling.

Sorcerer smiled saying, "it is good seeing you two again. Both of you are looking nice as ever."

Paula smiled saying, "can I fix you guys a drink?"

Sorcerer smiled saying, "please, Scotch and water for me."

Paula said, "what about you Maria, what can I get you?"

"Soda and gin will be fine," Maria said smiling.

Gena said, "so how long have you two been married?"

"Exactly twenty-four years today," Sorcerer said smiling.

"Damn that's a long time," Gena said.

Shawn said, "it sure is, and I hope y'all see twenty-four more good years."

Sorcerer held the glass in the air saying, "now I'll drink to that."

They all held their glasses in the air saying at the same time, too twenty four years."

Sorcerer smiled, "I'm enjoying myself already, and I haven't even been here thirty minutes yet."

Maria smiled, "so am I, my husband could'nt'uv given me a more better anniversary present than this. And look who's coming downstairs, oh my goodness, he has gotten so big since the last time I seen him. Come here Antonio, come give me a hug." He walked up to her. "You are so cute." She put her arms around him. "Do you remember me?"

"No," he answered.

"Well, I remember you, you and my little girl are around the same age. I should'ah brought her with us; then you would have somebody to play with."

Nighttime had finally set in and they sat around the dinner table cracking joke after joke, laughing their hearts out. Shawn said, "hay why don't we all go in the living room and listen to Richard Pryor tape."

They all marched to the living room. Sorcerer peeped out the living room window and said, "mannn it's dark outside, don't you guys have street lights?"

Gena said, "yeah they normally on, something must be wrong with the power tonight."

Shawn said, "I want you two honeymooners to sit in the loveseat and enjoy the tape. I'll make the drinks this time."

Sorcerer said, "I want you and Gena to come to Columbia on y'all anniversary so me and my wife can spoil the hell out'uv y'all like y'all spoiling me."

Shawn put the tape on and walked over to the bar to fix the drinks, but before he could sour the first drink gunshots started flowing through the living room window by the seconds. Shawn ducked behind the bar, Gena and Paula dived to the floor. Sorcerer threw his body over Maria when she hit the floor. They all laid on the floor waiting for the shots to cease. Finally after about three minutes of shooting there was silence.

Shawn crawled from behind the bar asking, "is everybody all right?"

Sorcerer said, "I'm hit, but it's not bad." He looked at Maria and screamed out. "Oh my God Maria!" Blood was coming from her chest. "Get an ambulance!" He cried out.

143

After Gena seen the blood coming from Maria's chest she screamed out, "oh my God is it bad?!"

Sorcerer went into a rage and said, "dammit just call an ambulance! Maria, darling, you gone be okay."

Five minutes later the ambulance arrived. They quickly placed Maria on the stretcher. Sorcerer kept telling her, "you gone be all right, hang in there!"

Sorcerer rode in the back of the ambulance holding her hand all the way to the hospital, and when they arrived at St. Joseph Hospital emergency room, Sorcerer wasn't allowed to go in the operation room, so he waited patiently in the lobby, hoping and praying his wife would be all right.

Shawn arrived shortly after the ambulance arrived. He paced back and forth in the lobby with Sorcerer, and was trying to figure out in his mind what was going on at the same time. "Why did this happen? Who would want to shoot up my home?"

Thirty minutes later, Shawn looked at his watch and said to Sorcerer, "she been in there two hours now, she got to be okay!"

The doctor walked up to Sorcerer saying to him, "I'm sorry, we did all we could!"

Sorcerer just held his head down looking at the floor saying, "whyyyy, whyyy, why did this had to happen to her. God knows what's best!"

Shawn tried to put his arm around Sorcerer to comfort him saying, "I'm sorry!"

If looks could kill, Sorcerer's eyes had death in them as he said, "oh I bet you are you mothafucka, you had me setup!"

"I would never do that to you man, you know me better than that!"

"I know nothing. What the fuck am I gone tell my kids, huh, tell me that? You son of ah bitch you had me setup. You'ah dead man Bomoski, you hear me, ah dead man. Now get the fuck away from me. You will pay for my wife death, and I want rest till I see you six feet under!"

Shawn's heart was filled with sorrow and regret, wishing he had a way to get Sorcerer to believe him. Instead of making things worse with Sorcerer he decided to go on home.

When Shawn got home Gena and Paula met him at the front door. Gena asked him, "how is she?"

"She's dead, and Sorcerer thinks I set him up, now he wanna kill me. The only one who knew Sorcerer would be here tonight is Alvin, and I know he wouldn't do no crazy shit like that. I hate I ever talked'em in to coming to Detroit. Would somebody please make me a drink. What did the police say about the shooting?"

"All they did was take slugs from the walls and off the floor. Investigators suppose to be here after something like this happen I thought."

Wednesday, Mar 31, 1978 2:00 P.M.

Four days later Sorcerer stood over Maria's casket with tears running down his face saying to her, "don't worry Maria, I will avenge your death. He will pay for what he did to you, I promise you they all will pay!"

Shawn and Gena didn't attend the funeral, but had flowers sent to Sorcerer's home. When Sorcerer and his family got back from the funeral they started reading the names on the cards, seeing who sent what, and when Sorcerer spotted the card that said 'from the Bomoski family" he told one of his servants, "get this shit out my home, all of it!"

"Yes sir, right away," the servant answered. "And when you get done with that have my bodyguards to come to me immediately, that will be all for now."

"Yes sir, I go now," he answered.

The housekeeper did just as he was told. The bodyguard came to Sorcerer right away. He was in his middle thirties, deadly black looking eyes, six feet even, and dressed in all black.

The bodyguard looked Sorcerer in the yes and bowed. Sorcerer said, "I have a job for you, you gone need one more man to take with you. Y'all are going to America to do a hit for me. You the best man I got. Do not leave nothing breathing. You will leave today. I will give you the address to go too, ask no questions, just do your job. Go and choose you a man to take with you, and when you are done report back to me. You may leave now."

The bodyguard bowed his head and left, and when he returned to Sorcerer he had another bodyguard with him. Sorcerer said, "you two will have everything y'all need on the plane." He handed them the address. "Here's the address to the house y'all gone hit. I already told Shaka, and now I'm telling you, leaving nothing alive in that home. When y'all return, report back to me.

146

I'll have a bonus for the both of you. Y'all may go now, and me, I almost forgot, let the hit take place tomorrow at four o'clock their time."

The two bodyguards nodded their heads at the same time and walked out the door. When they left out Sorcerer said to himself, "I wish Maria could see you die Shawn Bomoski. My wife is dead because of you, and now you must pay!"

Meanwhile Shawn and Alvin were talking on the telephone to each other. Shawn said, "man you know he want rest until I'm dead, and there's no way he'll talk to me, what can I do?"

"If you know he gone kill you why don't you go somewhere else and live where he can't find you?"

"I'm not gone hide from'em, especially when I didn't do anything to'em."

"Well I guess you know what you doing, but if I was you I would pack my shit and leave Detroit before it's too late. What about Chicago? I have a few cousins there; they could show you the town."

"Thanks man, but no thanks, I'll take my chances here."

"That's on you man. Well I'm about to take my ass out to Southwest Detroit. I got some business to take care of; I'll try to call you back later on."

"Okay Alvin, I'll be here."

Thursday, April 1, 1978 9:30 A.M.

The next day the two hit-men left the Holiday Inn driving the car they rented at the airport. They drove straight to the address Sorcerer had given them to check out the scene.

Shaka said, "it's a good thing, I know how to read maps. This his house, we come back at four and take care of business. It is twelve o'clock now, we gone get food in stomach, then come back and wait in the car till time come."

While Shaka drove, Kayo spotted a donut shop. They stopped in and grabbed a table, and the waiter came over asking, "what will you boys be having?"

Shaka did the talking. "We'll have two coffees and two hamburgers."

The waiter smiled, "I haven't seen you two around here before, where you boys from?"

Shaka smiled, "we not from America, we from another country. I like other countries better."

"Well why do you come to America if you don't like it here, and what country are you from?"

"We fromm Columbia, never cold like this country."

"Well I definitely couldn't go somewhere I don't like."

After they were done eating, Shaka asked the waiter, "where can we go have a drink?"

"We can't, I'm a married lady," she said smiling.

Shaka laughed, "no, no, no, I was speaking of me and my partner. We would like to go somewhere where liquor served."

"Ohhh I'm sorry, I misunderstood you. It's a bar a couple'uv blocks from here called the Happy Tavern. I go there all the time when I leave work. When you leave here go left, you can't miss it."

"Thank you, you have been great help."

When Shaka and Kayo got to the car they both ordered Cognac on the rocks. A few white men sat at the table behind them, and one of the men yelled out to the bartender saying, "hay Bill, I didn't know you served niggers." Everybody at the table laughed at the joke.

The bartender said, "I'm not into discriminating. You fellas don't pay them no attention."

One of the men at the table said, "you two color boys need to be taught a good lesson about drinking our fine whiskey. Now why don't you boys leave peacefully before we get real upset."

The two hit-men just sat there holding their peace, and another man said, "I don't think you two boys hear too well, we don't like nigga company at all."

Shaka turned around and said to them, "why do you call us name, we not fuck with you, don't fuck with us. Excuse me bartender, where is restroom?"

"Right over there," the bartender said pointing his finger to the direction of the bathroom.

Shaka said to Kayo, "I'll be right back," he said downing his drink.

The three white men got out their seats and followed Shaka into the bathroom. Kayo saw what was going down and said to himself downing his drink. "God help them!"

149

After one out of the three men walked out the bathroom, the other two stayed to mess with Shaka. Shaka shook his head in a no motion and said, "why do you two come in here? I did nothing to you. I come here to have drink, that's all."

Shaka walked up to the toilet and one of the men walked over to the toilet next to Shaka, and as Shaka stood peeing the man took his penis out and peed on Shaka's shoe. The other man stood laughing.

Shaka zipped his pants up and said, "I see you America boys don't have respect. I teach you to fuck with me. We play yoe way, this game is called, let's see who die quickest." Shaka pulled his forty-five magnum out and placed the silencer on it. "You two ever play this game before?"

The man that peed on his shoe said, "please, please sir, we didn't mean no harm, don't kill me, we was only joking."

Shaka said, I know, I played your game, now you play my game, lay on your backs."

They laid on their backs begging for their life. Shaka spit on both of them and headed towards the door to leave, but before he could get to the door one of the men jumped up. Shaka turned around saying, "see that's not the way we play, you wasn't told to get up, and you have knife in hand." Shaka shot him right between the eyes. "It would be a shame if friend didn't have somebody to laugh at his jokes." Shaka shot'em in the head and rushed out the bathroom to get Kayo.

"Let's get out of here, this place stinks!" Shaka said storming out the door.

The bartender watched them leave out and said to himself, "where's Calvin and Frank?" He quickly rushed to the men's room, only to find both Calvin and Frank dead. He ran out the bathroom yelling. "Somebody call the police, Frank and Calvin just got killed; that foreigner killed both of them!"

The bartender ran outside to see if he could spot them, but they were nowhere to be seen, As Shaka drove he said, "we go wait at house we to hit, we have one hour left."

Five minutes later Shaka was parking the car a few blocks away from Shawn's house. He pulled out his binoculars and could see a car pulling into the driveway, and when he saw who it was getting out the car he couldn't believe his eyes and said out loud, "I be damned, it's Shawn Bomoski we have to kill. I hate to do this to you Bomoski, but job is job!"

"Are you sure it is Bomoski?" Kayo asked grabbed the binoculars, but too late, Shawn had went inside the house.

"I know him anywhere, he Sorcerer number one man in America. I guess he fuck up like Montana we had to take out some years ago. Get weapons ready, it is time we do this. Remember, no questions, we just kill!"

They had oozie machine guns that let out a hundred rounds a minute. Gena and Paula were sitting in the living room stoned on dope. Shawn was sitting in the living room in his favorite chair watching television, and Antonio was in the kitchen playing with his toy cars.

When Shaka and Kayo got to the house, Shaka pushed the doorbell, and Gena answered the door. "Who is it?"

"Is Mr. Bomoski in?" Shaka asked.

After Gena heard the name Bomoski she opened the door saying, "may I help you?"

Shaka and Kayo just cut loose on Gena with their oozies, making their way into the home. Before Paula and Shawn could make a move their bodies were being filled with lead. Antonio thought he was hearing firecrackers going off in the living room and stuck his head out the kitchen door, and as soon as they spotted the door moving they turned their oozies loose in that direction hoping to kill whoever was behind it, but Antonio ran straight downstairs to the secret hiding place where he knew he couldn't be found. Both Shaka and Kayo followed the stairs that led them down to the basement, but they was unable to find anyone, so Shaka said, "it was little boy."

"How do you know?" Kayo asked.

"I see face, we go now, the boy don't mean nothing, we got our man."

As they were leaving out they checked the bodies to make sure they were all dead, but when they got to Paula she was still breathing. Kayo lifted her head up by her hair and pumped a few more bullets in her head. Shawn and Gena were dead as dead. Shawn laid across the arm of the chair with blood streaming out of his mouth. Gena lay by the door with her eyes wide open, blood running out of her nose and mouth.

Hours passed, and Antonio was still hiding in the secret hiding place too frightened to come out. When the paperboy got to Shawn's house he noticed the door wasn't all the way shut and called out as he pushed the door open. "Mrs. Bomoski, your paper!" As the door opened wider he screamed and ran down the street.

Mr. Cash spotted the paperboy coming towards him running and said, "what's wrong Mark?"

"It's the Bomoskis, they all dead."

"What?" Mr. Cash said in shock. "Let me go and see what you talking about son."

When Mr. Cash got inside the house he couldn't believe his eyes. "Oh my God," he said staring at the bloody bodies.

Mr. Cash checked all the bodies and after he saw that they were all dead he called the police, and twenty minutes later the police along with the news reporters were swarming all over the house. The homicide department couldn't believe it; two execution killings within one hour apart.

The new caster Diane Lois stood in front of the house saying, "Detroit has become the number one murder capital in the world. I'm standing at the crime scene with the man who discovered the bodies. He had identified the neighbors known as Mr. Bomoski; he says that Mr. Bomoski has a son, but police are still unable to find the child. The child name is Antonio Bomoski. Here is a picture of what the child looks like." They showed his picture. "If you have seen this child please dial 911 immediately. Please, if you know where this

"I do that sometime, it's nothing, gone finish yoe homework."

Alvin called the morgue to arrange for the bodies to be cremated, and when he was done talking to the funeral director he called to tell Paula's mother the bad news, but before he could get a word to her ears, she was crying in his ears.

Alvin said, "I'm sorry about your daughter. I just wanted to let you know I was taking care of the burial. I'm having the bodies cremated. I'll bring her ashes to you. You okay? I can come out there if you like me too?"

"That's okay, I'll be all right. Did you tell Stan yet?"

"N'all not yet, I'll tell'em later."

"Thanks for calling. I'm fix'n to lay on down for a while. I'll talk to you later."

"Okay then, now are you sure you don't need anything?"

"N'all baby, I'm all right, talk to you later." Sharen hung up and laid on the couch crying her heart out, and saying over and over 'Lord" that was my only child. You took my baby from me. Why Lord? Why Lord?!"

As the day grew older, nighttime had finally set in. Stan was on his way to the bathroom to take his bath. Alvin walked up behind him saying, "befoe you get in the tub I got some very bad news to tell you son. Look man, something bad happened today to your mother and yoe Uncle Shawn and Gena."

"What happen to-um?" He asked.

Alvin put his hand on Stan's shoulders and looked him in the eyes. They were killed today!"

"Somebody killed them?"

Well let's ride then."

When they got to Shawn's house, Alvin had to force his way in the front door by kicking it in. The lights in the house were still on, and once they were inside the house they could see from the drawing of the chalk where the bodies laid. Alvin said, "come on son, show me where he at so we can get out'uv here."

When they got to the basement, Stan took Alvin straight to the hiding spot, and sure enough there was Antonio, balled up in a knot shaking like a pair of dice.

Alvin picked him up saying, "come on son everything gone be okay."

Antonio recognized Alvin and held on even tighter when he saw Stan standing behind Alvin.

Alvin drove straight home and fixed Antonio something to eat, and after Antonio had eaten, Alvin had him to sleep in Stan's room with Stan for tonight.

Alvin laid down in his bed thinking to himself. "Now I got two sons; I'll raise Antonio like he was my own, Bomoski would like that. I'm glad he escaped the hit, thank God for that. Stan has a brother now. I won't send you to school tomorrow; you got enough on your mind right now." The telephone started ringing, "hello."

"What's up man, this Dino?"

"I know yoe voice, what's up with you man?"

"Nothing man, you tell Stan the bad news yet?"

"Yeah, he took it better than I thought he would, and guess what?"

"What?"

"I have the kid with me."

"What kid?"

"The kid the police looking for."

"That's cool, where was he?"

"Stan took me straight to'em. Why don't you come out here tomorrow and I'll tell you about it, and I need you to help me do something."

"Gone get you some rest, I'll see you tomorrow."

"Yeah okay man, later."

Chapter XII

The next morning Alvin woke up and called Dino to let him know he was going out to Stan's school to try to get Antonio enrolled. After Alvin was done talking to Dino he woke Stan up saying, "if Dino come by before I get back let'em in, and you feed Antonio when you get up. I'll see you in a few."

When Alvin got to the school he went to the principal office. He spotted the gray headed man sitting down reading the newspaper, and said to him, "excuse me sir, are you the principal?"

"Yes I am, and how may I help you?"

"Well sir, I'm gone get straight to the point. A good friend of mine got killed in'ah shootout, and in this shootout his wife was also killed. They have a son and I'm the godfather. The kid needs to be in school, and I was hoping you could help me out."

The principal smiled, "I definitely can help you son, what's the boy's name?"

"You see sir that's where the problem comes in. I don't want everybody knowing this kid name. See people who killed his parents may wanna kill him too."

"I see, so what exactly do you want from me? Hold up, let me guess, what you want me to do is keep this boy's name from the public?"

"Exactly sir, and I can pay you let's say five hundred thousand not to mention his name."

158

"I'll do it, but for the record what is this kid name?"

"Antonio Bomoski."

"Well I'll be damned. I know exactly who you talking about; the police are looking for him as we speak."

"Yeah I'm aware of that, now can I trust you to keep this between us?"

"Of course you can, you just me your full name and address and we can do some business."

Alvin spotted three photos sitting on the desk. "Who are these three men on these pictures here?"

"Oh them my three sons."

Alvin smiled, "how long the one in the middle been'ah police?"

"Bout fifteen years now."

"Bout fifteen years huh. Thank you for your time sir, but that's okay about what we talked about. You have a good day."

"If you change mind, you know where I'm at."

"I'll keep you in mind, have a nice day sir."

"You too son, be seeing'ya."

The principal's name was Mr. Rose, and Mr. Rose decided to play police and follow Alvin, and Alvin had no idea he was being tailed. Mr. Rose followed him all the way home and wrote down the address, then drove to the nearest payphone and called the police. Sergeant Brice answered the phone. "Third Precinct, Sergeant Brice speaking."

159

The sergeant wrote down all the information Mr. Rose gave him and sent a swat team out to Alvin's home. Fifteen minutes later, police were swarming around Alvin's house.

Dino and Alvin were inside the house talking business. They had no idea the house was surrounded by sharp shooters until the chief police spoke into the megaphone saying, "you in the house, this is the chief of police speaking."

Dino said, "man did you hear that? It's coming from outside." He looked out the window. "Man police everywhere out there."

Chief said, "you in the house come out with your hands in the air."

Alvin said, "I'll be damned, that punk ass principal. I thought somebody was following my ass. Don't worry man they want me." Alvin opened the door, "I'm coming out don't shoot."

Dino called the kids down from upstairs so the police could see that they were okay. "Y'all gone outside behind Alvin so they won't hurt'em."

Alvin stepped outside. "What's the problem? I ain't done nothing wrong."

The chief said, "who them kids?"

"The black one is my son, and the Italian one is my godson. Both their mothers were murdered yesterday; they my responsibility now. Why don't you ask the kids who I am?"

The chief said, "you can put your hands down now." He yelled out, "at ease men. You know the police are looking for the Italian boy right now, and unless you have legal papers stating you the guardian, we gone have to take'em with us."

"But his parents are dead sir. I shouldn't need no legal papers; I'm the boy's godfather."

"I have o follow the law sir, and right now I got to take the child with me and make sure he gets proper care."

"Well what I got'ah do to get custody of him?"

"You got to get with the social service department and tell them you want to adopt the boy. If they let you the boy is yours. Excuse me sir, Sergeant Brice put the boy in the car."

Antonio started crying, and Alvin said, "don't worry lil-man, I'll be to get you, I promise!"

The chief said, "good day sir, and I hope you all the luck in the world with this boy."

"Thanks," Alvin said putting his hand on Stan's head walking back in the house.

Stan said, "where they taking Antonio dad?"

"Don't you worry son, he'll be back with us soon."

Dino said, "man you know social service ain't gone turn that boy over to no black man."

Alvin smiled. "Money talks and bullshit walks; remember that and you'll always get what you want in life. I'm going down there first thing Monday morning and get Antonio, and that I do know."

Monday, April 5, 1978 9:00 A.M.

Alvin made it to the social service department around nine that morning, and he was being orientated by Mrs. Steiner, and she read out each step to him on how to adopt. "First you must be an owner of your own home, and the home must have at least three bedrooms. Second, you can't have a criminal history background. So…if you meet all of these requirements you can adopt a child.

Alvin said, "I have a son of my own that I'm raising, and this little boy that I want to adopt is like a son to me already, I'm his godfather. I'll be honest with you up front Mrs. Steiner, I been in trouble once with the law, and that was years ago. I'm a different man now with a new attitude about life. Can you please help me adopt this child? I have my own home, and I have plenty money. I'll pay you whatever you want. Please let me adopt this boy!"

Mrs. Steiner let out a sigh. "Well since you were honest about being in trouble with the law before, and you do own your own home, and have a child already, I see no need why you can't raise this child."

Alvin smiled. "Thank you so much, how much do you want?"

"I don't want anything from you, except you give that child plenty love. That'll be enough pay for me. Now here are the adoption papers, he's all yours now."

"Thank you so much. I'm still gone send you some flowers or something to show my appreciation. You been so kind to me."

Mrs. Steiner smiled, "you get out'uv here befoe I changed my mind. Take care of yourself and your new son. If you need any tips feel free to call me."

Alvin smiled, "I'll do that, you have a good day Mrs. Steiner."

Alvin took the papers she gave him straight to the adoption center where they were holding Antonio. After Alvin showed the lady at the desk the paperwork she got on the phone and had Antonio brought to the front desk.

When Antonio got to the front desk and saw Alvin he started smiling, and Alvin smiled too and said, "what's up man, you ready to go home?"

Alvin stopped by the flower shop and bought a card and a dozen of roses for Mrs. Steiner! Alvin put a thousand dollars in the card. They took the card to her office, and Alvin opened the door to her office saying, "it's me again, this is the little boy you let me adopt. We brought you some flowers and a card to show our appreciation."

Mrs. Steiner smiled. "Ohhh he's so cute. Thank you both for the flowers and card. You'ah nice young man and I'm more than sure you'll make him a good father!"

"Well we got to get going now, say goodbye Antonio."

"Bye," he said.

Mrs. Steiner smiled, "bye sweetheart."

As soon as they left the office Mrs. Steiner opened the card up. Her eyes got big as a fifty cent piece as she smiled saying, "God bless his heart, he's a nice young man."

163

Friday, May 7, 1987 2:00 P.M.

Stan and Antonio both attended school at Southwestern High. Alvin had bought Stan a 1976 candy apple red Camaro for his sixteenth birthday. Stan was parked in the school parking lot smoking weed, waiting on Antonio to get out of school. The school bell rung at two-thirty and Antonio walked slowly toward the parking lot where he knew Stan would be waiting for him.

Before Antonio could get to Stan, three boys started bullying him, pushing on him, knocking his books out his hand. When Antonio bent down to pick up his books, one of the boys punched him in the back of his head. The blow caused him to fall on his chest.

When Antonio raised himself up, he saw Stan standing in front of him staring straight into his eyes with rage.

Stan shook his head saying, "what's wrong lil-broh, these punks fucking with you?"

"Yeah, they been messing with me all day in school, calling me scarface, punk bitch, shit like that."

Stan walked over to the bullies and said," yo man, why y'all keep fucking with my lil-brother?"

One of the boys said, "man fuck that mixed bitch!" Another boy said, "yeah fuck'em, he ain't yoe brother no-way."

"Oh he my brother, and I tell y'all what, the next time I catch y'all hoe motha fuckaz messing with'em again somebody going to Stinson Funeral

Home. I hope I make myself clear, now get the fuck away from here before I really get mad!"

Stan was two years older than the boys messing with Antonio, and the three of them knew they couldn't do anything with Stan, and Stan's reputation alone they feared.

After the boys walked off, Stan started yelling at Antonio. "Look man, you gone have to stop being'ah punk, you got to start fighting back. I'm not gone always be around to help you man, you got to learn to strap yoe nuts on!"

After they got in the car, Antonio thought seriously about what Stan said to him. Antonio could smell the weed still in the car, and Stan knew it, and he asked Antonio, "you want'ah joint man?"

"N'all I can't stand weed. I've been thinking about what you said man. From this day on out, win, lose, or draw, I'm not backing down from nobody else, not even them three chumps!"

"Now that's what I'm talking about lil-broh," he said taking a drag from the weed.

When they got home Alvin was in the living room talking with one of his employees, and after the man handed Alvin the briefcase he left. Alvin turned his attention to Antonio and Stan, "saying, 'what's up fellas? Y'all sit down, I wanna rap to y'all about something. Listen to me and listen good. One day a man told me to look up in the sky at the flying saucer. I looked up and he threw a paper airplane in the air and said, "did you see that flying saucer?" I said, no sir." Then he said, "I did that to tell you this, don't believe everything you see son. It don't always have to e what it appears to be." Now do you two understand what I'm trying to say?"

Stan said, "I think so." Antonio said, "yeah I got you."

Alvin said, "so what y'all do in school today?"

Antonio said, "I got into it with some boys today, but thanks to my big brother here I didn't get beat down."

Stan said, "all you got to do is start fighting back. Ain't nobody walking on this earth I wouldn't throw down with. You not included dad!"

Alvin laughed. "Lucky me, you definitely my son though."

The doorbell ringed, Antonio got the door, and it was Tangela. She smiled saying, "hi Antonio, is Stan home?"

"Yeah he here, come on in, he in the kitchen."

Alvin and Stan came out the kitchen; Alvin smiled saying, "hay Tangy."

Stan said, "what's up oh big head girl?"

Tangy smiled. "Forget you boy, hi Mr. Stone."

Alvin said, "I'm about to go to the store, anybody want anything while I'm out? Come ride with me Antonio, and we will be right back so you two behave yourselves."

Stan smiled, "take your time dad."

As soon as Alvin drove out of sight, Stan started undressing Tangela. She didn't resist the opportunity. They made love on the living room couch. When Stan got ready to burst inside of Tangy, she pushed him off saying, "boyyy you came in me?"

Stan said, "and?"

"And you know I'm not on the pill. I told you not to do that in me, dang!"

"I'm sorry baby, you just feel so damn good when I'm in you."

"You ain't getting no more."

"All baby, don't be like that."

"I ain't playing with you Stan, you know better. Suppose I get pregnant, then what?"

"Well, we'll just have'ah little Stan or Tangy running around the house."

"Well I ain't ready for no lil Stan or lil Tangy!"

"I am baby."

"Since you can't seem to control yourself, we want be doing it no-moe."

"All girl if it'll make you happy, I'll buy some condoms."

"That's more like it then, that's all you had to do from the start."

"I know girl, give me some sugar. You know I love you."

"Yeahhh and I love you too."

"'Fix yoe hair girl. I don't want my old man to think we been doing something in his house."

When Alvin and Antonio got back home, Alvin asked Stan, "when was the last time "That's more like it then, that's all you had to do from the start."

"I know girl, give me some sugar. You know I love you."

"Yeahhh and I love you too."

167

"'Fix yoe hair girl. I don't want my old man to think we been doing something in his house."

When Alvin and Antonio got back home, Alvin asked Stan, "when was the last time you had your tires and oil checked?"

"I don't know."

"Well I think you better do that today before you mess around and blow your engine man."

"I'll take care of it in a minute."

Antonio said, "I'll be glad when I'm old enough to drive. I wanna get me'ah Porsche, I love the way them babies drive."

Tangy said, "I want me a smooth riding Mercedes, just like yours Mr. Stone."

Stan said, "you like that car?"

"Yeahhh boy that's the ride."

"My Camaro is the ride. Come on girl let's go get this oil checked."

When Tangela stood up, Alvin even gazed at her ass, and he thought to himself, "damn that girl built, I'll fuck the shit out'uv her."

As Tangela was leaving she said, "have a nice day Mr. Stone, take care Antonio. I'll see y'all later. Yoe son look just like you Mr. Stone. Stan you look just like yoe daddy."

Alvin smiled saying, "is that good or bad? I hope it's good for your sake."

"Oh it is," she said pushing Stan out the front door.

Antonio shut the door behind them and said, "I wish I had'ah girlfriend."

"You'll find you one in due time son. You'll probably have so many girlfriends you won't be able to keep up with them."

"Since we talking, I keep on having these bad dreams about what happened to my mom and dad. It's kind'ah scary too. I wish I could stop dreaming about them."

"They'll go away son, but you got to realize you saw something kids don't normally see, and it's gone be on yoe mind for a long time. One day the truth gone surface, and when it does hopefully you'll be able to take care your business. Right now you too young to do anything. But I know for a fact, if you got your old man blood in you, you gone be'ah beast. And one more thing son, when you get your driving license, you'll get that Porsche you want."

Antonio smiled, "for real?"

"For real my son, and all I want you to do is stay your butt in school and make something out yourself. Now let's go find us something to eat I'm starving."

Two-hours-later Stan came walking through the door, eyes barely open from smoking weed. Alvin looked saying, "what's up with you boy, you look fucked up? You been smoking that weed shit again? That shit gone destroy what lil-brains you do have. What you do with Tangy?"

"I took'er home."

"She'ah nice young lady, you be good to her: a good woman is hard to find these days."

"Don't worry, she gone be my wife one day."

"So I take it you love'er then?"

"Can't you tell dad?"

"Hell I can't tell, you never tell me about her."

"Well I love'er, where's Antonio?"

"He probably upstairs doing his homework, something you never seem to have, but you'll see boy, you gone need that diploma. You ain't gone e able to get'ah dishwashing job without a diploma, you watch and see. I'm telling you something for your own good. I don't want you to grow up and be like me."

"What, a man that sells dope for a living? And I don't really see anything wrong with that."

"That's just what I'm talking about man," he started smiling. "You don't have to listen to me man, I know your head is like steel, but you make sure you don't fill Antonio's head up with yoe weed and shit. I want him to be something in life, I..." Antonio stopped doing his homework and went to the top of the stairs to listen. "I want you to be something too, but you got your head in your ass. One day you'll remember me telling you this shit!"

Stan said, "I'm gone be somebody."

Antonio thought to himself. "Alvin really cares about me. I'm gone make him proud of me."

Alvin said, "okay we'll see, wash your hands before you go in that food, ain't no telling what you been doing with yoe fingers, and I know you know what I mean too."

Stan laughed, "you'ah trip dad."

Alvin smiled. "Yeah dad was yoe age before." Antonio came downstairs. "Yoe brother is back, high as usual. Whatever you do, you don' mess with that weed, it ain't good for your brain."

""Don't worry, I can't stand the smell of weed."

"That's good, I'm about to step out for a lil-while. I'll see you later on."

After Alvin left Antonio went to the kitchen to see what Stan was doing, and said, "what's up Stan, see you got the munchies again."

"Hell yeah, good weed make you eat boy, and right now, I feel like I can eat'ah whole cow."

"How come you smoke so much weed? Do you know what that stuff do to the brain cells?"

"Look lil-broh I already been through one lecture with dad. I really don't feel like hearing you bitch about me smoking weed too. As long as I'm not hurting nobody, let me do my thang okay."

"Yeah man whatever you say that is yoe thing."

"That's right, I heard dad's car starting up. Where he say he was going?"

"He didn't, he just said he'll see me in'ah lil-while."

Stan smiled, "do you know what he do for a living?"

"N'all what he do?"

"Dad'ah big drug dealer, how else you think he could afford a house like this one with no job."

"He don't act like no drug dealer."

"That's because he don't want us to know. He want us o be high school graduates and slave for our money, but me, I'm not slaving for no mothafucka. I'm gone get paid like him. He rich lil-broh, got money up the ass."

"He rich?" Antonio asked.

"Hell yeah."

"You think we can get rich too?"

"I don't think so, I know so."

"I wanna be rich too."

"Stick with me lil-broh and you will be. If I make it to the top lil-broh you make it, and that's how it's gone be, just wait and see. What time is it?"

"It's almost eight."

"Damn, let me call Tangy before it gets to late." He dialed the number. "Hello, may I speak to Tangy?"

Stan could hear the music in the background as Tangy's mother asked. "Who is this?"

"Stan," he said. "Hi Stan, today is my birthday, wish me a ha00y birthday."

"Happy birthday, if I would'uv known I would'uv bought you a present."

"Well I'm giving a birthday party right now. Why don't you come on over, and bring that fine looking daddy of yours with yo, I heard he look just like you."

"Well he ain't home right now, but I'll tell'em what you said."

"You do that, and come on over okay, here go Tangy."

Tangy got on the phone saying, "hi, baby, my mother'ah trip ain't she?"

"Yeah just like her daughter, I see where you get yoe sense of humor."

"Yeah, yeah, are you coming over or what?"

"I'm bringing Antonio with me, we'll be there in'ah few."

"Don't be all night getting here neither."

"I don't have no mother."

"Boy just hurry yoe butt up would you."

"On my way, see you when I get there."

Stan hung up the phone saying to Antonio. "What's up man, come go with me to this birthday party Tangy mama giving. It's some girlies there too; you might be able to pull you one."

Antonio smiled, "cool, let's go. I'll leave a note on the door, better yet on the TV, that way pops won't be worried about us."

When they got to the party Tangy opened the side door and let them in, they all made their way downstairs to the basement.

Tangy noticed one of her girlfriends checking Stan out and said, "damn Shannon, you like what you see?"

"Yeah girl, that boy knows he got some sexy ass eyes."

"I know he do, he my boyfriend."

"Oh excuse me girlfriend, I didn't know," she said smiling.

Tangy's mother Mrs. Clay walked up to Stan, and before she could say anything Stan handed her the birthday card saying, "happy birthday Mrs. Clay,

173

if I would'uv known today was your birthday I would'uv bought you a gift. Thanks to my girlfriend here for not telling me."

Tangy said, "boy don't start with me, I forgot too."

"Mrs. Clay I want you to meet my lil-brother, this is Antonio, Antonio this is Mrs. Clay, Tangela's mother."

"Nice to meet you Antonio, would y'all like'ah beer? Y'all do drink beer don't you?" She said smiling.

Antonio didn't drink, but he didn't wanna say no, so he said, "I'll have one."

Stan couldn't believe his ears and said to himself smiling, "I better write this day on a calendar, he don't know one beer can fuck'em up."

Tangy brought the beers back and gave them to them. Antonio chugged his down and quick. It made Stan say, "dammn man yoe sure you don't drink this shit behind my back?"

Antonio burped and smiled saying, "get me one more, I like the taste of that last one."

"Okay, but take your time with the next one man."

After the second beer Antonio was feeling high, that high made him feel like dancing. Antonio finished off the beer and walked over to the nearest girl in his sight. Stan and Tangy stood back watching Tony walk across the basement floor, and they both laughed when he staggered.

Antonio spotted what he thought would be the perfect girl to dance with. He approached her saying, "would you like to dance?"

174

child is give the police a call. I'm Diane Lois signing off for channel three news."

The investigators believed the killings were drug related, and that's how they wrote it on their reports.

Dino was at home looking at the news with his mother and said, "I know my man who got killed. That's Alvin friend, I wonder if Alvin know about this. Let me call'em right quick." Dino dialed the number and Stan answered. "What's up lil man, where yoe daddy at?"

"Right here, dad telephone."

"Yeah Stone speaking," Alvin said.

"What's up man, did you see the news?"

"N'all man I been busy helping Stan with his homework. Why, what's up?"

"Somebody killed yoe boy Bomoski."

"You bullshitting."

"N'all man, they killed his wife and the girl."

"Yeahhh right man, I know today is April Fool Day, try again man."

"I'm sorry my brother, but this ain't no April Fool here, turn yoe TV on channel nine. They are looking for the lil-boy right now as we speak."

Alvin turned the television on and said, "I'll call you back man." Alvin put his head down. "How am I gone tell this boy his mother is dead, and can't nobody find Antonio. That damn Sorcerer!"

"What's wrong dad, why you talking to yoe-self?"

154

The girl smiled saying, "no thank you I'm with somebody."

The girl's boyfriend walked up behind Antonio saying, "what you say to her man?"

"That ain't yoe business what I said to her."

"O punk ass nigga I'm making it my business, that's my woman, you got something to say to her sissy you can say it to me."

Stan said, "damn I had'ah feeling this was gone happen. Let me break that shit up before it gets out'uv hand."

Tangy said, "and please do just that my mama don't want no fighting in her house Stan."

Stan said, "if he don't start none it won't be none."

Stan walked up to Antonio asking, "what's the problem?"

The boyfriend said, "this lil pussy told my woman to fuck off. You better get his lil bitch ass befoe I break something off in his ass!"

Stan said, "I doubt if you do all that my man."

The boyfriend said, "you can get some to nigga!"

Stan said, "I'm not with all that bullshit talk, we can take this on the outside, you make the call!"

The boyfriend said, "we can go right here nigga, what you thought."

Stan swung and hit him so hard it sounded like a gun and went off, and when the boy hit the floor Antonio started stumping him in the head Mrs. Clay ran over to break it up saying, "I'm not having this shit in my house."

Stan said, "I'm sorry Mrs. Clay, but I'm not gone let nobody mess over my brother. You have a happy birthday. Come on Antonio we out'uv here, I'll call ou tomorrow Tangy."

Tangy was to mad to say anything back to Stan, and thought to herself. "You embarrassed me in front of my mother; I'll get you back one day."

When Stan and Antonio got in the car, Stan said, "hell yeah Antonio, that's what I'm talking bout, don't let nobody chump you out, fight even if you lose."

"Don't worry, I'll never let nobody else chump me off again, and that's a promise from me to you!"

"Fuck all that talking, we gone either fight or dance, and I didn't come to dance with his ass. I fired his ass up and you did the rest."

Antonio smiled saying, "he was wayyy bigger than me."

Stan laughed saying, "size ain't shit; it's all in the heart. Don't ever wait on your opponent to draw first blood."

"Man that beer got me fucked up."

"I told you man, beer ain't no joke, that's why pops drink it."

"Thanks man for coming over to see about me."

"Man that's what big brothers are for, now ain't you glad you come with me tonight?"

"I must admit it, I'm glad you brought me with you tonight. I experienced a lot tonight messing with you."

Stan smiled, "I bet you dad ass ain't home."

176

As soon as Stan turned into the driveway Antonio said, "you right, he out hanging, probably over some woman house. It's almost twelve o'clock and I ain't got a thing to do."

The telephone rings, Stan answered. "Hello, Stan speaking."

"I hope you happy."

"Girl what you talking about?"

"You broke up my mama party."

"Girl don't call my house talking that I broke up shit."

"You make me sick," she hung the phone up on him.

Stan listened to the dial tone and said, "fuck you too bitch, lucky I didn't slap yoe mama for getting in my face talking that stupid shit. I'm tired of women already and I ain't even seventeen yet. All they wanna do is fuck and argue."

Stan walked up the stairs saying, "I wonder where Antonio disappeared too?" Stan looked in Antonio's room; he was knocked out snoring like a bull. Stan smiled. "O'well I guess I'll turn it in myself, ain't shit else to get into tonight."

Saturday, August 5, 1987 3:30 P.M

Alvin was outside barbecuing in the front yard in the driveway. He had the smell of hamburgers and steaks in the air. Antonio was outside sitting in the lawn chair next to the barbecue.

Stan came outside and started bouncing his basketball saying, "what's up Antonio, you wanna go shoot'ah few jays with me?"

"N'all man I don't feel too good."

"Dad if Tangy call me tell'er I'll call'er back when I get back. I should be back befoe seven; I'll catch you two later on."

Stan burned rubber pulling out the driveway; Alvin shook his head saying, "that boy ain't playing with'ah full deck at all."

An hour had passed since Stan left; Alvin noticed a car pulling into his driveway and said to Antonio, "I wonder who could this be?"

"Look like Tangy," Antonio said zeroing in on the car. "It is Tangy."

Tangy got out the car smiling and said, "hi Antonio, Mr. Stone, where's Stan?"

Alvin answered. "You just missed him, he went to shoot some basketball, he'll be back around seven he say, but you know how that knuckle head boy is when he gets in them streets."

Tangy smiled, "you don't mind if I wait here for him do you?"

"Course not, you welcome here anytime. Do you like steak?"

"Yes," she answered. "Good, its one on the grill for you if you want one."

Antonio said, "I don't feel too good, I'm going to lay down for a lil-while, it's got to be the heat."

"Okay son, drink you something cold that might help."

"Think I'll just lay on down."

Tangy said, "I hope you feel better when you get up."

Alvin smiled saying, "so Tangy who car you got?"

178

"That's my mama car, she out of town for the weekend, and that give me a chance to keep it all to myself. She say gone give it to me when I graduate."

"That'll be nice, I hope she keep her word," he said smiling.

"O she will, she don't like for me to be mad at me."

"Why you say that?"

"Cause, if I don't speak to her it irritates her, and she can't stand being irritated, especially by me."

Alvin laughed, "I see."

"Mr. Stone you mind if I use your bathroom right quick?"

"Look Tangy, you don't have to ask me to use no bathroom, you welcome to use anything in my house."

"Excuse me for'ah minute, I'll be right back."

"Take your time young lady." As she walked away his eyes were glued on her ass. He shook his head, "man that girl got'ah ass on her."

Tangy went upstairs and used the bathroom, and when she was done she came downstairs and started searching for the remote control to the television, and as she was looking on top of the television she spotted a pile of money and started counting it. When she was done counting the money she said, "fifteen thousand dollars, damn that's a lot'uv money. I ain't never seen so much money at one time."

Tangy put the money back on the television and went back outside. Alvin was flipping the burgers over on the grill. Tangy smiled saying. "I was looking for the remote control, but I couldn't find it. I couldn't help, but to notice all the money on the television."

"That ain't no money, that's chump change," he said smiling.

"Shood fifteen thousand dollars ain't hardly no chump change."

"Ohhh so you counted it?"

"I couldn't help it."

"It's okay, I was just wondering how you knew the exact money."

"What I wouldn't do to have fifteen thousand dollars of my own."

Alvin smiled, "well, tell me what exactly would you do to have your own fifteen thousand dollars?"

"Anything, but kill for it."

"Now I know you wouldn't do anything."

"Yes I would, do you know what I could do with all that money. I could get my own car, and you know."

"N'all I don't know, I asked you what would you do to have the money you just saw?"

Tangy smiled, "you name it, I'll do it. I can't put it no better than that."

"Would you sleep with somebody for it? I can't hear you, what's the matter cat got yoe tongue?"

"Shood I sure would."

"Would you sleep with me for that kind of money?"

"Yeah, I guess so."

"Well if you sleep with me right now you can have all that money you saw on the television."

"What about Stan?"

"I'm not gone tell'em, and I know you not gone tell'em!"

"What about Antonio, he upstairs sleep."

"As long as he sleep he can't hear nothing or see nothing."

"Come on we better hurry up then."

Alvin didn't bother taking the meat that was still cooking off the grill. They both hurried to Alvin's bedroom and got undressed. Alvin turned the radio on, and got in the bed with Tangy. They started making love. Antonio woes up and as he headed to the bathroom he could hear the sound of a woman's voice coming from Alvin's room saying, "fuck me, fuck this pussy, yes, yes."

Antonio said to himself, "damn I know that ain't who I think it is in there."

When Antonio finally made it outside he found the meat burning up on the grill, and saw that Tangy's car was still in the driveway. He shook his head saying, "that girl upstairs fucking the old man, she ain't shit!"

Antonio sat on the porch with his head down until he heard the sound of Stan's car pulling up. Stan parked on the street since Tangy had taken his parking spot.

Stan got out the car drinking a pop and saying, "what's up man, you look like you worried about something."

"N'all man I'm all right."

"Where dad and my girl? I see her mama car here."

"I guess they in the house, I don't know I just woke up."

Stan opened the screen door and looked back at Antonio, and said to himself, "that boy tripping off something." He stepped in the house. "Damn it's quiet down here, Tangy probably got her ass upstairs in my room waiting on me. Dad ass probably sleep," Stan headed up the stairs calling Tangy.

Tangy said, "oh shit that's Stan."

Alvin said, "hurry up and get out'uv here befoe he come up here."

It was too late for them, Stan had made it to the top of the stairs when Tangy came running out of Alvin's room with no top on trying to make it to the bathroom.

Stan couldn't believe his eyes and said, "what the fuck is this shit bitch. I know this ain't what I think it is."

Tangy was speechless and scared out of her mind as she stood staring at Stan. Stan opened Alvin's door and saw him trying to get dressed and said with a raging voice, "you ain't shit man!"

"Man let me explain."

"Fuck you man!" Stan stormed out of Alvin's room. Tangy was still trying to button her blouse. Stan looked at her with hate in his eyes. "Bitch you still here?!"

Tangy said, "I can explain, I didn't mean…" Before she could get another word out Stan was punching her lights out. She started screaming, "please Stan!"

Alvin stormed out the room saying, "you not gone hurt this girl under my roof boy!"

"I hate your fuck'n guts man, I thought I had'ah caring father, but I see you ain't shit. From now on I ain't got no father, and you can have yoe mothafuck'n roof. I'm out'uv here! I don't never wanna see you or your fuck'n roof again. I hate both you dirty ass no good tramps, don't ever cross my path again, and I mean that from the bottom of my fuck'n heat!"

Stan ran downstairs and grabbed his keys and jumped in his car and took off like a jackrabbit. After Antonio saw Stan kick over the barbecue grill he didn't bother saying anything to Stan.

Two minutes later Tangy came out the house crying. She said goodbye to Antonio, but Antonio was too upset with her to speak back, and said in his mind, "just leave bitch you done broke up the family. I hope I never see you again in my life."

Alvin came to the front door and saw Antonio sitting with his head down and said to him, "I hate what just went down. I should'nah done that too my son. I was dead wrong. Damn, I lost'ah son over some stanky ass pussy!"

Alvin saw that Antonio wasn't responding so he went and sat on the couch to try to collect his thoughts. Antonio got on up off the porch and went inside where Alvin sat and said, "you all right old man?"

"Yeah I'm all right, I fucked up though!"

"I know I saw Stan when he was leaving. He didn't bother to say nothing to me. You think he'll be back?"

"I don't think so, he hate for what I did, and I can't blame'em!"

"It ain't yoe fault she wanted to sleep with you. She got'ah mind of her own, she knew what she was doing. It ain't like she didn't know what she was doing."

"I'm glad you understand son. I'm just sorry it went down the way it did"

Chapter III

Friday, June 18, 1990, 6:00 P.M.

Three years later, Antonio graduated from high school just like he said he would. Alvin was very proud of him; he loved watching Antonio walk across that stage to his cap and gown. Every time Alvin looked at Antonio, he thought about Stan. Years had passed by and he still hadn't heard from Stan. He knew Stan had went to stay with his grandmother Sharen, and would often call out to Sharen's trying to speak with Stan, but Stan refused to hear his voice.

After Antonio came off the stage from receiving his diploma he looked at Alvin and smiled saying, "so what you think of me now?"

Alvin smiled, "I'm proud of you son, you did it!"

"Yeah I did, and thanks again for the ride."

"You deserved it man. Now sit down for'ah minute I wanna talk to you about something, and I'm only gone tell you this once. You see Antonio, you is like m own son, and I love you like you was my own. Now is the time for you to make your own decisions. You'ah grown man. I never told you this before because I thought you were too young to understand. I won't beat around the bush. I'm not'ah high school graduate. I didn't go to school. I always hustled my way through life. What I'm trying to tell you son..."

"You don't have to explain to me. I already know you deal drugs, and I don't knock what you do. In fact I admire you very much because you waited till you thought I would be able to understand, and I appreciate that, I wanna be like you!"

"You wanna be like me? What I do is a dangerous game son!"

"Life itself is a dangerous game."

Alvin smiled, "You smarter than I thought, but what do you know about selling drugs man?"

"I know about seventy-five percent of my school was getting high off drugs."

"Mannn you'ah high school graduate now, you can go to college, and make something out yourself."

"I'm not going to college. Look, I finished high school to make you happy. I'm not spending the rest of my life slaving for somebody else enjoyment!"

"Well just what do you wanna do with your time out here?"

"I wanna be like you, do what you do. For reason reason I feel like I was meant to be'ah dope man."

Alvin smiled. "So you wanna sell drugs. Well if that's what you wanna do I'm the best teacher in the world for that, and your first lesson is to never trust no-one, and I do mean no-one. That's number one. Number two is simple: you got to have'ah a cold heart, or people will shit on you every time. Third and the last of all don't ever use no type of drug. You cannot get high on your own supply and expect to stay successful in the dope game. If you follow these three steps you'll make it to the top. And don't forget this here; you can never get bigger than the big man himself. So once you in, you are in, there is no getting out. Now do you follow me so far?" Antonio shook his head in a yes motion.

"Good, because one day you'll probably have to run my business, and I want you to be on top of your game."

"I know plenty people who wanna buy dope right now."

"I tell you what son, I'm gone give you a couple've kilos and you can do whatever you want with them. This just to see where your mind is."

Antonio smiled, "cool, I have this friend, his name Veno."

Alvin cut him off, "never ever give the person you dealing with name out."

"My bag, I got'cha, let me give him a call." Antonio dialed the number, somebody answered. "Yeah Veno in?"

"This Veno, who this?"

"What's up Veno, this Antonio."

"My main man Antonio, what's up?"

"I got'ah couple'uv keys I'm trying to get rid of, can you help me out?"

"No problem man, can you be at the viaduct on Schaefer Road in an hour?"

"I'll be there," he said hanging up smiling at Alvin. "Look at that, my first customer."

"Look here son, you gone need'ah heater, you never know what might go down!"

"This my boy, I trust'em."

"Didn't I just tell you not to trust nobody? Go upstairs and look in my top dresser draw, take the thirty eight special, you can have it, it's yours. Don't take it if you scared to use it."

"I got one question."

Alvin smiled saying, "I already know what you wanna ask me. The kilos go for fifteen thousand ah piece, but they yours now, you can sell'um for whatever you want too, since they yours now."

"I'll be back in'ah few minutes."

"You be careful man, and if you have to don't hesitate to blow'ah son-of-a-bitch head off!"

"Don't worry I'll be okay."

"I'll see you when you get back."

Veno went and picked up his friend Lando, and as Antonio got closer to the viaduct he thought about what Alvin said to him. "Don't trust nobody. Don't be scared to use your gun."

Antonio picked the 38-special up saying to it, I'm not scared to use this baby." Antonio drove under the viaduct and checked the scenery out. He spotted the TRANS-AM. "That's got'ah be Veno."

Antonio drove up to the vehicle, Veno was sitting on the passenger side and rolled down the window smiling and saying, "what's up Antonio?"

"What's up Veno, you ready to do business?"

"Yeah man, you got the stuff?"

"You know I do."

"Well what you waiting on? Bring it over and my man can check it out."

Antonio had the dope in a brown paper bag. Antonio checked his gun making sure it wouldn't slip out his pants. When he got out the car Veno smiled saying, "this is my friend Lando."

Lando reached over Veno and shook Antonio's hand. Antonio noticed the dragon tattoo with the word cobra inscribed in it. Lando smiled saying, "so my man you wanna get rid'uv some birds. Let's see the yaeo."

Antonio handed the hag to Veno, and he passed it to Lando and yelled, "drive man, drive."

Lando pushed the paddle to the floor and Antonio grabbed the latch on the passenger door with his left hand, and gripped his gun with his right hand and the car started driving off. Veno was trying to knock Antonio hand loose, but when Antonio finally got control of the thirty-eight special he started firing shots into the car before turning the door latch loose.

Antonio thought he had broken his arm, but after he saw that his fingers was moving he said, "it's not broke, I don't need no doctor. Damn, they got away with my dope. Veno I swear, if I ever see you or your man again, y'all dead meat. I learn from my mistakes."

Meanwhile, Lando was driving and laughing and saying, "we did it, you was right, that punk is soft as hell." Veno wasn't responding back. Lando glanced over at him; he could see Veno's head was titled over. Lando pulled in the nearest alley and saw that Veno had been shot in the neck. He opened the passenger door and kicked the body out his car. "God be with you my friend. Thanks for the dope, I'll see you one day, adios amigo."

Antonio drove around in Mexican Town hoping he could spot Veno. After driving in circles for thirty minutes he decided to drive home. When he got home Alvin was in the living room watching television. Alvin could look in Antonio eye's and see that something was wrong. Antonio let out a big sigh and said, "I blew it man, I'm sorry."

"You ain't got to be sorry, it was yours to blow. They took off on you didn't they:"

"Yeah."

"Why didn't you smoke they ass?"

"I tried, but I couldn't get'ah clear shot off. I was holding onto the car door and trying to shoot at the same time. I hope I run into Veno again. I'll see'em again, he can't hide forever."

"Forget about it for now, you hungry? It's some pizza on the stove, wash yoe dirty hands too."

Alvin wasn't mad at Antonio for messing up. He could tell by Antonio's clothes that he tried to get to them, Alvin went in the kitchen behind Antonio saying.

"I'm having'ah meeting here tomorrow and I want yo to be there. I think if you hang around Dino for a few days you can learn a lot from him. As a matter of fact let me call'em now and he won't have no excuse not to be here tomorrow."

Saturday June, 19, 1990 3:00 P.M.

Dino brought Chico and two more of the Ecorse gangsters out to Alvin's house. Alvin opened the door smiling and saying, "I see you fellas are here at three on the nose. It's plenty to drink so y'all make y'all selves at home. Dino I got something I need you to do for me. I want you to take Antonio with you for'ah few days under yoe wings, show'em how the business is ran. Okay everybody, I called this meeting today for one reason only. Listen and listen good, if anything happen to me, I want Dino and Antonio to hold the fort down!"

Dino said, "man that's automatically, you know I got yoe back man!"

"I know man, and I have you to death for that. I just need you to teach my son here the game."

Dino said, "you can consider that done. When I'm through with him, won't nobody be able to touch'em. Speaking of sons' man, when the last time you heard from Stan?"

"Well I haven't," he sadly said.

Dino quickly changed the subject saying, "so you want me to turn Antonio into a gangster?"

"That's right, and make'em cold as ice, like me."

Dino laughed, "you know we can't turn nobody into another Stone."

Alvin laughed, "then turn'em into another Dino," they all laughed.

191

Antonio sat back sipping on a Budweiser listening to all the gangster talk that seemed to flatter him. Antonio thought to himself, "what went down yesterday will never happen to me again."

Dino said, "all right nephew get ready, you coming with me. I'm gone show you how to be like yoe godfather and me."

Antonio said, "yeah I can't wait, let me grab'ah few things right quick."

When Antonio came back downstairs, Alvin said, "leave yoe car here and ride with Dino."

"Okay, we out'uv here."

When Dino got back in his neighborhood he stopped by Rollins Party Store. "Nephew you want anything out'uv here?"

"Yeah bring me back'ah nice cold six pack of Budweiser."

As soon as Dino walked away from the car a girl from the hood came walking pass the car smiling at Antonio. Her name was Cat, a well built pretty black girl with pretty jet black hair to go along with her pretty black eyes. She was five feet eight, around seventeen years old. Antonio liked what he saw, and when Dino came back to the car he asked him, "what's on yoe mind man?"

Antonio said, "that chick that just went inside the store digs me man."

"Man you don't want none of these sluts out here in this hood."

""""Man that's just what I'm looking for, ah slut, I'll be right back."

Antonio got up enough nerves to walk on in the store. Dino just laughed at him saying, "it's yoe dick, don't say I didn't warn you when it fall off. These bitches out here will burn you in'ah heartbeat. I hope he know what he getting into."

Antonio came out the store smiling and holding a piece of paper in his hand with Cat's phone number on it. When he got in the car Dino said, "I see you scored. I wish I was yoe age again. I see so many young bitches till it's a shame."

"Yeah man it's something special about that girl I like. I told her I'll get back with'er in a few days. She say she only live'ah few blocks from here."

Dino smiled. "I'm glad you found you'ah lil lady you like, but do be careful my man, these girls out here will set you up in'ah heartbeat."

"I heard that, I'll be careful, trust me."

"Well let me take you around'ah few blocks; show you how the niggas the whities be chasing after that cocaine shit. You won't believe how much money comes through here'ah day. This is one of the fastest money making operations in the world. No, no. let me rephrase that, this is the fastest money making operation in the world. And the best part about it, we supply the supplies. You gone be the man one day, that's why Alvin wants me to school you. He believe in you nephew. Alvin is the man who got me on top, and I love that black man to death. I'll kill the dead for him. He's ah good man." As they continued driving, "you see all them buildings coming up here, yoe old man own all of them. You see that street there, Bassett Street? That's where Stan grandmother stays. Yepp, that's yoe god-brother street."

"I knew he stayed out here somewhere, but I never knew what street. That shit that happened with him and the old man was fucked up."

"Yeah it was, Alvin never did have good dick control," they both laughed.

"You know nephew, you okay for an Italian boy, I like you."

Antonio smiled, "I like you to man, I can see it's gone be fun hanging with you."

"Later on we gone cruise down the hoe stroll where the hoes hang out."

"Where the hoe stroll?"

"You mean to tell me you don't know where the hoe stroll is nephew?"

"N'all man I don't."

Dino smiled, "Woodward Avenue man, everybody know where the hoe stroll is."

"Everybody but me."

"When I'm done with you nephew, believe me you gone be hipped to'ah lot of things from fuck'n with me nephew."

"I heard that," Antonio said smiling.

"Pass me another beer man."

"Damn you can drink man."

"That's why I paid for it," Dino laughed and he popped the cap off the beer. "I'm fix'n to take you on Seventh Street to the pool room. When we get there show no signs of fear. First of all can you shoot pool?"

"I ain't got no table at home for nothing, hell yeah I know how to shoot."

"Good, cause these boys like to bet big money, and I love taking it from'um. So if anybody in their wanna bet you gone and bet, I got you covered."

Antonio was a pretty good pool shooter. When they got inside the pool room he won his first three games. They were playing a hundred dollars a game. When Antonio was done shooting he said to Dino, "I won three hundred."

Dino smiled. "That's cool, but you ain't ready for me yet nephew."

"Ain't, but one way to find out," Antonio said smiling.

Dino said, "rack man, rack'um up man, and I'm gone let you break the balls first nephew."

Antonio didn't make a ball on the break, and Dino got his pool stick and ran the table. When Dino sank the eight ball he smiled saying, "like I said nephew, you ain't ready for me yet, but you keep on practicing and maybe one day we'll play for that pretty Porsche you got parked back at yoe house."

Antonio could tell by the way Dino was talking that he was a stone hustler. Antonio smiled saying, "n'all man I don't think I'll ever get that good."

Dino smiled. "You learn fast nephew, I like that. Well we killed about four hours bullshitting in here, it's about ten something. Let's make that ride I was telling you about earlier, and I can use another beer."

"Yeah me too."

After they got in the car Dino said, "here man, here yoe money back."

"You won that money fair and square."

"Yeah I know man, but I knew you couldn't do nothing with me on that pool table. I been shooting that shit every since I was five years old."

"Yeah, but how did you know you could beat me?"

"When you were playing them other fellas, you missed too many shots, and a guy like me don't miss too often."

"In other words you hustled me?"

"Nope I taught you something. If you wanna b better than somebody else in what you like to do always observe the person you trying to outdo moves. I observed yoe moves. If you don't want him to be better than you don't show him what you know."

"Man you really schooling me."

"That's the mission I'm on, now let's go get on a six pack and cruise the hoe stroll for'ah minute. Not unless you ready to turn in or something?"

"Hell n'all, I ain't had this much fun since Stan took me to that basement party with him."

"You know I'm taking you through this for a reason don't you. I'll tell you about when it's all over if you don't catch on yourself. Whoo weee that's one ugly motha fucka coming this way."

Antonio looked at the man and burst out laughing and saying, "you'ah trip man, you should be'ah comedian."

"N'all Antonio, my man, dope pusher is all I'm gone be. I don't know anything else, I'll probably die selling dope, but at least I can say I died'ah rich nigga."

"I heard that, but we got'ah long way to go befoe we cross that dying bridge."

Dino smiled, "I hope so nephew."

When they got to Woodward Avenue, Dino started pointing at different hoes saying, "if you see one you like nephew let me know, I'll pull over so you can take care yoe business."

Antonio smiled. "Man why you trying to test my ego. I'm not going for this one. I know you just testing me. Damn man, pull over, I know that girl there from somewhere."

"You sure man, I can back up if you want me too."

"Yeah back up." Dino backed the car up. "Hell yeah, that's the bitch Stan use to mess around with, that freak selling pussy now, I'll be damned."

Dino laughed, "wait'ah minute nephew, you mean to tell me that, that's the girl Alvin and Stan fell out about?"

"That's her man."

"Mannn cuss that bitch out."

Antonio called her over to the car and said, "what's happening Tangy, so you selling pussy now?"

Tangy recognized him, "ain't you Stan brother?"

"Yeah bitch, I don't see what he saw in you, I always knew you wasn't shit. Here's a dollar for your time, that's all'ah slut is worth. Man let's ride befoe this hoe make me throw up."

Dino was cracking up. Tears rolled down Tangy's face as she watched them pull off. Antonio said, "did I break it to that bitch or did I break it to'er?"

"You told that nasty ass slut off. Bitch caused my boy to lose his son. I should go back and buss'ah cap in her stanky ass, old stanking bitch!"

"Man fuck that girl, let's ride. I'm not into fucking hoes so you might as well find us something else to get into."

"I don't care how desperate you get, never take'ah hoe home with you. Ah woman is sometimes considered to be man's weakness. A lot of men try to use the woman to set'ah man up, if you know what I mean."

"I know exactly what you mean. I learned a lot from you today. I see why the old man wanted me to hang with you for'ah few days. I seen enough for one day I'm ready to take it in, call that lil lady I met earlier and see what's up with her."

When they got to Dino's house he said, "you got to be extra quiet man, I don't wanna wake my mama up." They went downstairs to the basement. "We downstairs, make yoe-self at home."

"I just wanna use the phone. I'm gone call this girl anyway, they can't do nothing, but cuss me out for calling so late."

"I doubt that, these people around here go to bed till late anyway and I mean late. Most of us up all night chasing that crack shit, looking like vampires and shit." Antonio laughed. "You laughing man, but I'm serious as hell, you'll see."

"I believe you, you ain't told me nothing wrong so far."

"And I'm not gone tell you nothing wrong, you my nephew. Now gone use the phone, I'm fix'n to take me'ah shower."

Antonio dialed the number Cat had given him. A male voice answered the phone, "hello."

"May I speak to Cat?"

"Yeah hold on. Cat....telephone."

"Ask who it is."

"She said who calling?"

"Tell'er Antonio."

"Antonio," he yelled out.

Antonio could hear Cat's voice in the background saying. "Oow I been waiting on this call all day." Cat got on the phone. "It took you long enough, what you up too?

"Sorry about that. I'm not up to nothing right now, how bout you?"

"I'm just sitting around the house hoping you would call."

"Actually I didn't know if it was cool to call this late or not, but the beer I was drinking said go right ahead they can't do nothing, but cuss you out."

Cat laughed, "we be up late around here, so where you stay?"

"I stay in Romulus, and I went to Southwestern High School out this way."

"Oh yeah, I went to Rouge High, and I graduated this year."

"Square business, I did too."

"So do you know'ah lot'uv people in Southwest Detroit?"

"N'all not many, my god brother do."

"What's yoe god brother name?"

"Stan Stone."

"I know him, my girl like him, he look good. Ah lot'uv girls out here wanna get with him. I see him all the time. Ain't his father a big drug dealer?"

"I don't know about all that, but I do know he own a lot'uv businesses out here. That might be why people think he a drug dealer. Anyway when will you be available for'ah movie or something?"

"Shood I'm available tomorrow for a movie."

"Can I pick you up at your house or what?"

"Sure you can."

"I'm not gone run into yoe boyfriend am I?"

"N'all because I don't have'ah boyfriend, not unless you gone be."

"I wouldn't mind being your boyfriend. I like what I saw today."

Cat smiled, "I like what I saw today too."

"Hold that thought baby, I'm not much of'ah talker on the phone, we'll finish this conversation tomorrow over dinner and a movie. Give me yoe address right quick." Cat gave him the address. "So how does three o'clock sound?"

"Sound good to me."

"Good, I'll see you at three then."

Dino had got out the shower and made his way back to Antonio. He looked at Antonio and smiled saying, "boy that girl must'uv told you something awfully good. You got'ah smile on yoe face that want erase."

"Yeah I'm taking her out tomorrow to dinner and then after dinner to the show."

"That's cool nephew, you can use one of my cars out there. I'm glad you met you somebody you like. If you wanna take her somewhere nice, take her to the Landsdown Restaurant. That's this lil ship on the riverfront, they serve damn good food."

"I'll keep that in mind. Where you keep your wash rags? I'm fix'n to hit the shower and take my butt straight to sleep."

"Well I'll see you in the morning nephew, cuss I'll be sleep before you get out the shower."

Sunday, June 20, 1990 2:40 P.M.

Antonio pulled in front of Cat's house and got out the navy blue Mercedes Benz. He looked at the address and walked up to the door and knocked three times.

Cat's mother came to the door saying, "hi, come on in, I'm Cat's mother Ms. Bell."

Antonio smiled, "nice to meet you Ms. Bell, I'm Antonio."

"Nice to meet you Antonio," she called for Cat. "Cat... somebody here to see you," she said smiling."

201

"I'll be right down," Cat said yelling down the stairs.

Ms. Bell smiled. "Have'ah seat, she'll be with you in'ah second."

Antonio could see Cat coming down the stairs, and when she got to the bottom of the stairs he smiled saying, "you look lovely, I wish I would'uv brought my camera with me."

Cat smiled, "you like this old gold dress?"

"Yes I do, gold is my favorite color next to green."

Ms. Bell said, "I told you he'll like it. Now you make sure you take care my lil girl Antonio."

"Oh I will, you don't have to worry, she's in good hands. She'll be all right with me, I promise you."

"Okay then, y'all have fun and I'll see y'all later," Ms. Bell said smiling.

Antonio said, "we will, it was nice meeting you Ms. Bell."

"Nice meeting you to baby."

After Antonio and Cat got in the car, Antonio said, "I'm taking you to the best restaurant in Detroit."

"And where is that?" She asked smiling.

"The Landsdown baby."

"I heard it was nice."

Antonio smiled. "Can I ask you a question?"

"Sure," she said smiling.

"Where did you get the name Cat from?"

"Oh that's just short for Cathy."

"Cathy is a pretty name."

"Thank you, is Tonio short for Anthony?"

"N'all Tonio is short for Antonio."

Cat smiled, "I was gonna say Antonio first."

"I bet you were," he said smiling.

"I'm serious, honestly I was."

When they got to the restaurant they were seated at a table for two, candles burning on each side of the table. Antonio smiled saying, "order anything you want baby."

"I'll have the lobster dinner special and a kiss to go with it if you don't mind?" She said smiling.

"Not at all," Antonio said smiling and leaned over to kiss her. "You have soft lips. I guess I'll have the same thing you having."

After they were done wining and dining they took a walk down the waterfront holding hands. They were walking and started kissing. Antonio smiled saying, "I got to be honest with you. You the first girl I ever been with!"

Cat just smiled. "And you make sure you keep it like that too, I wanna be with you Antonio!"

Antonio took his gold chain off his neck and put it on her neck saying, "I don't want you to ever take this chain off!"

"I'll never take it off. I wish I had something to give you."

"Let's not worry about me okay. I just wanna make you happy. The main thing is we together."

"Yeah I'm so glad I decided to walk to the store. I was thinking about sending my lil brother and something said girl get yoe lazy butt on up and go yoe-self. Lucky for me I did, or I would'nah never met you."

"Let's go catch us a movie."

"What's playing?"

"It don't matter to me, as long as we together. I think Death Wish is playing though."

"Yeah it's playing, I seen previews of it yesterday."

"Good, Death Wish here we come."

Antonio started thinking to himself. "I just wanna be with you Cat, I don't care what's playing. I know I'm not gone sleep with you on the first date anyway. I wouldn't disrespect you by even asking on the first date. As soon as the movie is over I'm taking you straight home."

After the movie Antonio did just that. He drove Cat straight home, and walked her to the front door and kissed her goodnight, and said, "I'll call you when I get home. Tell yoe mama I said goodnight and thanks for trusting me."

"I'll do that, drive careful."

"I will baby, gone on in now."

Chapter XIV

July 12, 1996 Six-years-later

Things were going very well for Alvin and Antonio. Sorcerer had grown to like Antonio very much. He gave Antonio a lot of respect on account of Alvin. Antonio had gotten to know Sorcerer's family very well during his trips back and forth from Columbia.

Sorcerer's daughter Tamara had fallen madly in love with Antonio, and every time Antonio would visit Columbia with Alvin, she would try to get Antonio to propose to her, but Antonio's heart was with Cathy.

Sorcerer could see that his daughter was falling for the handsome Italian and he confronted her about the matter saying, "I want to ask you something, and do not lie to me Tamara!"

"What is it father?"

"You have been seeing Antonio haven't you?"

"Yes father I have, why do you ask?"

"You leave him alone. I don't want you seeing him anymore, and I don't want to discuss it any further. Just keep away from him!"

"But father, I like Antonio."

"You my daughter, do as I say."

Tamara could tell by her father's face expression that he was serious, so she dared say anything else to him about Antonio.

Sorcerer watched his daughter storm out the room. He put his head down and thought to himself. "Antonio is a very lucky child; he should have died with his mom and dad. I'm gonna let by gone be by gone. He doesn't know anything about me, and as long as he is taking care of business in America, he'll always be all right with me. Other than that, I could care less about him. If he knew what I had done to his family he wouldn't give'ah fuck about me either!"

Friday, September 9, 1996 9:00 P.M.

Ms. Bell was sitting in her living room when she noticed Antonio pulling up. She called upstairs to Cat. "Come on in its open."

Antonio came in saying, "hi Ms. Bell, how you feeling today?"

"I'm feeling just fine Antonio, how you feeling today?"

"I'm okay, I haven't told your daughter yet, but tomorrow I wanna take you two out. I have'ah surprise for you."

"You have'ah surprise for me?" She said smiling.

"Yepp sure do, you gone love this surprise." Cat came downstairs. "Hi baby, I was just telling your mother I got'ah surprise for her tomorrow."

Cat smiled. "Boy you full'uv surprises, where we going tonight?"

"To the drive-in."

"Mama, I'll be back kind'uv late tonight don't wait up for me."

"I won't. y'all have'ah nice time, and do be careful out there." Ms. Bell watched them pull off. "I wonder what that boy got for me this time. He's always buying me something."

As Antonio pulled off Cat said, "we went to the drive-in yesterday Antonio, now where we really going?"

206

"To my house to watch a lil cable TV and make a lil love," he said smiling.

"Ain't you tired of sex?"

"Nope not as long as it's coming from you," he said smiling.

"It better not be coming from nowhere else, make me catch'ah murder case."

"Girl you know you the only love for me."

"So where's your godfather?"

"He's out of town."

"He'ah trip, I hope you be that active when you get that old."

"What you mean?"

"You know, just live."

When Cat said what she said, Antonio's mind flashed back to Stan and Tangela. "I love my godfather, but I wouldn't trust'em around my woman. That old geezer will have'ah man's woman in bed in'ah heartbeat especially a young woman. I shouldn't even be thinking like this about him. He has changed since Stan walked out of his life; that took a lot'uv him."

"What you thinking about?" Cat asked.

"Nothing really," he said pulling into the driveway. "Well we here baby, welcome to the house of love. Tonight is our night, just you and me."

"By the way, let me tell you now. I ran out'uv birth control pills yesterday so do be careful when you unload your gun."

"I'll keep that in mind."

Antonio dimmed the lights in his bedroom and walked over and undressed Cat. They made love while listening to Franky Beverly and Maze on tape.

After they were done making love, Cat said, "I know you didn't cumm inside of me?"

"N'all girl," he said smiling.

"You better not. I don't need no crumb snatchers right now."

"If you did get pregnant I would take care of mines, and you know this!"

"I know you would baby, but I'm just not ready. I mean, look at where I stay, it's barely enough room for me there, and Lord knows how my brothers feel, they share the same bedroom."

"All that's gone change baby, trust me. Now give me'ah nice big kiss with yoe pretty self."

"Boy you know I'm ugly," she smiled.

"Believe me baby if you were ugly you would still be at the store where I first saw you," he said laughing.

Cat grabbed his dick saying, "I want some more of this here."

They went at it again, and then hit the shower together, and made love in the shower. After they were done making love in the shower Antonio said, "I wanna ask you something, and I want you to be straight up with me!"

"What you wanna ask me?"

"Do you ever think about seeing another man?"

"Hell n'all and don't ask me nothing like that again. You must be thinking about seeing other women?"

"N'all baby, you enough woman for me!" Cat was really upset because she thought he was about to ask her to marry him. "Look here baby, we been together six years now, and I think it's about time you know what I do for'ah living."

"And just what do you do for'ah living?"

"I'm not gone beat around the bush. I'm a dope dealer, I sell drugs baby."

"I know that already, it don't take no genius to figure that out."

"You knew already?"

"Yeah I knew man yoe godfather is the big man around here. His name be ringing like Taco Bell, and yours too, you right behind'em. Look Antonio, I love you for you, not for what you do. What I'm saying to you is don't ever be afraid to tell me what's on your mind!"

Antonio smiled, "when tomorrow gets here I have something for you and your mother. You make sure your mother home till I get there, which will be at one o'clock on the nose."

Cat hugged him. "I can't wait to see what this surprise you got for my mother."

"I'll give you one hint. I spent a lot'uv money on them both. Gone get dressed so I can get you home, it's late as hell."

"I told my mama I was gone be'ah lil late coming home."

"I know baby, but I done got sleepy and if I don't take you home now you won't make it home tonight. Making all that love got me feeling the way I do."

"Let's go then, you make me sick."

Antonio laughed, "yeah I love you too."

Ms. Bell was at home watching television, and got up when she heard Cat and Antonio outside the door. She opened the door saying, "I thought I heard you two out there, what's wrong, y'all mighty early?"

Cat said, "ain't nothing wrong mama."

Antonio kissed Cat goodnight and said, "I'll see you tomorrow. Goodnight Ms. Bell, I'll see you tomorrow."

"Goodnight Antonio," Ms. Bell said.

"Call me when you get home," Cat yelled out as he walked way.

Saturday, September 10, 11:45 A.M.

Antonio called Cat to let her know he was on his way out to her house. She told him to stop by Coney Island and bring her something to eat.

Antonio wore his red Adidas jogging suit that matched his red Mercedes Benz. His Mercedes Benz was trimmed in gold with the gold rims to match.

Antonio drove straight to Coney Island drive through and ordered, and he waited for the food. His mind flashed back to his parents, "I wish y'all could see me now. Mannn I wish I knew who killed y'all!"

The waiter said, "that'll be six dollars and fifty cents sir. Sir that'll be six-fifty, what you death man?"

"I'm sorry, my mind was somewhere else. Here's a twenty, don't worry bout the change."

When Antonio got to Cathy's house she smiled saying, "it took you long enough."

"Girl, I'm thirty minutes early it's only twelve thirty. Where yoe mama?"

"She's upstairs getting dressed. Oh, and I told my mama what you do."

"What she say?"

"She said she didn't care, as long as you was taking care her baby. That's me of course."

"I'm glad that's out the way."

Ms. Bell hollered downstairs. "I'll be ready in one minute y'all."

Cat hollered back. "Okay mama, we know yoe minutes."

"I heard that Cat."

Cat laughed. "Dang that woman got some good ears."

When Ms. Bell got downstairs Antonio looked at her and said, "you look lovely."

"Why thank you Antonio, I can't wait to see this surprise of yours."

"Well as soon as Cat finished feeding her face we can go."

"I'm done now boy, let's go."

"How far do we have to go?" Ms. Bell asked. "Not too far I hope."

"We got to go to Romulus city, close to where I stay. It's not that far."

When Antonio finally made it to Romulus, Ms. Bell said, "It sure is nice out this way. I wish I stayed out here, so peaceful and quiet out here."

Antonio smiled. "You know sometimes wishes come true." He turned on Colgate Street. "Ms. Bell you see that big house over there to your right?"

"Yeahhh it's beautiful."

"Well that beautiful home you see is yours."

"You kidding me," she said smiling.

"Nope, and that thing parked in the driveway is yours baby."

Cat smiled, "Antonio you didn't! I love you so much!"

"I love you too baby, the keys are already in the car, and here's the keys to your house Ms. Bell."

Ms. Bell said, "somebody pinch me, I know I got to be dreaming."

"N'all you wide awoke, this is your wish come true. Let's go inside and look around."

When Ms. Bell opened the front door she couldn't believe it. "You already furnished it too."

'Yepp, all you got to do is move your family in. You can give your furniture to somebody you know out that way."

"Give mama ah hug," he hugged her and smiled. "Thank you so much Antonio!"

"You welcome, come on let's go see what Cat doing. And Ms. Bell, I want you to know that I love your daughter very much!"

"I know you do son."

"If it's okay with you I would like to marry her."

"That's good Antonio, you have my blessing. She loves you too, you the best thing that ever happened to her."

Cat was outside sitting in her brand new 1996 Ford Escort, and when she saw her mama and Antonio coming she got out the car and walked up to Antonio and kissed him saying, "I love you so much. Mama how you like my car?"

"It's beautiful. How you like my house?" She said smiling.

"I love it, it's definitely a dream house," she said smiling.

Antonio said, "baby you got your own wheels now, and if you two don't mind I got some business to attend too, but I will see you two later on."

Cat kissed him. "I love you, you be careful. And I hope this business don't take you all night."

"It won't baby, it'll be shortly. I promise. Now gone in there and see the inside of the house"

Antonio had droved about a mile down the road before his beeper started vibrating. He checked it and said, "damn, that's the old man code, he must be back in town. I ain't, but five minutes away.

Alvin was standing in the driveway by the garage when Antonio pulled up. Antonio got out the car saying, "what's up, I wasn't expecting you back till Monday."

"Yeah I know it didn't take me as long as I thought it was gone take to take care business. Here's the list to all our outer town communities just in case something happen to me you'll have their names. This way you'll know exactly where to collect our money, and how to get the dope to them. Where you been man?"

"I've been shopping. I bought my woman mama a house and my woman ah car. That was cool wasn't it?"

"Man you do what you want with yoe money, that's yoe money not mines, yours. I can't tell you how to spend yoe money. That's cool, you looking out for yoe woman. You really love'er don't you?"

"Yeah I really do!"

"Well why don't you marry her, she the right one for you. You've been with her over five years now. I can tell she loves you, gone tie that knot man. I ain't never told you about the girl I was in love with did I? I was young, not as young as you though. Anyway she was white, and to make'ah long story short, somebody didn't like us being together so they killed her. She was'ah beautiful woman. Right now today I still think about'er. What I'm trying to say man, Cat is a very beautiful black woman and I think you should marry her befoe somebody gets jealous of you like they did me!"

"I get the message. You might not believe this, but I was on my way to the jewelry store to get her a ring right befoe I got yoe beep on my beeper. I came here first to see what was up with you."

"Don't let me hold you up son, gone take care yoe business. And whatever you do don't lose that list I gave you, if you do we both might end up broke as hell."

"Don't worry I want, I'll see you in a few."

"Be cool man, and bring me back a steak dinner."

Antonio drove straight to Meyers Jewelry and bought Cathy a diamond clustered engagement ring. Antonio couldn't believe Alvin was actually pushing him to get married. It was four o'clock when Antonio returned to Ms. Bell's house. He knocked on the door saying, "hello…. is anybody home?"

He could hear Ms. Bell's voice saying, "we in the kitchen come on in."

Antonio made his way to the kitchen and Cat said, "you back kind'uv soon ain't you/"

"Yeah I am, and I have something to ask you."

"What now Antonio?"

Antonio reached in his pocket and pulled out the ring. "Will you marry me?!"

Cat looked over at her mother, and Ms. Bell said, "he talking to you girl, not me."

"Yes, yes Antonio. I'll marry you!" She said smiling and kissing him.

Antonio shouted. "Yes! We can set any date you want."

"Any day is fine with me. Why don't we get married on your father birthday in November?"

"That's a good idea, we'll be celebrating two things in one," Antonio said.

Ms. Bell smiled. "I can't wait to see my baby in that wedding gown."

Antonio smiled. "Neither can I, I'm about to go rent'ah hall right now for that day. You know the old man is on the seventeenth. Here baby take this money and buy yourself the prettiest wedding dress in America. You know my size baby, get me'ah tuxedo to match whatever color you get. As a matter of fact get twelve more tuxedos the same color of yoe wedding dress. I got to stop back at my house to take the old man a steak dinner and tell'em the good news. I'll see you later on."

When Antonio got to the house and handed Alvin the steak dinner he told Alvin the good news, and Alvin congratulated him, then said smiling, "oh yeah man I brought you something back from New York."

"Oh yeah, where is it?"

"Look on the television."

Antonio looked on the television and said, "I like this, my own license plate with my name on it. Thanks man."

"I'm glad you like it, I got one for me too. When you get ready to leave out again look at my plates, they say Al Stone."

"Yeah, I'm about to put mines on right now. Why don't you hang out with me the rest of the day?"

"I would son, but I'm beat from that trip. You go on, I'll be all right especially when I get this steak in my belly."

"Well I'm out'uv here.'"

"Okay son, tell Cat and moms I said hi, and be careful man1"

"I will, so by the way, we getting married on your birthday."

Alvin smiled. "That's cool with me, we gone have'ah ball. I'm fix'n to call Dino right now and tell'em the good news."

Antonio made it back home around eleven o'clock that night, and when he got comfortable he decided to give Stan to call to see if would be his best man. Stan was all for it until he asked, "is my old man gone be there?"

"Of course he is man."

"I can't be yoe best man then. I'm not gone never be caught with that man again in my life, not even a funeral home to view his body especially after what he did to me. I'm sorry man, I hope you understand where I'm coming from!"

"Man all that's in the past now!"

"Yeah lil-broh, but it's still on my mind. I'll never forgive that man for that shit he did to me. Look here man I hear my ride blowing, I'll get back with you, you take care yourself."

Antonio hung up saying to himself, "I know ain't nobody outside blowing for'em, he just said that to get off the phone. I can't make him do what he don't wanna do. I guess Dino will be my best man."

Alvin came downstairs saying, "damn I slept my ass off. I see you home early, what's up?"

"Ain't nothing up, I'm just tired from all the running around today."

Alvin sighed, "yeahhh that'll do it to you every time. I been meaning to ask you son, have you found a house for you and Cat yet?"

"Yeah, I came up with the perfect idea. We decided that we gone build onto this house, sort'uv like turn it into a baby mansion. And we won't be in your way. I already hired the people to do the work; they estimated that it would take them eight months. And while they building, me and Cat will be gone away for about a year."

"I'm happy for you son, when you get back I'll throw y'all a nice coming home party. I'll rent'ah suite at the Renaissance Tower. We gone party all night long there," Alvin said smiling.

"That sounds good. You know if it wasn't for you I don't know where I would be, I owe you my life!"

"You don't owe me nothing son, just when y'all start making babies try to name one after me."

"Antonio smiled. "You got that coming."

"I always dreamed of having a bunch of grandkids running around here getting on my nerves. Mannn I bet that feels good and you gone stick around here and make that dream come true for the old man. You look like you tired man, gone get you some sleep, I'll kick it with you tomorrow when we get up."

"Yeahhh I'm beat."

Wednesday, November 17, 1996

That day was very cold, it seemed like everybody in Detroit was at the wedding, and after the wedding reception Antonio and Cathy went on their honeymoon. They decided to spend their honeymoon in Las Vegas. They spent most of their day at the casino and in between the sheets.

After being in Vegas for over four months, Cat went to see the doctor and found out she was pregnant. Antonio was very excited about becoming a father. The baby wasn't due till August.

After months of staying in the Richmond Hotel and gambling and lovemaking they were finally ready to go home.

Cathy was now in her eighth month of pregnancy; her stomach stuck out like the size of a watermelon. She couldn't wait to get back home to surprise her mother with the new life in her belly. Antonio nor Cat called home since they left the wedding reception. The house had been finished being remodeled in May.

Friday, July 2, 1997 9:30 P.M.

When Antonio and Cat got home Alvin and Dino was there to greet them. Alvin smiled saying, "well it's about time y'all brought y'all tails home. I've been worried about y'all. Y'all could'uv called, anyway what y'all bring me back?"

Antonio smiled saying, "I brought you back a t-shirt with your name on it, and Cat brought you, well just look at'er stomach and you'll see."

Alvin smiled, "well I'll be damned, y'all did it, I'm gone be'ah grandpa Dino."

Dino smiled, "yeah I see, look like you ready to drop that load any day now Cat."

Cat smiled. "Yeahhh I got one more month."

Antonio said, "I see they finished the house?"

219

"Yeah they finished two months ago, and me and my mellow man have decided to give y'all another wedding gift, so we just took our poor selves to the furniture store and had the place where y'all gone be living furnished."

Cat smiled. "All… that was no nice of you two."

Alvin said, "yeah we know, gone check it out, see how y'all like it."

Antonio said, "I know you man, you got good taste in everything you buy. I can imagine how everything looking. Come on baby, let's go check our new furniture out along with our new home."

Cat said, "they really did a good job on the house. I like it, you two sure did pick some beautiful furniture."

Dino smiled. "Let me call my mama and let'er know I'm back, she probably worried to death about me."

Alvin said, "tell'er I said hi, and invite her over for the fourth of July, I'm giving a cookout."

"I'll tell'er," Cat said dialing the number

Dino said, "well my man I'm out'uv here, you got Antonio and Cat here to bug the hell out of now. Beep me if something comes up."

"Okay then take yoe ass on."

Dino laughed, "see how you putting me out, any other time it would'uv been, come on man stick around'ah few moe minutes. Son and daughter here now, you don't need a Dino."

Alvin laughed. "Yeah right, I'll see you the fourth."

Cat got off the phone saying, "baby my mama told me to tell her son-in-law to come over right now, and bring yoe daddy with you. She said how we think we can stay gone for almost ah year and come back in town and not come see her. She told me to tell you just what she said."

Antonio laughed. "Well we better get our behinds over there. You coming old man?"

"I guess so, I can use the night air."

After they got over to Kate's house they sat around laughing and joking. Kate had a crush on Alvin, but Alvin wasn't interested in her sexually. They all talked for hours until Alvin yearned saying, "I don't know about y'all but I'm beat. It's time for the old man to turn in. We'll all get together on the fourth and do it just like this again, I really enjoyed myself Kate."

Kate smiled. "Me too, Cat you call me when y'all get home so I won't be worried if y'all made it back or not!"

"Okay mama! I will."

Monday, August 16. 1997 11:30 A.M.

Cat was due to drop her load any day now. Personally Antonio thought she was overdue. Tony and Cat was still in bed when they heard the big commotion coming from downstairs. Antonio said, "did you hear that baby?" He could hear Alvin yelling out, "what's this shit?" Antonio jumped up and put his robe on, but before he could make another move their bedroom door was being kicked in.

221

All they could hear was "don't move motha fucka, freeze asshole, get on the floor you son of' ah bitch. I should yoe fuck'n head off."

"What's going on?" Antonio asked.

One of the F.B.I agents put his forty-five magnum to Antonio's head saying, "shut the fuck up we ask the questions, not you punk!"

Antonio was full of rage and said, "hey motha fucka I don't know who the fuck you think you are, but if you ever put yoe hands on me again I'll have yoe fuck'n head cut off, and I swear yoe own mama want recognize you when I'm done, that I promise you!"

The detective put his gun on Antonio's head and said, "I should waste you now then you piece of shit!"

Cat cried out. "Please don't hurt my husband," she grabbed her stomach. "Antonio, my stomach, my stomach!"

Antonio said, "she pregnant, she in labor, she bout to have'ah baby."

Cat screamed out again. "Antonio I think it's time!"

"Hang on baby, I got to get her to'ah hospital now."

The F.B.I agent said, "ma'am we gone get you to'ah hospital, but you going to jail Mr. Stone!"

Cat cried out. "Please….somebody help me please!"

The F.B.I agent said, "get'ah man and drive her to the hospital."

Antonio said, "if my wife loses that baby you boys better find somewhere else to work, cuss Detroit won't be big enough for all of us!"

222

The officer in charge said, "somebody read him his rights and get his ass out'uv here. Don't worry ma'am we gone get you to'ah hospital right now."

"What's gone happen to my husband?"

"Your husband is going away for a long time, he better have one hell of a lawyer."

They had already put Alvin in the backseat of the squad car, and when Antonio got in the car with him, Alvin said, "don't worry bout nothing man. I pay these assholes good money to leave my family alone. They probably want us for tax invasion shit."

"How you know it's not for drugs?"

"Because they would'uv tore the house up searching for that shit. Just relax son I got everything under control. All we got to do is pay'ah fine. I've been through this same old shit befoe. They gonna try to make the fine sky high hoping we can't pay so they can throw our ass in the pen. We might have to spend all day down there, but we will get out. How's Cat holding up?"

"I believe she in labor, they taking her to the hospital."

"When we get down to the station don't answer no questions period. We let our lawyer do all our talking for us."

"To you ten dollars is'ah lot of money, I can tell by yoe uniform."

Officer Smith pumped Alvin the phone and said, "don't forget to dial nine first and don't forget you only get one call!"

"Yeah that's all I need is one, and if you ever feel like getting ah real job come and see me, I can always use you."

223

Officer Smith just smiled and said, "I'll keep that in mind."

"Yeah you do that," Alvin said dialing his attorney number.

"After Alvin got off the phone from talking with his attorney he said to Antonio, "don't worry son he on his way."

"I'm not worried about this lil shit, I'm worried about my wife!"

"She'll be okay son, and we'll be out of here before you know it."

"I hope so, I hope she don't have the baby befoe I get there."

Alvin smiled, "just hope he or she is fat and healthy."

"Yeah I hope it's a boy, it's a boy I can feel it."

Three hours later the lawyer had finally made it to the police station and when he got to Alvin and Antonio he said, "here's the deal, we got to pay some back taxes an'ah fine. And they want their money within sixty days or you two go to prison. Well I just laughed in the judge's face and said to myself, "hell in sixty days, they'll owe that much again."

Alvin said, "so how much it's gone cost us?"

"Five million and you two talk right out the door."

"Well you know what to do man."

"Give me one hour and I'll have y'all out of here in no time."

After the attorney Mr. Loeb left out Antonio said, "man where you find that lawyer at, he seem like he down for his work, he on his J.O.B."

"Yeah he ain't no joke, that's why I hired him. In this game you just remember this one thing; money talks and bullshit walks."

It was six in the afternoon when Tony and Alvin were finally released and on their way out the door. One of the officer's said, "hay Stone next time y'all won't be so lucky. We'll triple fine next time around!"

Alvin sighed, "you do what you got to do. There ain't ah number in the world you can come up with that I can't match and don't forget that. Like I said befoe, if you ever need'ah job come see me. Now you boys have'ah good day."

When Tonio and Alvin got outside, Tony said, "I see you talk any kind'uv way to them."

"Fuck them whose, they can't touch us. They lucky I don't come back and blow this punk ass precinct off the map with all they ass still in it!"

Tonio laughed, "you'ah bad man."

"You'll feel just like I do once you get to know them bastards. Damn, where the hell is that cab?"

"Here it come now," Tonio answered.

After the cab dropped them off at home, Tony asked, "you going to the hospital with me?"

"Well yeah, I'm going, I wouldn't miss this for nothing in the world."

"We can take my car."

"You drive yoe car son and I'll drive mines. I got'ah few stops to make tonight and I know you gone be at the hospital with your wife for'ah while."

When they got to the hospital, Cat had already given birth to a seven pound baby boy at four-twenty-five. They walked in Cat's room smiling.

Cat smiled saying, "what took y'all so long to get here? Here's yoe son," she said handing the baby to Antonio.

Antonio said, "what we gone name'em?"

Cat smiled, "I tried to squeeze both y'all name in, I named Altonio."

Antonio smiled, "that's ah slick name, I like it."

Alvin smiled, "yeah I like that name. Now let the god father hold his godson."

Tony smiled, "here man, take this joka, he heavier than me."

Alvin takes the baby saying, "damn, he sure is heavy. How much he weigh Cat?"

"Seven pounds exactly."

Alvin smiled, "look I'm gone leave you two alone. I got some business I got to attend too. I'll see you when you get home son. Cat you take it easy."

After Alvin left Cat said, "you know I been thinking about us. We have'ah child to raise now, you have'ah good head on your shoulder, you graduated from high school, and you still young. There is plenty things you can do with your life besides selling drugs. You can go to college or something. I'm worried about you baby, think about our son's future!"

"Look baby, ain't nothing to worry about, ain't nothing gone happen to me. I love you too, I love my son, but I ain't about to spend the rest of my life doing something I don't wanna do. I make more money in five minutes than lawyers and doctors do in five years. Now you knew what I did for a living befoe I married you, and you didn't complain then, so don't go changing on me now. You do have'ah choice. You can keep on loving me or you can leave me, it's yoe call!"

"Baby you know I don't wanna leave you. I just don't want anything to happen to you' that's all!"

"We live day to day baby, ain't no guarantee we'll see tomorrow. Let's not worry so much about me okay. You look sleepy, try to get you some rest."

"I can rest now that I know you all right."

"When can you come home baby?"

"The doctor said tomorrow, at least that's what he told my mama when she was up here earlier. Oh yeah, she said that boy look just like his daddy."

Tony smiled, "he do, he got your eyes."

Cat laughed, "that's all he got of me, everything else take after you."

Visiting hours were up. Tony kissed Cat on the lips saying, "I'll see you first thing tomorrow baby."

Tuesday, Sept 2, 1997, 10:30 A.M.

Ms. Bell was sitting at home watching the Barbara Walter special updates and the special was on Lost Claims Inheritance.

Barbara took her seat saying, "if anybody know the where bouts of any of the names on the screen please call us toll free at the number on the bottom of the screen. Today's show is about millionaires and billionaires, and these people names' you see written on the bulletin board are actually millionaires and billionaires, but they don't know it yet. Why? Because we haven't been able to catch up to them. I'll read the names off and if you out there know any of these people please contact us. Mr. Robert Wage, he's ah millionaire, Bryan Givens, he's ah millionaire, Sherry Dean, she's ah millionaire, Antonio Bomoski, he's ah billionaire. These people can contact us by calling the number on the screen for their claims."

Ms. Bell said, "my goodness, I wish my son-in-law name was Antonio Bomoski instead of Antonio Stone."

Barbara closed out saying," again the number is on the screen along with the address. We thank all of you out there for tuning into the 20-20 Barbara Walter Special."

"Good luck whoever you are Antonio Bomoski."

Ms. Bell's oldest son walked in saying, "what you watching mama?"

"Some man's father left him ah billion dollars,"

"Damn, Rodney said.

228

"Watch yoe mouth boy!"

"Sorry mama, that's ah lot'uv money mama. Wish I had one percent of that."

"I know, now wash yoe hands and make mama some lemon-aid please."

Tony and Alvin were at home having a serious talk. Alvin said, "look son, I been thinking man, you have'ah fine baby boy to raise and ah lovely wife to support, why don't you get out the game, settle down, raise yoe family the right way son. I know you don't want Altonio growing up in this kind'uv environment."

"I understand you being concerned and everything, but let me decide what's right and what's wrong for my family. Maybe one day I will get out the game, but right now I'm not ready too. All I want is my family to be happy!"

"Do you actually think Cat is happy about what you do for a living?!"

"She knew what I was about before I married her, and she do have options!"

"Yeah and so do you. Look man it's gone come a time when it's gone be too late for you to get out the game, like it is for me."

"What you saying?"

"I'm saying I wanted to get out the game but, now it's too late. I'm in too deep. Sorcerer would kill me first befoe he let me walk away. I know too much!"

"Why would you wanna get out anyway? You got everything a man could dream of!"

Alvin shook his head. "You just don't get it do you; look man when you get my age material things play out. I been everywhere and seen everything, but it don't mean nothing to me no-moe. We not playing softball my man, we playing hardball now and Sorcerer holds the bats. It's up to you, you'ah grown man, you make yoe own decisions, just don't say I didn't tell you beforehand. One day I'm gonna get out the drug game. I come too far for me not to enjoy the rest of my life on the beach laid back watching the ladies pass by my way in their skin tight bikinis."

"Yeahhh that do sound good. Look, I know how you feel about me, but it's in my blood to sell dope. I don't know why I feel that way, but I do."

Alvin thought to himself, "I know why you feel that way, you just like yoe father Montero. It's in yoe blood, and one day you'll find the truth."

Cat was upstairs calling for Antonio and Antonio said, "she probably wants me to get the baby. I'll chat with you later on, but as far as me getting out the dope game, that's ah no-no."

"Well son I'm about to cruise out to Ecorse, I'll catch you later on."

When Alvin got out to Ecorse he spotted Dino at ROLLINS party store talking to Jitt. Alvin pulled up hollering out the window of the car, "what's up you two players?"

Jitt said, "what's up slick Al?"

"You got the best hand lover boy."

Dino said, "man let me holla at you in private for'ah minute. Excuse me for'ah minute Jitt."

Jitt said, "yeah, I got to make'ah quick run anyway. I'll catch up with y'all two later on."

Dino got in on the passenger side of Alvin's car saying, "this about Stan."

"What's wrong man?" Alvin asked.

"Main I hate to tell you this."

"Come on man, give it to me straight."

"Stan was talking to this lil babe on seventh street, the babe ex old man shows up while Stan was over there. Man you know yoe son got'ah temper like yours, he just like you when it comes to taking care his business. Anyway the nigga and Stan got to arguing, the nigga left and came back with another nigga. The girl kept telling the young nigga it was over between them, the nigga wouldn't accept no for an answer, he started saying, "bitch ain't nothing over, tell that punk ass nigga to bring his bitch ass outside. I'll fuck'em up." The girl mama said she told Stan to speak out the back door. Stan told her he wasn't running from them and when he got ready to go he was leaving out the front door the way he came in. The girl hollered out the front door again telling her ex-boyfriend to leave her alone. The ex-boyfriend said,"send that nigga out here then I'll leave." Stan got mad and said," fuck this shit, let me out'uv here." The girl and her mama tried to hold him back, but they couldn't. Stan broke through the front door saying, "what's up here I am. I wish one of you tough mothafuckas run up on me, come on I'm right here." The ex-boyfriend said to the other boy, "come on man let's beat this nigga ass." Soon as they started

231

toward Stan, Stan pulled his thirty-eight special out and went shooting crazy they say. He in Ecorse jail right now for first degree murder and attempted murder, one of the boys lived. We know it was self-defense, but the law don't!"

"How much is his bond?"

"If I'm not mistaken a half million."

"Whatever it is pay it, don't let'em know I had something to do with it. Better yet, tell'em I got'em out and I still love'em no matter what. Tell'em don't worry about going to prison, my lawyer and judge over there is best of friends! Put'ah few thousands in his pockets."

"Consider it done man."

When Alvin got back home Antonio could see in his eyes something was wrong and asked, "what's wrong old man, you don't look like you did when you left here earlier."

"Its Stan, he in jail out in Ecorse. He killed ah boy over some girl out there. I sent Dino to get'em out."

"Sit down and let me fix you'ah drink. I'm sure he gone be all right."

10:00 P.M. Tuesday night

Dino bonded Stan out of jail and waited patiently for him in the lobby to be released.

Stan spotted Dino sitting down reading a Jet magazine and said, "what's up Dino, I know my brother had something to do with you getting me out of here."

Dino laid the magazine down. "Actually he don't even know you in here, yoe old man sent me down to get you out'uv here. He still loves you, you know. He told me to tell you not to worry about going to prison."

"Well, you tell'em I wish I could say the same for him. Tell'em thanks for getting me out, but I still feel the same way about'em!"

When they got in the car Dino said, "here, put this in yoe pocket."

Stan looked at the money, "it's from him ain't it?"

"Yeah man."

Stan shook his head in a no motion and said, "I don't want it," Stan looked away in sorrow.

Dino pulled out the parking lot saying, "one day man you gone miss yoe old dude and it's gone be too late. If I was you man I would forgive and forget!"

"It ain't that easy Dino."

Dino got angry, "what you mean it ain't that easy? Look man you ah grown man, and I know you know the difference between right and wrong. Now I admit your father was in the wrong for doing what he did, but you got to look at the situation like this, he didn't put no knife to that girl throat and make her do what she did; she did what she wanted to do. I'll never let'ah tricky ass woman break up my happy home. All I'm trying to say is this man, women make their own decisions when it comes to opening and closing them legs. Let me ask you'ah questions and I want you to answer me with the truth. If it wasn't for that pretty lil girlfriend of yours, what's her name Scarlet? Anyway, you wouldn't be in this shit you in now. Am I right or wrong?"

"You right man, I wouldn't be in this shit if it wasn't for her."

"Now you see what I'm trying to tell you man. Look man it's time you grew up, let's face it, these women will set'ah brother up in'ah heartbeat and you know it's the truth, just like that pussy selling broad that fucked you and yoe old man relationship up."

"Pussy selling," he said in disbelief.

"Man you mean to tell me you don't know that girl you use to have sold pussy for'ah living? Damn where you been? As a matter of fact that bitch is working right now. You got'ah few minutes, I'll take you straight to her spot, then you can see for yourself with yoe own eyes."

"Yeah I got'ah minute, show me this shit. I got to see this with my own eyes."

Dino got straight on 1-75 and drove straight to Woodward Avenue, and once they got on the stroll Dino started cruising. Dino yelled out, "damnnn look at the freaks down here, they wasn't lying when they said the freaks come out at night."

"Stan my man you crazier than yoe old man was when he was yoe age," Dino laughed. "Now take'ah good look at that freak coming this way."

Stan looked like he had seen a ghost. He couldn't believe his eyes and said, "so this is what that bitch life amounted too?"

"You got eyes man, need I say anymore. You wanna say something to'er while we down here."

Tangy stood on the corner with her red dress on, the high heel shoes catching. Stan said, "n'all man, fuck that hoe, I hate I ever met that bitch."

"Why don't you give yoe old man a chance to say he sorry!"

"Dino man I appreciate what you trying to do, but my mind is made up man. Who knows maybe one day I'll forgive him, but right now things stand the same."

"You know what man, you and yoe pops could go for twins. You look just like that nigga; well nephew let me get you home man."

When Dino got in front of Stan's house he said, "here man, take this money."

Stan laughed, "you just don't give up do you? I'll take it under one condition."

"And what's that?"

"You tell the old man I love'em, but I just can't forgive right now!"

"I'll do that; he'll be glad just to know you still love'em. Peace out, and do stay out of Ecorse for'ah while."

"I will man, and thanks for coming through for me."

As soon as Dino got home he called Alvin and told him about everything that happened. Alvin was satisfied just to know his son still loved him.

As soon as Stan got in the house he went and took a shower, and when he got out the shower he called over to Scarlet's house. Her mother answered the telephone, "yes may I speak to Scarlet?"

"Scarlet has company right now, who's calling?"

"Stan."

She was surprised and shocked to be hearing Stan's voice. "Stannn, where are you?"

"I'm at home. If you don't mind I would like to speak to your daughter."

"Hold on, I'll get'er."

Stan could hear Scarlet's mother in the background saying, "I don't know how he got out'uv jail, but I know he out and he wanna talk to you."

Scarlet got on the phone. "Hi Stan, are you at home?"

"Yeah I'm at home, and I see you got company."

"Yeah it's just my cousin and her boyfriend. When did you get out?"

"Not long ago."

"I called down to the police station and they said yoe bond was a half million dollars, and you know ain't nobody around here got that kind'uv money."

"Well evidently, you don't know who my father is, he laying like that."

"I heard about him, but I didn't know he was laying like that at all."

"It's a lot you don't know about me and my family, and it's a lot I don't know about you and yoe family."

"My mama said you got'ah very bad temper and she don't see how I put up with you."

"Wait'ah minute girl, put up with me? I'm the one who had to shoot his way from yoe house. If it wasn't be for you that boy would still be living. Yoe mama got'ah lot'uv nerves and so do you bitch!"

236

"I'm not no bitch Stan."

"You what I say you is. I'm through fucking with you and yoe sack chasing ass mama; both y'all can kiss my black ass. My godfather was right about you trick ass whose!"

"I'm not no hoe Stan."

"Bitch let this dial tone be the last thing you remember about me!" He slammed the phone down in her face.

Scarlet was to brokenhearted to say anything to her mama about what Stan had said and did, so she just smiled and played it off by saying, "that boy is so crazy mama. I'm through messing with him. I told him it was over between us; he begging me not to leave him. If he calls back tell'em I'm not here, it's over between us!"

"Well, I'm glad you finally came to yoe senses girl, you should'uv been on left that nut alone. You give a man ah little yoe goodies and they think they own you. I don't need no man in my life especially one that's ready to kill the whole world just because ah ex-boyfriend shows up over your house."

Thursday, May 20, 2002 1:30 P.M.

Cat had made a new year resolution that she was going to church every Sunday of 2002, and she even tried to talk Antonio into coming with her some Sundays, but he would give her the same old response. "I'm not into church baby, take Altonio with you." Cat would respond to him with words like, "I'm praying for your soul Antonio. I'm not gone stop asking you to come to church with me until you come. God answers prayers you know," Tony would laugh

237

and say, "I hope he'll answer my prayer." Cat asked him, "what are you praying for?"

"I'm praying that you would leave me alone." Cat threw the pillar at him and said, "you are a trip boy, I'm not gone say nothing else to you about it." Tony folded his hands together saying, "thank you Jesus."

Antonio sat around the house watching his big screen television, and Cat came up to him asking, "you ready to eat?"

"N'all not right now. By the way baby have you decided what you gone wear to the cabaret tomorrow?"

"Nope, and I shouldn't go, ain't nobody gone be there but'ah bunch of drug dealers from all around the country. It's the same old thing every year."

Antonio smiled, "don't talk like that baby, you know I want you there with me, and besides we haven't moved our bodies on a dance floor since last year, and looking at you, you can really use the exercise baby."

Cat smiled, "don't even try it, my body is in good shape. Ain't nothing wrong with my body."

"I'm just joking baby, don't jump on me. But I do think you would look beautiful in that red dress I bought you for your birthday."

"If it'll make you happy I'll wear the red dress Antonio."

"It most certainly will, thank you. One more thing baby."

"And what's that?"

"You may not know it but, it's gone be more than just drug dealers there. I arranged for a couple'uv celebrities to drop in on us."

"Oh really, like who?"

"Like Toni Braxton and Teddy Pendergrass, and ain't no telling who else the old man invited. We gone have'ah ball tomorrow night. Now come here and give me ah lil sugar."

Cat smiled, "nope, because you know once we start kissing you can't control yourself, and you ain't setting none today. Now the joke on you."

Antonio smiled, "that's okay, I love you too baby."

"Alvin and Altonio is banging ain't they?" She said smiling.

"Yeah ain't no telling where them two at. Knowing my godfather he probably took yoe son horseback riding or something," he said smiling.

"That old man know he love himself some Altonio."

"Yeahhh that he do baby. You know if it wasn't for him I don't know where I would be today. He saved my life, I owe him the world for that. I love'em like he was my real father. I have a lot to live for now!"

"Yes you do, that's why I want you to come to church with me just one time. I bet it would change your way of looking at life. Come with me one time Antonio."

Tony sighed saying, "one day baby I just might go, but let me make up my own mind okay."

"Okay, I'm not gone ask you no more, I promise you that Antonio."

Friday May 21, 2002, 9:00 P.M.

Alvin had already reserved ten tables in front of the stage for all his guests and when Cat, Antonio, and Alvin arrived Kate was already in her seat.

239

When they approached Kate she smiled saying, "how's everybody, I thought you three wasn't gone show up. What y'all do with my grandson?"

Cat said, "his bad butt at the babysitter. You look nice mama."

The music conductor came on stage saying, "ladies and gentlemen, Ms. Toni Braxton and her newest single, "Love Should've Brought You Home Last Night."

Kate smiled, "that girl can sing her ass off. I didn't know she was gone be here tonight."

Antonio smiled saying, "where's my brother-in-law?"

"He sitting in the back, back there somewhere with his friends. You know that boy ain't gone miss this for nothing in the world. Can't you see'em over there? Cat you know how that boy like to party."

"Yeah, and he can't dance ah lick," Cat said laughing.

Antonio said, "speaking of dancing bay, may I have this dance?"

"You sure can," Cat said smiling.

"Excuse us for'ah minute mother law."

Alvin smiled and said to Kate, "you know we can't let them outdo us young folks, would you like to dance?"

Kate turned to see who was talking to her and happily said, "Alvin, you know I would love to dance with you."

As Alvin and Kate danced to the music Kate smiled saying, "you know Alvin I been meaning to ask you something."

"And what's that Kate?"

"Do you think I'm attractive?"

"Sure I do, I think you are a very beautiful woman!"

"Well, why is it when I see you, you act like you don't even see me. It's like you scared of me. You not scared of me are you?"

"It's not that I'm scared to talk to you, it's just that I don't wanna hurt you. See I have'ah bad habit of loving women and leaving them, and you much better than that. Now I hope you don't dislike me for telling the truth about me."

"Oh no, I respect you for telling me the truth. Look Alvin, all I want you to do for me is make love to me just one time. You can leave; I'm not looking for no commitment and definitely no husband."

"Do you always speak this way when you want something?"

"Only when I'm this close to what I want, "she said pulling his body tighter.

"Well shall we leave now?"

"Only if you promise me you want leave until the job is done."

"That's a promise I think I can keep. I'll tell Antonio and Cat we going for'ah drive."

"We grown folks, they'll figure it out on their own. Let's get out'uv here."

Alvin and Kate crept on out and went straight to the (THUNDER BIRD) motel, where they spent the rest of their night making love.

Meanwhile Teddy Pendergrass was back at Cobo Hall performing on stage singing, "It's so good loving somebody when somebody loves you back."

Cat's older brother Michael came over to Antonio's table saying, "brother law I need to holla at'cha for'ah second it's about business."

Antonio said, "I'll be right back baby."

Antonio pulls him to the side asking, "what's on your mind Michael?"

"I got somebody sitting over there at the table wanna do some business with you. That's if the price is right."

"Well you introducing him to the right man, let's go meet this friend of yours."

Michael walked Antonio over to the table and introduced him to his friend, saying, "man this dude here runs all of Mexican land. He says he only got one problem."

"What's the problem?" Antonio asked.

"His supplier is always running out of dope."

"Well he'll never have that problem fucking with me, and you know that. If it goes well he'll deal through you and you only."

"This dude is cool man, you'll see."

When they got to the table Michael said, "I want you to meet my brother law, he able to supply you with all the dope you need."

"You hear good," Antonio said smiling. "We can meet at my warehouse to discuss this further if you can find time in yoe schedule to meet me there tomorrow."

"Of course I can, any day is a good day for business when it come to making money my friend."

"Good, Michael have him at my warehouse, sayyy three o'clock."

Michael said, "no problem we'll be there."

Cobra said, "it's been'ah pleasure meeting you Antonio."

"Same here," Antonio said extending his hand to shake Cobra's hand.

Cobra stuck his right hand out to shake Antonio's hand, and Antonio's mind went into a rage when he recognized the tattoo on Cobra's hand. "Pleasure meeting you to Cobra."

As Antonio walked back to his table he thought to himself, "that's the son of'ah bitch that beat me out them two kilos. I want that punk hand cut off and thrown to the rats in the alley. I knew we would meet up with they ass sooner or later. I wonder where Veno hiding his punk ass self."

"Sorry it took so long baby," Antonio said smiling.

"That was quick."

"Well you know I can't stay away from you to long baby," he kissed her. "I guess the old man and yoe mama slipped out'uv here."

The announcer said, "ladies and gentlemen we bout to say good night, but before we go we gone turn off the lights with Mr. Teddy Pendergrass."

Cat could tell something was eating away at Antonio's mind as she asked, "what's wrong, something bothering you, and don't give me that nothing bull!"

Antonio smiled, "you think you know me don't you. I was just thinking about the time I was tricked out'uv my dope, the boy that got me for it had'ah

243

tattoo on his hand just like that guy Cobra had on his. It's been awhile, but I'm positive it was him, but I could be wrong."

"Baby we here to enjoy tonight, not daydream about the past."

After the show was over Cobra ran into Antonio again and smiled saying, "I'll see you tomorrow my good friend."

Antonio nodded his head, "just make sure you bring plenty pasos with you."

Cobra was a man with lots of heart. He stood about six feet even, dark black eyes, and jet black hair to give his Mexican heritage complexion.

Cobra smiled, "don't worry my friend, I have lots'uv pasos."

"Remember you deal through Michael only, and bring no one else with you. I wouldn't want our business to go sour befoe we even got started."

"Don't worry, I'll come alone, just me and Michael," he said smiling.

"See you then," Antonio said leaving him and Michael behind.

.On their way home Cat said, "I wonder where my mama and Alvin disappeared too?"

"Come on baby you not that blind I know, you mean to tell me when we passed by the THUNDER BIRD motel you didn't see the old man car?"

"I sure didn't. Well at least we know where they at and you know what they doing. I know mama, she got to have hers."

"And I gots to have mines to Mrs. Stone," he said smiling.

Antonio drove straight to the babysitter and picked Altonio up, and from there they went straight home. Him and Cat made love and fell asleep in each other's arms."

Saturday, May 22, 2002, 10:00 A.M.

Alvin checked out of the motel and took Kate home, and drove straight home from her house. When he got inside the house Antonio and Cat was still sleep. Altonio was up watching cartoons. Alvin asked him, "where yoe mama and daddy at lil man?"

"They still sleep."

"You ate breakfast yet?"

"Yepp."

"Good, I guess I'll watch me ah lil TV with you if you don't mind."

"I'm watching, He Man, I like He Man he strong."

Alvin smiled, "strong like me?"

"Yepp, you can't fly like him."

Antonio finally woke up, and he didn't bother to wake Cat. He looked at the clock and said, "I got plenty time, it's still early."

Antonio got in the shower and after he was done taking his shower he went downstairs to check on Altonio, and was surprised to find Alvin home.

Antonio smiled at Alvin and said, "what's up old man, when you get home, not that it's any of my business."

Alvin smiled, "not long ago, why?"

"You must'uv had a busy night."

245

"You know me son, I been good loving, body rocking all night long."

Antonio laughed, "I knew that, I just wanted to see what you were gone say."

"How you know?"

"Well the Jeffrey expressway was closed down last night, and that left us with no choice, but to take Fort street so we could hit 75 south. So you know we had to pass by the Thunder Bird Motel on Fort Street to get home, and that's where I saw yoe car parked."

Alvin smiled. "Say no more son, you damn sure saw what you saw. That damn Jeffrey freeway," they both laughed.

"Yepp that's what busted you so how was it?" Antonio asked smiling.

Alvin smiled, "I got to get me another shot of that thang. I mean quick fast and a hurry. Cat don't know do she?"

"Yeah she know, but she don't care in fact she told me she knew her mama had to have hers. Cat had been told me her mama wanted to get with you."

"Well since she know now I ain't got be sneaking and creeping now."

"I hear you, I see Altonio got you watching that cartoon stuff."

"Yeahhh man, me and lil man got to have our cartoons."

Three-hours-later 2:15 P.M.

Antonio sat patiently at the warehouse waiting for three o'clock to pop up. He laid his sixteen gauge shotgun on the desk and leaned backwards in the black leather chair staring at the clock on the wall until he saw a mouse run across the floor.

Michael and Cobra arrived at the warehouse three on the nose as planned. Antonio opened the door up saying, "I see you two are right on time."

Alvin sat down and Cobra said, "well my man, I'm ready to wheel a deal."

"So am I and I don't know how to thank Michael for bringing you to me. Pull up'ah chair gentlemen. I'm not gone waste yoe time Cobra. Let's see the money in the briefcase or do you trust me?"

Cobra smiled, "sure I trust you Antonio, you Michael brother law ain't you. Of course I trust you, I trust Michael, and a friend of Michael is a friend of mine."

Antonio said, "that's all good, now let's see the cash."

Cobra opened the briefcase saying, "this is half million dollars, and there's plenty more where it came from. I'm serious about what I do Antonio."

"I see, and I'm serious about what I do too. Let me ask you something personal. You can answer it or don't answer it, but how long have you had that tattoo?"

"I say about twenty years now."

"Twenty years now, that's a long time. I got one more question for you. Do you remember how one of these sound?"

As Antonio held the sixteen gauge shotgun in his hand, Cobra said, "hay man what's this shit, I go now!"

Antonio fired the shotgun and blew half of Cobra's arm off. Michael jumped back in shock, and shook like a leaf on a tree.

Cobra cried out, "man what are you doing?"

"You remember my good friend Veno?"

Cobra cried out, "I didn't kill'em man, he was shot by some punk in my car. I didn't kill'em I swear to you man!"

Blood was running out of Cobra's arm and tony said, "you talk too much, that punk was me."

Antonio pumped the shotgun one more time and Cobra cried out, "please don't kill me, please Antonio!"

"I'm not gone kill you, take yoe money, and yoe one arm, and get the fuck out my face. Wait'ah minute, let's see, back then kilos went for twenty thousand. I'll take fifty thousand out'uv here and we'll call it even, If you make it to the hospital in time they might be able to sew that arm back on."

Michael said to himself on the way to Receiving Hospital, "Antonio is one crazy motha fucka, I got'ah maniac for a brother law."

Cobra's arm was barely connected. He passed out before Michael could get him to the emergency room. Meanwhile, back at the warehouse Antonio said to himself, "yeah got my money back and some for waiting so long. I feel good enough to go to church with my wife in the morning. Think I'll surprise her in the morning."

Chapter XVI

Sunday May 23, 2002 10:00 A.M.

Cat was the first to awake. She opened Altonio's door saying, "it's time to get ready for church Altonio."

When Cat walked back to her room Antonio was up smiling and said, "I'm going to church with you today."

Cat smiled. "Thank you Jesus, now I know you can do anything, but fail. I know mama gone be shocked when she see you in church today."

Cat was running late getting to church, but they made it just in time to hear the choir sing their last song, "we shall overcome."

When the choir was done Reverend Bannon took his place behind the pulpit, saying, "yes, yes, yes we shall… overcome. Today I wanna preach about addictions. Yesss Lord we have all kind of addictions in this world today. A lot'uv people are addicted to the wrong addiction." The people were shouting and hollering preach Reverend! "A lot'uv folks are saying to themselves, what you talking about Reverend? Some of us are addicted to the wrong addictions, and I'm not talking about no card playing addiction, or no cigarette addiction, or no television watching addiction. No, no, no, some of us are addicted to some far worse addictions. But what they don't know. These…. Addictions will cause us to lose our friendship with the Lord. Amen now! Boyyy when you lose yoe friendship with Jesus, yoe addictions become ten times worse. Y'all don't hear me. I said yoe addictions become worse. And when you dislike yoe brother or yoe sister for any cause, you are addicted to the wrong addiction. What you saying Reverend? I see brothers selling dope on the street corners to their

brothers. And, and I see sisters on the corner selling their bodies to buy drugs

from the brother selling drugs on the next corner. And, and they ain't doing

nothing, but destroying what God... created. I'm telling you people here today,

we are addicted to the wrong addictions. Once a man put'ah gun in his hand and

shoot that gun, he starts to carry that gun everywhere he go. In fact he takes the

gun with him, and leaves his wife at home every time he leaves out the house.

That man is addicted to the wrong addiction. Some of us even start our kids off

with some of these bad habits. Wanna smoke pot because he seen daddy

smoking pot. Wanna shoot the gun because he see daddy shooting the gun. That

kid just don't know, one day he gone be addicted to the wrong addiction. That's

why we need something and someone to help us get rid of these addictions. And

I wanna introduce y'all to'ah man, ah man who is able to help you get rid of any

kind'uv addiction you can think of. This same man was tempted with every

possible addiction in this world. Yet, he was able to hold fast to what he

believed in, and who he believed in. Let me introduce y'all to this man. His

name is Jesus, y'all don't hear me. I said his name is Jesus. I want every

woman, man, boy, and girl in here today to just try'ah little of this Jesus I

guarantee you you'll be back for some more. And when you get some of this

Jesus in yoe system then you will know you are addicted to the right addiction.

See when you get addicted to this Jesus you don't think about hurting yoe

brothers and sisters. When you get Jesus on your side you don't have to worry

about no gun, nor the person with the gun, because this Jesus will fight yoe battles for you. When you become addicted to Jesus yoe bad habits leave you, and the new addiction takes over. All I'm trying to say to you people in church today is a lot'uv us is addicted to the wrong addictions. Amen! Now will the church please bow their heads in a moment of prayer as we close out today's service."

After the church service was over Ms. Bell smiled and said to Antonio, "I'm so glad you came to church today Antonio."

Tony smiled, "I'm glad I came too. I enjoyed the message. And that's why I'm taking my mother law and wife to Red Lobsters for dinner."

Cat said, "Reverend Bannon really preached his tail off today."

"He sure did," Ms. Bell said smiling.

Antonio took the family out to Red Lobsters and while they sat eating and talking, Cat laughed and said, "I started to name Altonio, Rex."

Antonio laughed. "I'm glad you changed your mind. Rex, sound like'ah roach spray don't it mother-law?"

Ms. Bell laughed, "it sure do, so speaking of names, I remember looking at one of Barbara Walter's 20-20 specials. And I'll never forget this name either. They was looking for a guy named Antonio Bomoski, they say he's ah billionaire. I can't remember which one of my sons' was in the house with me, but I told him I wish my son-in-law last name was Bomoski. Anyway they've been looking for this Antonio Bomoski for over five years. They say his father left him his inheritance. I wish yoe name was Antonio Bomoski instead of

Antonio Stone. You would be one rick you know who. I wonder did they ever find'em?"

"I don't think so, because that man wouldn't be that hard to find if they were really looking for'em."

Cat said, "why you say that, evidently they can't find the man, or why else would they put his business on television like that. And I'm sure they done found him by now."

Antonio smiled, "I doubt it baby."

"Why you doubt so much Antonio?" Ms. Bell asked wiping her mouth with the napkin.

"Because Antonio Bomoski is…. Me!"

Cat laughed, "and I'm Elizabeth Taylor."

"I'm not kidding, let me explain it to y'all first befoe y'all go to laughing. Baby you know Alvin adopted me, and after he adopted me that changed my name from Bomoski to Stone. My real father last name is Bomoski. He was killed when I was just'ah kid. That's how I ended up in a center for little kids until Alvin adopted me. I guess God is a good God because tomorrow I'm a rich man."

Ms. Bell said, "Well Lord have mercy, I'm happy for'ya. Maybe you can send oh mother law on'ah vacation when you get your inheritance," she said smiling.

"Mother law if what you say is true you most definitely got that coming and much, much more," Antonio said smiling.

252

Cat smiled saying, "I'm so happy I can hardly eat my food. My man is'ah billionaire. Altonio yoe daddy is'ah rich man."

Altonio said, "what's that?" They all laughed at his question.

Antonio said, "I can't wait until tomorrow gets here. If all of this is true baby I'm leaving the drug business alone."

Cat smiled, "I hope to God that it's true. And just think about it Antonio, if you would'nah came to church with me today you wouldn't have no idea about this. I know God work in mysterious ways!"

Antonio smiled, "I got to give you ah Amen on that yoe baby. I know the old man ain't gone believe this because I don't quite believe it myself yet, and I'm not gone believe it till I get the money in my hands. I know you not joking with me mother-law, cause you would'uv told me by now you was kidding around."

Ms. Bell said, "n'all I wouldn't kid about nothing like that. Lord knows I wouldn't!"

When Antonio and Cat got back to the house Alvin was busy massaging his body in the whirlpool.

Antonio opened the door to the whirlpool and excitingly said, "old man tomorrow we the richest men in the world."

"What you talking about, run it down on me son."

"My father who I never really got the chance to know; well he left me'ah inheritance, ah billion dollars."

"Ah billion dollars, man that's'ah lot'uv counting, Alvin said smiling.

253

"I know, and you know what that mean?"

"N'all son, tell me just what that mean?"

"It means you and me splitting it fifty-fifty. It means we can do anything in the world we want with that kind'uv money including retiring from the game!"

"I'm with you on that one. I think we done made Sorcerer rich enough. It's time for the old man to resign, an as soon as you take care yoe business tomorrow we flying to Columbia. I'll tell Sorcerer face to face we want out. I think he trust me enough now to let me out. If not fuck'em. I can't wait to see his face when I tell'em."

"Yeahhh me too," Antonio said smiling.

Monday, May 24, 2002, 9:00 A.M.

When Antonio got to Triple A Insurance, he found out not only was he a billionaire, but he also owned casinos in Las Vegas.

After signing about twenty sheets of paper Antonio could finally could. He walked out the office saying to himself, "I don't have to sell shit else in life, fuck some dope."

Alvin and Cat was at home waiting patiently for Tony to arrive, and as soon as Antonio, stepped foot in the door Alvin said, "how did it go son?"

Antonio smiled saying, "we some rich motha fuckas."

"Hell yeahhh!" Alvin said as him and Cat shouted with joy.

"Call Sorcerer," Antonio said.

"Let me call that bastard right now to tell'em we'll be up there first thing tomorrow." Alvin dialed the number and Sorcerer's secretary answered the telephone. She told Alvin that Sorcerer wouldn't be back until July some time. "When he get back, you make sure you tell'em to call Stone as soon as he get in. You have a good day now," Alvin hung up. "We got to wait till July; that bastard ain't home, he want be back home till July?"

Antonio said, "that's no far away. Let's celebrate, I'll have'ah nice cold Budweiser."

"And I'll have the same," Alvin said.

Cat said, "two cold Budweisers coming up."

Cat went and got the two beers and herself a ginger-ale pop, and when she passed Antonio his beer he said, "I would like to make'ah toast." They all touched glasses. "To the billion dollar men."

Too the billion dollar men they all said. Cat smiled saying, "I would like to make'ah toast to you two leaving the drug business alone. No more drug-selling."

They all touched glasses saying at the same time, "no more drug selling."

Alvin smiled saying, "wait, I have one. Too Shawn Bomoski," they all said, "too Shawn Bomoski."

Cat smiled saying, "let's not forget about mama, after all she did make this day worth living for!" They all touched glasses saying, "too mama."

Friday, July 2, 2003, 2:00 P.M.

As soon as Sorcerer returned from his vacation he called Alvin two o'clock American time.

When Alvin answered the phone he recognized Sorcerer's voice and said, "Mr. Sorcerer, I been expecting yoe call. I need to see you as soon as possible. I'm hoping today will be okay with you."

"Of course, today is a good time, I'll be expecting you."

"Oh, I'm bringing Antonio with me."

"That's fine with me, see y'all when y'all get here. Good day Mr. Stone."

Alvin hung the phone up and dialed Antonio's number upstairs, and Antonio answered, "yeah what's up?"

"Okay I'm on my way down," Antonio kissed Cat. "I'll be back by tomorrow night baby. This ain't gone take long."

Cat hugged him saying, "you be careful, I love you!"

"I love you, I'll send Altonio in the house when we get ready to leave out. I'll see you shortly."

Alvin was already downstairs waiting on Antonio, and when Antonio came downstairs he called Altonio in the house. "Hey lil man yoe mama wants you. Go see what she wants. I'll see you when I get back."

Alvin said, "you be good lil man, I'll bring you something back okay."

Altonio said, "bring me'ah dog back."

Alvin said, "when I get back I'll take you to the pet shop and let you pick out what kind'uv dog you want. Is that cool?"

256

"Yeahhh."

Antonio said, "now gone in the house where yoe mama is okay."

Alvin said, "you drive son."

Alvin and Antonio made it to Columbia around ten o'clock America time, but it was still evening time when they arrived at the airport in Columbia. Sorcerer's security escorted them to the mansion.

When they got inside the mansion Sorcerer greeted them. "Gentlemen, good to see you two again. Look at you Antonio, the older you get, the more you remind me of someone I use to know. In fact his name was Antonio too. So tell me Mr. Stone what did you wanna discuss with me that you couldn't say over the phone?"

"I'll get straight to the point. I've been working for you for quite some time. And I'm not the type of man that'll bite his tongue for no one. I came here personally to let you know me and Antonio is getting out the dope game. I hope you understand!"

"Oh I understand, and I don't bite my tongue for nobody either. Now you listen and listen good. I told you once, and this will be my final time telling you again, no one get out the drug game, and I do mean no one. Once you in, you in, and you know this Alvin Stone. What do you take me for, a fuck'n joke, ah fuck'n fool? Now I suggest you two head on back to America and continue what you was doing before you came here today. Now there is a way out of this business I'm running. And you can purchase a ticket today if you like Mr. Stone. How about you Antonio, would you like'ah ticket out?!"

"N'all you can hold onto yoe ticket, you may need it for yourself."

Sorcerer goes into a rage. "You young Antonio, I take it you don't know me very well, if you did you would sit there and keep yoe fuck'n mouth shut because I do not joke! Now Alvin Stone is there anything else you wanna discuss with me?"

"I have spoken one way or another I'm getting out the game!"

Sorcerer smiled, "You know Alvin, I like you. I like you'ah lot. And that's why I'm gone pretend I didn't hear you say that. I'm gone have my guards to escort y'all back to the jet before I get upset and take the life that I gave you Mr. Stone!"

Alvin got angry. "Yeahhh like you did my good friend Shawn Bomoski and his!" Alvin cut himself off, he didn't want Antonio to know about Sorcerer having his mother killed.

Sorcerer was really angry. "Get these two out my face befoe I have them beheaded. Before you go Mr. Stone, I want you to know I'm serious about taking care my business. I'll be seeing you two. Have'ah safe trip back to America!"

Sorcerer said to himself after they left. "Alvin you'ah good man. I would hate to lose you, but I have to look out for my investments like any other business man would."

When Antonio got on the jet he asked, "what did you mean when you said like Shawn Bomoski?"

"Look man, you not'ah child anymore. I think it's time you know the truth about yoe family. When you was just'ah kid, Sorcerer put'ah contract out on yoe stepfather and mama!"

"Stepfather," he said in shock.

"Yeah stepfather, he married your mama and raised you like you was his own. Yoe stepfather messed up a big shipment of dope, and Sorcerer didn't like that, and when Sorcerer finally forgave Bomoski, Bomoski invited him and his wife down for dinner. To make ah long story short, Sorcerer got shot that night at the dinner and his wife got killed. Next thing I know Sorcerer had yoe whole family taken out including my son's mama. Stan's mama was yoe mama's best friend."

"Well tell me this, who is my real father?"

"Yoe real father's name was Antonio too, Antonio Montero. He used to work for Sorcerer too. Yoe father wasn't the type of man to take orders either, and that's why Sorcerer had him killed."

"You mean to tell me this motha fucka killed my mother, my father, and my stepfather?"

"Yepp that same son of'ah bitch you just saw. You remember him saying you look just like a Antonio who use to work for him?"

"Yeah I remember him saying that."

"Well he was talking about your father when he worked for him back in the days."

"I swear I'm gone kill that bastard. He murdered my whole family!"

259

"Wait'ah minute son, you got to promise me you won't try to avenge yoe people death, because I don't want nothing to happen to you. Sorcerer got too much power for us, we'll need'ah army to take him out. Now please son promise me you'll let it be!"

Antonio looked at him with grief in his eyes, and Alvin put his hand on Antonio's shoulder saying, "I know it's hard man, but you got to promise me you want try anything foolish, I need you man!"

"I promise, but if he ever do anything to you or my family I'm taking it too his ass, and that's ah promise!"

"Thennn you do what you got to do son, but for now let it go."

"Do you know I still have dreams right now today about my mother and father? And if it don't be for that secret hiding place and you I wouldn't be here today. That bastard would'uv killed me too!"

"That's for sure, it was all part of the contract, kill everything in the house. I want you to know one thing son, I will always be there for you when you need me the most, and that I promise you. From here on out I want you to be alert at all times. I don't trust Sorcerer no moe. He has the power to do ah lot'uv dirty shit to us!"

"We got just as much power as he do. If you go down, I go down too. I will die for you. I'm not afraid of nothing no more. That comes from being around you!"

"I feel the same way about you son. I would never let anything happen to you, you my son now. From now on out just be careful. I'll always be there for you, even when you think I ain't. I think I raised you up real well, and I'm sure you know me by now, I will never tell you anything wrong!"

"All I know is you ah good man. Who else would'uv took care me all these years like you did!"

Saturday, July 3, 2002 8:00 A.M.

It was eight a.m. the next morning when they got home. Altonio was up watching television, and as soon as he spotted Alvin he said, "are we going to get me ah puppy?"

Alvin smiled, "yepp, go put you some clothes on so we can go get you'ah puppy."

Altonio ran upstairs and changed so quick into his clothes. When he got back downstairs Alvin laughed saying, "damn you quick boy. Let's ride. We'll be back in'ah few son. If Dino call tell'em we still on for that cookout tomorrow.

"I'll do that; let me go check on my wife. I'll see y'all when y'all get back. While you out grab'ah few videos."

Sunday, July 4, 2002 3:30 P.M.

Alvin had a front yard full of friends and family over for fourth of July. They all were full of the fourth of July spirit. Even the puppy Alvin had bought Altonio was busy running from shoe to shoe playing with the company. Altonio named the puppy Chip, and when Chip started biting on Ms. Bell shoe she said, "oh isn't he cute." She picked Chip up and held him in her face. Chip licked her on the lip. She laughed, "let me put you down, ah kiss like that again I might

fall in love with you."

Alvin heard her remark and said, "don't fall in love like that," he

laughed.

Ms. Bell laughed. "You just hush up now."

Chico said, "hay Antonio where the Hennessy, y'all know I don't drink

nothing but, hen, "ne, say."

Alvin said, "damn Chico man I'm sorry. I thought I bought some

Hennessy, I bought everything but that. Don't worry my brother I'll be right

back. You just kick back and enjoy yourself. I know you can't drink no

galloon."

Chico said, "I can go to the store myself, just tell me how to get there.

Cuz I got to have my Cognac."

Alvin said, "I'll go to the store man, you just chill."

When Alvin got in the car Dino said, "where he going?"

Antonio said, "to the store, he'll be right back. You want another beer,

its plenty beer in the cooler."

Antonio and Dino watched Alvin as he turned the corner, and as soon as

he turned the corner his car blew up, and then burst into flames. When

everybody heard the big boom sound, that caught their ears' attention, they ran

to the direction of all the smoke.

When they got to the flames Cat screamed out, "O my God!"

All Antonio could see that was unrecognizable from the car was Alvin's license plate lying in the street. Antonio picked the license plate up and fell to his knees screaming out, "nooo, nooo!"

Dino held his cool and said to himself, "Lord why my brother? Who would wanna do this to him?!"

Ms. Bell took Altonio and Cat back to the house and called the police.

When the police and fire department got on the scene everything in the car was burned to ashes. One of the firemen said to Antonio, "even if we would'uv got here sooner whoever was in this car would'not of made it, but you might'uv had ah chance to hold ah funeral!"

Antonio watched the fire fighters put the car out and said to himself, "I'm gone kill you Sorcerer even if it cost me my life. You have killed yoe last man, now you must pay. You fucked with the wrong one this time!"

The channel 50 news didn't waste any time getting on the scene. The spokesman said, "good evening Detroit, I'm Barry Louis for channel fifty news update. I'm on the scene where a car blew up just minutes ago. So far it has been said that one victim was in the vehicle when it went up in flames. Witnesses said the black male known as Alvin Stone was driving the car at the time of the explosion. Fire fighters are still searching for a clue as to what caused the explosion. We'll have more information coming up later on this evening on our six o'clock channel fifty news beat, I'm Barry Louis signing off for channel fifty news beat."

When Antonio got back to the house he said to Cat, "I want you to stay with your mother for awhile, You and Altonio will be safe there. Don't ask me no questions just do what I say. Dino I need to talk to you in private, but first let me get my family out'uv here."

Ten minutes later Antonio watched his family drive off, and when they got out of sight he looked at Dino and said, "look man, you my uncle, and ain't nothing in this world I wouldn't do for you. Now I came across a huge piece of money, over ah billion dollars. Me and the old man had made up our minds to leave the dope game alone. So we flew to Columbia day before yesterday to tell Sorcerer we was through dealing, we wanted out. He said no way, then the old man made'ah couple'uv smart remarks to'em. Now this shit happened. Look now I'm telling you I have all the money we need to live on for the rest of our life man. Just help me take Sorcerer ass out. I'm only gone ask you once. Are you in or out?!"

"Look man, I don't want yoe money. Alvin was my brother. I'll never forget this day. I'll do anything to get the punk who did this to him. I'm in, and so are the Ecorse gangsters!"

"Meet me here tomorrow night at nine. That'll give you enough time to get your men together. I'll see you there. Oh, and make sure yoe men are ready to die because it's gone be'ah lot'uv bloodshed!"

"My men are always ready to die for what they believe in. You get you some rest, I'm out'uv here."

After Dino left the house Antonio sat back on the living room couch thinking about all the good times he had with Alvin and then said to himself, "I wish I was never born!"

Dino stopped by Stan's house on his way home. Stan opened the door saying, "I already know man. It was on every news on television."

"I'm sorry man. He loved you. If you need me you know where I'm at. Take care yourself!"

Tears slowly ran down Stan's face as he watched Dino walk away. After Dino drove off Stan went in his bedroom. His grandmother wanted to say something to him, but decided it was best not too. Stan put the Marvin Gaye tape on he knew his father loved so much, and as he listened to the song he started crying.

Sharen was in her room drinking her cognac, and said to herself, "that Alvin Stone was'ah good man. Even the good have to die someday. This just don't seem real to me. Whatever happened to folks dying in their sleep? I guess it ain't no certain way to die. We live to die. By car to bullet we got to take that journey one day. Damn I wasted my drink."

Monday, July 5, 2002 9:00 P.M.

Dino and the Ecorse gangsters set up at Antonio's house as planned. Altogether, fourteen gangsters were going on this mission. Antonio explained to them how many guards would be at the airport, and at the front entrance of the mansion.

265

Antonio said. "we'll use silencers only going in, and after we get in I want everything living destroyed. Once we get through the gate. Chico I want you to take yoe men west. Don't worry about me. I got something personal to take care of. Now, is everybody ready to do this?"

Dino said, "let's do this shit."

Chico said, "I ain't never been moe ready in my life. I can't wait to send them Cuban motha fuckas to hell."

Antonio said, "you fix'n to get yoe chance. My pilot is waiting on us, let's ride."

When they got to the jet Antonio said, "men, it's gone be piss dark when we get there, make sure y'all don't lose sense of y'all direction. When we land the way starts right then!"

All the way there the flight was quiet until the pilot said, "we bout to land boss man."

Everybody started saying, "hell yeah, let's kill us some Cubans."

Antonio said, "remember now, use yoe silencer till we get in!"

As soon as they landed the jet, four of Sorcerer's men approached the jet. Antonio said, "here we go, open the door."

As soon as the pilot opened the door up Dino said, "y'all looking for this?"

When the guards looked up it was too late. Antonio and Dino was chopping them down with their M-16 machine guns, killing all four men instantly.

Antonio marched the men to the front gate. One guard was operating the gate. The guard recognized Antonio and said, "Antonio, where is Mr. Stone tonight?"

"In his grave where you bout to go!" Antonio shot the guard in the head. "We in, I'll meet y'all back at the jet when I'm done."

"Got'cha," Dino said.

As soon as Antonio and the gangsters got in the gate the war began. Sorcerer's men were everywhere, and the Ecorse gangsters were killing them like flies.

Antonio made his way inside the mansion and when the two bodyguards saw him walking their way they thought nothing of it until they saw the 45-magnum in his hand. Antonio shot one of them in the head, and the other one straight in the mouth and neck.

Sorcerer was busy laid back in his whirlpool watching his big screen television. He had one of his bodyguards posted outside guarding the door, but Antonio sneaked up on the guard saying, "you did yoe job, is he in there?"

The guard stared at the barrel of the gun and said, "yeah, he inside."

"Good and good night." Antonio shot the guard right between the eyes and eased the door open.

Sorcerer had his back turned away from the door watching television. Antonio walked up behind him. Sorcerer turned his head around saying, "who let you in here?"

"I wouldn't worry about that if I was you," Sorcerer focused in on the .45 magnum in Antonio's hand. "Alvin Stone was good to you."

"What about Alvin Stone?"

"You have murdered for the last time. I hope you still holding onto them tickets," he said with hate in his eyes.

"I don't know what you talking about Antonio, I didn't kill Alvin. This is my first time hearing about this. I'm sorry, but it wasn't me Antonio!"

"Yeah it's never you, you have somebody else do yoe dirty work. Just like you had my father killed!"

"Yoe father, I don't even know yoe father."

"Antonio Montero was my father!"

Sorcerer's eyes got big as he said, "I should'uv guessed. I can see the resemblance, I use to call him Scarface."

Antonio pointed the .45 magnum directly between Sorcerer's eyes saying, "yeah motha fucka I'm here on his behalf today. This for Alvin," boom, shooting him in the chest. "My father," boom. "My mother," boom. "Bomoski," boom, "And this for me," boom. "I wish I could kill you again."

Antonio watched the bloody body float on top of the water in the whirlpool for a few seconds, and then went to join Dino and the gangsters.

Antonio got on the jet saying, "how many men we lose?"

Dino said, "three, did you get that bastard?"

"I got that bitch, he want be no trouble for us no-moe. Our mission is completed. Get this baby in the air Mack."

268

Dino said, "that was ah piece of cake man."

Antonio said, "I appreciate yoe help man. I could'nah done it without you!"

"Anytime for you nephew. If you ever need me you know where I be!"

Chico said, "I don't know about y'all, but I can use me ah nice shot of Hennessy."

Antonio said, "push that button behind you Chico, that's where all the liquor at. And pour me ah drink to while you at it. Let's drink to our victory."

Chico downed his drink and laughed saying, "this is my first time getting high in the sky, and love it too."

"Chico you just like to drink," Dino said laughing.

Chico said, "I feel like Alvin would still be here with us if it wasn't for me. He was going to the store to get me my Hennessy drink!"

Antonio said, "its not yoe fault Chico, you can't stop what's meant to be. Don't nobody blame you for what happened to the old man!"

Chico said, "yeah I know man, but I still feel like part of it was my fault!"

Tuesday, July 6, 2002 1:00 P.M.

As soon as Antonio got home he turned the television on and called Cat. He told Cat that it was okay to come home.

While he waited on Cat and Altonio to get home he laid back on the sofa watching the news. Antonio listened joyfully as the news spokesman spoke about the massacre in Columbia.

The news spokesman said, "it has been said that the killings in Columbia was done by professionals. One of the world's most biggest drug suppliers' was found floating in his whirlpool shot to death. The mayor says that whoever was behind this slaying did the United States a big favor. The man, the brain behind the Columbia drug Mafia, again, was found floating in his whirlpool shot to death. There has been no clues as to who done these brutal killings. We'll have a news update coming up later on, on our channel seven action news. I'm Rick Copeland signing off for channel seven action news."

Antonio turned the television off and fell asleep on the sofa, and as he slept he began to dream, and in his dream could see a body walking closer and closer towards him. The closer the body got to him he could see Sorcerer's face and hear Sorcerer saying, "it's me Antonio, you didn't think the dead could come back so quick did you? Did you? Did you? You must come with me Antonio."

Antonio started talking in his sleep, "please… let me live. Let me live."

The voice of Sorcerer kept saying, "you must come with me Antonio," Sorcerer pointed the .45 magnum at Antonio's head. "There's no other way Antonio."

As Sorcerer began to pull the trigger, Antonio cried out. "Nooo, nooo!" The voice was saying there's no other way Antonio.

Antonio was tossing and turning when Cat got inside the house. Cat could hear him hollering, "nooo." She quickly woke him up saying, "its me baby, you okay? You are having a bad dream."

Antonio hugged her saying, "yes, I, was. I'm glad you came home when you did. Somebody was trying to kill me in my dream. Damn I need'ah drink."

Altonio said, "can people kill you in yoe dreams daddy?"

"N'all son, but some dreams seem so real sometimes."

Chapter XVII

Friday, October 22, 2002 3:30 P.M.

Every since Alvin's death, Antonio sat around the house trying to drink himself to death.

Cat came home from the grocery store and sat the groceries on the floor saying to him, "why you wasting yoe life like this, you've been drinking for three months straight now. I can't this much longer, you destroying yourself, you destroying us. I know Alvin getting killed been on your mind, but drinking ain't gone bring him back Antonio! I know you hurting. You finding out about your real father, the way your family were killed. It's enough to drive ah person insane, but I can't take it no more. You wake up drinking, you go to sleep drinking. When it gone end Antonio? I try talking to you; you act like you don't hear me half the time. We steady arguing now. You don't even care what yoe son think about you!"

Antonio put his glass down on the table and said, "fuck that shit! All day I listen to yoe bullshit talk. I'm sick and tired of hearing the same oh shit day after day!"

"Listen to me Antonio, you drunk."

"I'm not drunk bitch, you the one drunk. Why can't you leave me the fuck alone? I don't need you telling me how to live my fuck'n life. Why don't you just leave bitch if you don't like what the fuck I do! I'm not gone stop for you or no fuck'n body. This is me, Antonio Stone, and whoever don't like it can kiss my ass!"

Tears ran down Cat's face. "I'm out'uv this house. I'm taking my son with me. I'll be at my mama house till you come to your senses. Don't bother calling me because I don't need no alcoholic in my son life!"

Antonio threw his glass of liquor at the television. "Get the fuck on, I don't need you. I don't need nobody. I got all I fuck'n need. You ain't gone yet?!"

Cat cried even more as she stormed out the house looking for her son. Altonio was in the front yard playing with his basketball.

Antonio looked out the window at drive off with Altonio. He took another big swig out the liquor bottle. "I don't need you. I don't need nobody." He threw the liquor bottle into the wall. The bottle broke when it hit the wall. "I came in this world alone, and I'm leaving out alone, I'm not worried. She'll be back!" He started crying. "Alvin, Alvin, why you had to die man! You said you'll be here when I needed you the most. You lied to me!" He walked over to the bar in the living room and grabbed another bottle of brandy.

When Ca got inside her mother's house Ms. Bell looked at her and said, "girl what is wrong with you? Come here Altonio and give yoe granny ah kiss."

Cat said, "me and Antonio got into it again. I'll be staying over here till he come back to the Antonio I use to know."

"He under ah lot'uv pressure baby. The boy just lost somebody he loved very much. I'm sure he'll come around soon. Give him some time alone. He'll be all right."

"I don't think so mama, he been drinking himself to death, and it don't make no sense."

"He loves you Cat, and this boy here. Just give'em ah little time to himself and I guarantee he'll be calling over here for you to come home."

"I hope so, where's Michael and Lonnie at?"

"I don't know where Lonnie is, Michael at some girl house. N'all I'm lying on the boy. He took some girl he met the other day to the show. And please don't ask me what they went to see, coss I do not know. Boy what yoe mama been feeding you, you getting so big."

"My cereals make me big," he said.

"They do, well grandma need to start eating cereal, especially if they make you gain weight like that."

Stan called out to Antonio and Antonio answered sounding drunk. "Who, who dis?"

"Its me man, Stan, yoe god brother."

"My, my, my god brother. Its, it's good to hear yoe voice."

"What's wrong man, you sound like you drunk or something."

"I'm not drunk man, talk to me. Where you been? You all right?"

"I'm cool, how bout you? Why you ain't call me man and tell me something? He still was my father you know!"

"yeah I know man, I just couldn't for some reason. I didn't wanna believe it myself, but I did holla at the punk who did that to'em."

Stan was very surprised to hear Antonio say he took care of those punks. "That shit that happened in Columbia that was you?"

"Killed all them Cambodian bitches, they all dead!"

Stan smiled. "I'm glad you took care of business. I feel much better now. Even though my old man did what he did to me I still loved him!"

Antonio put his head down. "I know you did man!"

"Look man, I got to make ah quick run. I'll be in touch. Peace out my brother."

Antonio slowly laid the phone down and poured himself another drink. He forced himself to eat a sandwich he had made for himself before Cat left.

Thursday December 23, 2002 5:00 P.M.

Two days before Christmas, Cat called Antonio to ask him about spending time with his son. Antonio answered, "I'm not in the mood to spend time with anybody. I ain't got the Christmas spirit Cat."

"Tony, you need to leave that drinking alone. Its driving you crazy. I can't believe you don't wanna spend one day out the year with yoe only son. He needs you!"

"I ain't got to listen to this shit you talking."

Cat started crying, "you sure don't," she slammed the phone in his face.

Antonio put the phone down. "That bitch is crazy. Fuck'ah Christmas, I wanna be alone. Can't she see I don't wanna be bothered with nobody? I don't understand women."

275

After Cat hung the phone up in Antonio's face she fell down on her knees and started praying. "Lord, help my husband. He need you, I can't do anything, but I know you can Lord!"

Ms. Bell peeped in on Cat and saw her on her knees praying, and she said in a low voice. "Lord, please help her, she need yoe help Lord!" She walked away. "Everything gone be all right!"

Antonio just sat around the house drinking and talking to himself.

Friday, December 24, 2002 2:00 P.M.

After six months of being in the hospital, Cobra was finally being released. The surgery he had on his arm left it much shorter than the other one. As soon as Cobra stepped out the hospital door his first words were, "I'm coming Antonio, you son of ah bitch you'ah dead man. Don't nobody do this to me and live to tell about it. Nobody! Now I got to catch up with yoe brother law. When I'm done with you, you gone wish you would'uv killed me my frien!"

Cobra took a cab to Mexican land where his brother Rico ran a diner that sold Mexican food only. Cobra said to the driver, "you see the sign on left that say Rico Restaurant, stop there." The cabdriver pulled in front of the restaurant. Cobra put a fifty dollar bill in the slot. "Keep the change my frien."

When Cobra stepped inside the restaurant Rico hollered from behind the counter. "Hay, hay everybody, my little brother has finally come home. Come, come, give yoe big brother ah hug," they hugged. Rico pushed him away, "can you use yoe arm my brother?"

"I can't do shit with it. I'm lucky to have it the doctor say."

Rico got real angry, "when do you wanna do this motha fucka?!"

"I want both his arms today!"

"Then today it will be. I'll get our men together. Do you know where this punk stay?"

"No, but I know who do. And if it wasn't for his ass I would still have full use of my arm. I know just where he live."

Rico gathered up four cars of men, five men to each car. Cobra led the way to Michael's house.

When they got to Michael's house Cobra and Rico got out the car at the same time. Rico signaled for the rest of the men to stay in their cars.

Michael was in the den watching television. Ms. Bell answered the knock on the door. "May I help y'all?"

Cobra smiled. "Yes madam, is Michael home?"

"Yes, hold on," she called for Michael. "Michael, some men here to see you. Y'all come on in, he'll be right with y'all."

Michael was very surprised to see Cobra. Michael smiled saying, "what's up Cobra?"

Rico pulled his gun saying, "you know what's up motha fucka."

Ms. Bell couldn't believe what was happening and said, "what's going on?"

Cobra said, "not here Ramone. Let him take us to Antonio."

Rico put the .45 glot to Michael's head saying, "come on nigga, you gone show us where this punk live!"

Michael was trembling from head to toe saying, "man I ain't done nothing to y'all!"

Ms. Bell cried out, "please don't hurt my son!"

Cobra said, "I know you ain't done nothing. All we want you to do is show us where this Antonio lives. Now move yoe ass."

Cat could hear the commotion going on outside after being awakened by the sound of her mama voice crying out. "Please don't hurt my son."

Ms. Bell grabbed Rico's arm that was holding onto her son, "let me son go."

Cat ran to the door just in time to see Rico strike Ms. Bell across the head with his gun. The blow knocked her out instantly. Cat ran out the house screaming out, "noooo, mama...!" Cat took a good look at the cars driving off. "Mama, mama, please Lord help me!"

Ms. Bell came too. "I'm okay, Call the police they gone kill Antonio. Please Cat hurry, they gone kill my son, I know it," she said crying.

Cat ran in the house and called the police, and after she called the police she called Antonio. Antonio sounded drunk to her as usual. "Who talking?" He asked.

Cat was breathing hard. "Antonio, you got to get out'uv that house, some men on they way there to kill you!"

"Who, who on they way here?"

278

"Antonio you got to listen to me, they got Michael with them, they wanna kill you. Leave the house now Antonio," she cried out.

"I'm not going nowhere. They wanna kill me, let'um come. I'm not scared to die, I'll be here!"

"Antonio please don't do this, think about yoe son!"

"Today is my lucky day, I get to die, thanks for warning me."

"Antonio please....!"

"What the fuck is wrong with you? You don't hear to good. I'm not leaving my fuck'n house for nobody. I'm sick and tired of yoe trying to tell me what the fuck to do."

Cat cried even harder, "you can at least save yourself!"

Antonio squeezed the phone tight as he could. "I'm ready to die!" He slammed the phone in Cat's face and ran to his gun cabinet. "I want run. They wanna fuck with me. I'm ready to die. I'll be right here when they get here. I want run, I be here!"

Antonio grabbed two M-16 machine guns out the cabinet, and then put on his bulletproof vest. He sat on the couch waiting patiently for them to show up.

Ms. Bell asked, "did you call Antonio?"

"Yeah mama, but he wouldn't listen to me. He said he wanted to die. I believe him too. He's gone crazy. I got to face it mama, the man done lost his mind. He gone get killed. You saw all them mens!"

"I hope the police make it there in time Lord knows I do!"

Antonio could hear the cars pulling up. He peeped out the living room window and saw Cobra and his men getting out the cars. As Antonio counted the men he said, "I should'ah killed that bastard when I had the chance, but today its him or me. I'm ready to die, and I hope they are too."

Antonio sat back on the couch with his two machine guns on each side of him waiting for them to make their move. "It's twenty of them to one of me. I'm ready for war!"

Cobra lined all the men up and said to Michael, "go knock on the door, see if he home."

As Michael started walking towards the house Cobra said, "if that door open kill'em!"

Michael knocked on the door, "Antonio, it's me Michael."

Antonio got up saying, "yeah."

"It's me Antonio, Michael, let me in."

Antonio could tell by the sound of Michael's voice that he was scared out of his mind. As soon as Antonio opened the door all he could hear was guns going off. Michael fell straight on the living room floor. Antonio pulled his body all the way inside the house and shut the door saying, "hang in there man, don't worry I got yoe back now." Blood was running out of Michael's mouth. "Hang in there!"

Michael spoke slowly, "don't, go, out, there. They will, kill, you!" Michael's head titled to the side. Antonio checked his pulse, he was dead.

Antonio could hear Cobra calling out to him. "Come on out Antonio, I might let you keep one of yoe arms. I don't wanna kill you Antonio. I believe in the arm for ah arm. You should'uv killed me Antonio!"

Antonio pushed the remote for the garage door to let up, and then grabbed both of his machine guns. Rico yelled out, "get ready he coming out the garage!"

While Cobra and the men were watching the garage door raise up, Antonio was coming out the front door saying, "here I am motha fuckazzz." Antonio's machine guns was smoking as he turned them loose on them and hollering at the same time. "I'm right here motha fuckaz, y'all can't fuck with me, I'm already dead."

The more they shot Antonio, the more he talked. "What's the matter with you bitches, kill me," he turned his machine guns loose again.

Cobra yelled out, "that son of ah bitch got'ah vest on, shoot for the legs."

Antonio was still standing and shooting saying, "y'all fucking with the wrong man, I kill."

Before Antonio could say another word he got struck in the leg, and that caused him to fall to one knee. Antonio was struck again, this time causing him to drop his machine guns, but he was still talking. "I'm still living. You can't kill the dead."

Antonio was down on both knees, and as he was talking he could see a cab coming his way. Cobra and his men didn't pay the cab no attention as the shooting ceased. Rico finally noticed the cab and said, "who the fuck is that?"

Cobra said, "just some old man getting out cab, Antonio, as you can see I have allowed you to live."

The old man had the cabdriver to pop the trunk. The cabdriver said, "mannn, you see all them down there shooting them guns, you better get yoe ass back in this cab so we can get the hell out'uv here."

The old man put his bulletproof vest on and grabbed his machine gun out of his luggage, saying, "here's fifty dollars, have'ah nice day."

The old man started walking towards Cobra and his men, and when he got close enough he yelled out. "Surprise motha fuckazzz." He let his machine gun do the rest of the talking as he shot everything in his sight moving.

A bullet caught the old man, but he acted like he wasn't hit and kept on firing the machine gun.

Antonio watched this old man drop Cobra men like flies, and thought to himself. "Who in the hell is this old man? Should I play dead? Fuck it, I'm already dead."

After the old man was done taking care Cobra men he pointed his machine gun at Antonio and started walking towards him. When he got to Antonio, Antonio asked, "who the fuck is you?"

The old man looked down and said, "don't you know me? My name is." The man started pulling the fake gray side burns off his face. Then he snatched the gray and black wig off. "Didn't I tell you when you needed me the most I would always be there, I'm."

Antonio said, "Alvin Stone."

"Yeah that's right son, Alvin stone."

"Man I thought you were dead."

Alvin smirked, "dead, didn't I teach you not to believe everything you see."

Soon as Alvin leaned over to help Antonio up the police was everywhere. They picked Antonio up and put him in the backseat of the squad car along with Alvin.

Antonio looked over at Alvin and said, "I just wanna know one thing; where the hell you been all this time?"

Alvin smiled, "do you know who you look like when you was down on yoe knees?"

"N'all who?"

"THE SON OF SCARFACE."

TO BE CONTINUED

SONG BY: FRANKIE BEVERLY AND MAZE

I'M SO HAPPY TO SEE YOU AND ME BACK IN STRIDE AGAIN.

www.ingramcontent.com/pod-product-compliance
Lightning Source LLC
Chambersburg PA
CBHW070855180626
46817CB00003B/777